THE LOST BOY

NYES LANDING CRIME MYSTERY

S. F. WILLIAMS

Copyright © 2024 S.F. Williams

All rights reserved.

Published by Intrigue Press

No part of this book may be reproduced, stored in a retrieval system, or transmitted in any form or by any means, electronic, mechanical, photocopying, recording, or otherwise, without express permission of the publisher.

ISBN-13: 979-8-89342-116-3 (paperback)

ISBN-13: 979-8-89342-124-8 (e-book)

Copy editor Eliza Dee of Clio Editing Services

Cover designed by 100covers.com

This is a work of fiction. Names, characters, organizations, places, events, and incidents are either products of the author's imagination or are used fictitiously. Otherwise, any resemblance to actual persons, living or dead, is purely coincidental.

ACKNOWLEDGMENTS

Writing a novel takes a village. I own an enormous debt of gratitude to many people. Donna Ison, who inspired me to embark on this journey into fiction writing twenty years ago. Teri Monahan, my loyal cheerleader, who finds the bright spot in even the messiest manuscript. Beth Hallo, who tells me the truth, even when it hurts—every artist needs a friend like her. My unofficial continuity editor, Wende O'Reilly, who spots narrative inconsistencies and makes insightful observations about my characters. Dawn Roberson, my unofficial agent, who spreads the word about my books, for which I'm most grateful. Elizabeth Forst, thank you for your astute insights regarding plot holes and factual errors. Thank you, Jackie Jenkins, for your love, support, and grammatical expertise. Thank you, Paul Buzinski, for sharing your knowledge of lawnmowers and saving me from embarrassment. Thank you, Jeff Paul, for your encouraging words. Timothy Harris, your heartfelt response to my characters and story left me speechless, and that is no easy feat. My copy editor, Eliza Dee, and proofreader, Winni Troha, saved the book from becoming a grammatical mess. Any errors that remain are mine. My cover art designer and project manager at 100covers.com were prompt and professional. I am thankful for the members of the New York City Writer's Critique Group, whose camaraderie when I wrote my first novel kept me focused, and for the many talented thespians who have produced, directed, and performed my plays over the years. Most of all, I am grateful for my loyal readers, without whom I would be shouting into the void.

MAKE AN AUTHOR HAPPY TODAY!

If you enjoy *The Lost Boy*, please consider leaving a review on Goodreads, Amazon, or the bookstore platform of your choice. Even a sentence or two would be a tremendous help and most appreciated.

Sign up for my newsletter at https://sfwilliamsauthor.com and I will notify you about upcoming book releases and giveaways.

If you think your followers might enjoy *The Lost Boy*, please spread the word on your social media platforms. You can find me at @sfwauthor on Facebook, Instagram, and Twitter.

*Dedicated to my son
Francis Williams*

CHAPTER ONE

As I rush up the stairs out of the subway station, I collide with a scruffy homeless man who reeks of piss and gin. The unsteady fellow loses his balance. I break his fall before he cracks his head open on the pavement. He shrugs off my kindness and shuffles away, cursing under his breath. There, but for the grace of Mama Libby and Papa Frank, go I.

The hissing brakes of a city bus at the curb aggravates the pounding in my head from too much whiskey last night. I need caffeine, but I am running late for the third morning in a row, so I don't have time to stop at the breakfast cart on the corner.

A headline at the newsstand I pass catches my eye. Forensic searches through the rubble transported from the Twin Towers to the Fresh Kills dumpsite on Staten Island following last September's terrorist attacks will cease operation in three weeks. I, along with half the police force, worked twelve-hour days for months sifting through the debris. Forensics only identified a handful of the many remains we recovered, which was disheartening, to say the least.

My new Nokia cellular phone rings, startling me. I'm still getting used to carrying the clunky but convenient device.

"Where are you?" my partner, Ahn Tran, whispers. "Roll call is about to start."

"Almost there."

"Stop hitting the snooze button."

"Yes, Mom."

"I have two kids already, Nowak. I don't need a third."

Tran hangs up. I jog down the sidewalk and slip inside the precinct. Sarge is shouting at a cringing rookie I don't recognize. Better him than me.

Hustling downstairs into the locker room, I change into my ballistic vest and uniform, wipe the scuffs off my boots using spit and a tissue, and buckle on my duty belt. My flashlight needs batteries. I'll buy a pack while I'm on patrol. I strap on my Glock, which I cleaned after my trip to the firing range last weekend.

By the time I slip into the rear of the squad room, twenty pounds heavier in all my gear, Sarge has completed inspection and is briefing the team on a streak of robberies on Orchard Street. My cellular phone rings. Sarge glares at me. I silence the device. He shares descriptions of several suspects we should be on the lookout for and dismisses the team.

"Nowak," Sarge says. "My office. Now!"

I glance at Tran. She shakes her head. I follow Sarge into his office. He sinks into his desk chair and sighs. "What am I going to do with you, Nowak?"

I hope he doesn't expect an answer, because I'm out of excuses.

"I need your reports on my desk by the end of the day. And be sure they're legible."

"Yes, sir."

"The captain wants to see you."

My heart skips a beat. After patrolling the streets of the Lower East Side for five years, I applied for an open detective position on the domestic abuse task force. I've earned this promotion. I sprint toward the elevator. It's out of order again. I bolt upstairs, leaping two steps with every single bound. By the time I reach the sixth floor, I'm wheezing like I have emphysema, and I've never smoked a day in my life. That's what happens when I skip the gym.

"Come in, Nowak," the captain says.

I straighten my tie and step through the door. The captain rises. He stands eye to eye with me, and I'm six feet, two inches tall. Paperwork clutters his desk. He removes a box of case files from the only other chair in the room and waits until I take a seat before sitting himself.

"Impressive test scores, Nowak."

"Thank you, sir."

I studied my ass off for the detective exam. Even ditched the whiskey for a week.

"Your arrest record is exemplary."

"Highest in the precinct."

"But you have an alarming number of misconduct complaints."

"I have a short fuse for jerks who abuse women and children."

"We all do," the captain says. "But there's a right and a wrong way to put the scumbags behind bars." He sets my file aside. "I can't recommend you for detective, Nowak."

Story of my life. No matter how hard I try, I always get the shaft, and this time I'm certain I know why.

"The guys said you'd never promote a fag."

"Are you accusing me of discrimination, Nowak?"

"It's just—"

"I don't give a flying fuck where you stick your dick. So long as it's consensual. Do I make myself clear?"

"Crystal."

"Be discreet, though. Especially when you're wearing that uniform. Not everybody is as open-minded."

"Understood, sir."

"You're dismissed."

As I rush downstairs, tears blur my vision. I dry my eyes on my sleeve. The last thing I need is for another officer to see me crying. I'd never live down the shame.

The voice mail light on my cellular phone blinks. I press the play button.

Cal, it's me. Annie.

Annie and I dated in high school—before I came out. She's the kindest soul on the planet. One time, she stepped on a spider she feared might've been a mother like the spider in that children's book about a runt pig and cried so hard she hyperventilated. We searched for hours but never found any baby spiders. I haven't seen Annie since Papa Frank's funeral. Hard to believe that was seven years ago. She called me after the terrorist attacks last September, but we only spoke for a few seconds before I had to rush back into the chaos.

I don't mean to alarm you, but Mama Libby broke her wrist. Call me the first chance you get.

Mama Libby must be seventy by now. She and Papa Frank fostered my younger sister, Mary Catherine, and me after we lost our mother.

My radio crackles. "Ten fifty-two in progress, Nowak," Tran says. "Corner of Essex and Delancey Streets."

Eager to redeem myself, I sprint seven blocks to the intersection in question and spot Tran calming an emaciated young woman with a black eye and a bloody nose. Tran orders the gawking crowd of onlookers to step back. They do so without hesitation. My partner might be slight of stature, but she intimidates men twice her size. Me included.

"Everything that bitch says is a lie," a male voice shouts. I peer upward. A skinny white guy wearing a wife beater leans out a fourth-floor window. Neo-Nazi symbols sleeve his scrawny arms.

I rush through the open door of the apartment building and charge upstairs.

"Hold on, Nowak!" Tran shouts. "Don't do anything you'll regret."

Weapon drawn, I march up and down the fourth-floor hallway, banging on doors and shouting, "Police!"

"You're going to wish you'd kept your trap shut bitch," Wife Beater shouts, betraying his location. Finding his door unlocked, I burst inside. The smell of burnt plastic makes me suspect drugs may be involved, but I don't see any paraphernalia lying around. No weapons, either. Keeping an eye on the guy, I check the corners of the room and kick open the closet door.

"Clear!"

"You can't burst in here without a warrant."

"Shows what you know." I holster my Glock. "I'm collaring a suspect." I twist his arm behind his back. "That would be you." I wrench his elbow up between his shoulder blades and snarl in his ear. "Women aren't punching bags, asshole."

Wife Beater bites me. I fly into a rage. Next thing I know, Tran is hauling me off our suspect and shouting in my face, "Enough, Nowak!" Wife Beater lies curled up at my feet, sniveling that I'm crazy. I step back and throw up my hands.

"This is your lucky day, asshole."

Tran identifies and cuffs Wife Beater, tosses the prick for weapons and contraband, and reads him his rights as she marches his ass out the door. I follow my partner downstairs. Paramedics slide the battered young woman into the box of their ambulance on a stretcher and speed away.

Tran shoves our suspect into the rear of our squad car and hops behind the wheel. It's my week to drive, but I don't argue the point.

"I'm taking our suspect to the hospital," Tran says.

"Should've let me finish the job."

"This bullshit needs to stop."

"You saw what he did to that poor girl."

"Our job is to arrest the suspect," Tran says. "After that, his fate is in the court's hands."

"I know, but—"

"You're not the judge and jury, Nowak."

———

TRAN and I file our reports at the end of the day, change into our civvies, and walk five blocks to McDougall's Tavern. Founded in 1856 by Irish immigrants, the Lower East Side watering hole is one of the oldest bars in New York City. Says so right on the door.

Inside the tavern, photographs of politicians, sports stars, and entertainers collected over decades clutter the walls, and sawdust coats the floor—a nostalgic holdover from the days when men chewed tobacco. We belly up to the mahogany bar, nicked and scratched from a century and a half of abuse, but polished so glossy I can see my reflection in its surface.

"Your usual?" Mack asks. The Irish bartender with his waxed handlebar mustache appreciates cops, which is why we gather here. That, and the drinks are cheap.

"Make mine a double," I say.

Mack holds a rocks glass up to the light and wipes the rim. "Rough day?"

"I've had better."

Mack pours a pint of Harp lager for Tran and a double shot of Jameson Irish whiskey with a pint of Guinness stout for me. I raise my glass. "Bottoms up."

Tran grins. "Your favorite position."

"I wish I had a dollar for every time I've heard that one." I knock back my whiskey and chase the sweet burn with a gulp of beer.

"I can't keep covering for you, Nowak."

"Nice to know my partner has my back."

"That's not fair."

"Whatever."

Tran catches my eye in the mirror behind the bar and raises one brow.

"I hear you," I say. "Loud and clear." I crack open a peanut from a bowl on the bar, toss the nuts into my mouth, and dump the shells into the bucket beside the bowl. "I'm a lousy partner."

"Don't put words in my mouth."

"I don't need this crap right now."

Fleeing to the back of the bar, I step inside an old wooden phone booth and pull out my cellular phone. I find and dial Annie's number. She answers on the first ring.

"Cal, thanks for calling me back."

"How are you, Annie?"

"Fine."

She doesn't sound fine.

"Kit had better be treating you right."

"I'm fine. Kit's fine," Annie says with a little too much enthusiasm. "We're fine."

Annie's husband, Kit, has resented me since high school, when she chose to date me rather than him. As soon as I came out, he swooped in. He and I haven't spoken a civil word since our senior year, when we lost the state championship. I threw a pass in the last seconds of the fourth quarter that should've won us the game, but he fumbled the ball. Of course, he blamed my arm. He and his fellow bullies Oakley Reeves and Howie Clark jumped me after the game. By the time Coach pulled me off, Howie had a busted lip, Oakley had two black eyes, and Kit lay cringing on the ground, his arms raised in surrender, his handsome face a bruised and bloodied mess.

"And you?" Annie asks.

"Can't complain," I say, keeping my disappointment over not having made detective to myself. "How's Mama Libby?"

"Driving her nurses nuts."

"How did she break her wrist?"

"Tripped over that darn dog of hers. She's lucky she didn't break her neck. After she gets released, she'll be in a cast for weeks and will need help."

"Can she get a home healthcare aide?"

"Her doctor suggested that. More like insisted. But she refuses to let a stranger into her home."

"She and Papa Frank took in dozens of foster children over the years."

"She claims this is different. I was hoping you might talk some sense into her."

"Give me the phone number for the hospital and her room number."

I scrawl the information on a cocktail napkin. We say our goodbyes, and I return to my bar stool.

"Everything okay?" Tran asks.

"Yep."

Tran swigs her last swallow of beer and tosses six singles onto the bar. "I have to pick up Liam and Cara from the YMCA and figure out what we're having for dinner."

Soon after we became partners, Tran kicked her deadbeat husband to the curb.

"Look, Nowak. I know you're disappointed—"

"Spare me the lecture."

"Be that way."

Tran leaves. I order another round.

Officer Fagan plops down on the bar stool Tran vacated. With his saggy jowls and permanent snarl, he resembles an overweight Rottweiler. He even slobbers when he gets angry, which is often the case.

"Told you they'd never promote a fag." Officer Fagan cracks open a peanut and tosses the shells onto the floor.

"Mack puts that bucket on the bar for a reason," I say.

Officer Fagan picks up the bucket and dumps the shells inside onto the floor.

"Pig."

Officer Fagan rises. "What'd you call me?" The brawny brute has been spoiling for a fight since our days at the academy.

"You heard me, Fagan." We square off. I'm taller and leaner. Although I won't be much longer if I don't get my ass to the gym. I stick out my chin. "Take your best shot."

Officer Fagan backs me against the bar. I shove the prick off and raise my fists. He steps back and throws up his hands.

"What's the matter, Fagan? Afraid you'll get your ass kicked by a faggot?"

"Internal Affairs is already crawling up my butt over a trumped-up sexual harassment charge. If they hear I kicked the shit out of a cock—"

"You know the rules, boys," Mack says, stepping between us. "Take your beef outside."

"That's okay, Mack."

I toss thirty dollars onto the bar and chug my last swallow of beer.

"Sit," Mack says. "Have another round on me."

"Rain check, Mack. Your clientele tonight stinks."

"Screw you, Nowak," Officer Fagan says.

"In your wet dreams." I blow Officer Fagan a kiss. He clenches his fists. I duck out the door and hop on the crosstown bus to my favorite dive gay bar in the West Village, hoping to get drunk and laid.

CHAPTER TWO

FRIDAY MORNING, I slink into the precinct a half hour late, drenched in after shave to mask the whiskey sweat seeping from my pores. I wish I could say my hangover was worth the misery, but the hot-as-hell construction worker from Philly who I picked up last night passed out on top of me. I need coffee, but the pot is empty. Just my luck.

Tran leans back and folds her arms across her chest. "You get hit by a bus?"

"Sure feel like I did."

"Nowak, get your ass in here!" Sarge shouts from his office. "Now!"

I pop a fistful of breath mints into my mouth and face the music.

"You look like hammered shit," Sarge says.

"Rough night."

"You're your own worst enemy, Nowak."

"So, I've heard."

"Take some time off."

"I'm fine, sir."

"That's not a request. We'll be lucky if that piece of human garbage you and Tran collared yesterday doesn't sue the department. You're on administrative leave until you get your head on straight."

"But, sir—"

"No arguments, Nowak. I'm doing you a favor. The captain wanted your badge. Speaking of which—"

I toss my badge onto Sarge's desk and surrender my duty belt and service weapon.

"They'll be waiting for you when you return," Sarge says.

On my way out, I slam the door. Tran ignores me. So much for loyalty. I gather my personal effects, head downstairs into the basement, and change out of my uniform into my civvies.

———

As I step through the door of my apartment, I stub my toe on an empty whiskey bottle. My place is a mess. Dirty clothes overflow the laundry bag. Pizza boxes and fast-food bags litter every surface. My alarm clock rests wedged between the chest of drawers and the wall where it landed after I threw it across the room this morning. Too hungover to give a shit, I tumble into bed and drift off into a restless sleep in which I'm thirteen years old again and running for my life through the tangled woods in the middle of the night. Pounding on my door wakes me.

"Shut the hell up, freak," Miss Tawanda LaRue shouts. "I can't hear myself sing."

"Sorry," I say. I must've cried out in my sleep again.

"Batshit crazy po-po," Miss Tawanda LaRue mutters. The clomp of her heels recedes. Her door across the hallway slams shut.

My stomach rumbles. I need sustenance, but all I have in my refrigerator is mustard, ketchup, and a dried-up lime. I venture outside into a sunny May afternoon. The bell at the high school around the corner rings. Raucous teenagers spill out onto the sidewalk. Several swarm inside the deli on the corner. I weave my way through the chattering mob outside and purchase two slices and a soda from the pizzeria down the block. On my way home, I stop at the liquor store and buy a bottle of whiskey.

As I bound upstairs, Miss Tawanda LaRue and her neurotic poodle trudge down the stairs. I step aside and allow the pair to pass. The burly drag queen whose platinum-blond bouffant wig clashes with her rust-red beard moves slower than a three-legged tortoise. The poodle bares her teeth and snarls. I recoil against the railing.

"If that mutt bites me, I'm charging you with assault."

"Pig."

"Oink, oink."

Retreating inside my apartment, I chase down my slices of pizza with gulps of soda and toss the bottle into the recycling bin, along with three empty whiskey bottles. I stuff the fast-food sacks and containers into a plastic garbage bag and throw away my busted alarm clock. My life is a mess.

I find the cocktail napkin with Mama Libby's information and call the hospital. The receptionist transfers me to her room.

"Hello?"

"Mama Libby?"

"No, Cal. It's Annie."

"I had to break my wrist to get that boy to call me," Mama Libby says.

Miss Tawanda LaRue belts out Bonnie Tyler's 1980s ballad "Total Eclipse of the Heart" in her husky baritone. Like it or not, I have time off, and Mama Libby needs my help. A few days away from the city might do me good. "I'm coming for a visit," I blurt out before I change my mind. "Can you pick me up at the bus station?"

"Of course. When?"

"Tonight."

Annie shrieks and shares the news with Mama Libby.

After we hang up, I call Mary Catherine. I haven't spoken to my sister since I dropped off Christmas presents for my niece and nephew last December. A year after our mother's death, a middle-aged couple from the city who couldn't conceive adopted my sister. Although she wants nothing to do with her past, she should know Mama Libby is in the hospital. After five rings, her answering machine picks up.

"Hey, MC. It's me, Cal. Mama Libby broke her wrist."

Unsure what else to say, I hang up. Seconds later, I receive a text on my cellular phone.

Got your message. I'll send flowers.

After everything that Mama Libby did for us when we were traumatized adolescents, my sister will send flowers. I'm disappointed in her.

MY BUS PULLS into the Nyes Landing station at ten o'clock on Friday night. I step off into a cool breeze, pungent with the odors of freshly mowed hay and cow manure from the pasture next door. The smells of my childhood.

Annie throws her arms around me. She's put on a few pounds since we last saw one another. As have I. We're not teenagers anymore.

"I'm glad you're here, Cal."

"Me too," I say, although I'm not sure about that. Coming home unsettles me. I retrieve my duffle bag and gun case from beneath the bus and follow Annie to her car. "How are you doing?"

"I'm fine."

"Are you really?"

"Yes." Annie buckles her seat belt. "Although I had quite the scare today."

"What happened?"

"One of my students wandered off the school grounds."

"Your students?"

"I teach second grade at the elementary school," Annie says. She looks both ways and pulls out of the parking lot. "Thank goodness Chief Harris found Evan and not some maniac. The boy wouldn't say where he'd gone or why."

"I'm glad he's okay."

"I hope so. At the beginning of the school year, Evan was one of my brightest students. This spring, all he does is sulk. His parents finalized their divorce last year and they fight over custody. If you ask me, neither of them is a fit parent."

"That's rough."

"Last summer, a local boy went missing," Annie says, "and no one ever found him. So, I worry."

"As you should," I say. "Too many missing children never come home."

I got lucky. When I was thirteen years old, a police officer rescued me from the old, abandoned paper mill where I'd hidden from my mother's killer for five of the longest days and nights of my life.

A deer leaps into the road. Annie slams on the brakes. I brace for impact. The deer bounds over the hood and disappears through the trees. We breathe a collective sigh of relief and continue on past Virgil's Bait and Tackle and the clapboard Baptist church. A faded billboard welcomes us to Nyes Landing.

"How's Kit?" I ask.

"I seldom see my husband these days," Annie says. "He's always on the road. And on those rare nights when he is home, he's preoccupied with his work."

I suspect Kit is having an affair. In high school, he and his fellow bullies, Oakley Reeves and Howie Clark, treated getting laid as a sport.

"We talked about starting a family," Annie says. "But Kit

decided we should wait. He's always working, and I'm out of sorts."

"Out of sorts?"

"My doctor thinks I have a chemical imbalance."

"You're one of the most well-adjusted people I know."

"You've been gone a long time, Cal."

We cruise down Main Street. Vintage clothing and antique stores, art galleries, and gift shops have replaced many of the local businesses from my childhood.

Annie brakes at a stop sign. "You remember Helena Potter?"

"The goth girl with the spider tattoo on her neck?"

"That's her gallery." Annie nods toward a somber gray house on the corner with a steepled turret and immense bay windows. "Weekenders up from the city spend a fortune on her ceramics."

We drive past Clark's Automotive Repair. The shingles have peeled off the tar roof. Rundown vehicles litter the parking lot. Stacks of worn tires line the rusted tin walls. The local garage has seen better days.

"Howie inherited his father's business," Annie says. "He and Elena Martinez got married last year. Six months later, they separated. Neither said why, but I suspect there's a story there."

What an odd couple. Class President Elena Martinez, sweet and unassuming despite her brains and beauty, and Howie Clark, who got held back twice and carried a chip on his shoulder the size of Texas. Given the way his old man knocked him around, it's no wonder. He and his brothers spent time in foster care with Mama Libby and Papa Frank, too, but he and I avoided one another.

Fans pack the high school stadium for the ninth inning of a varsity baseball game.

"The Fisher Cats might make the playoffs this season," Annie says.

I played second base, but football was where I excelled. My

record for touchdown passes thrown in a single season held for a decade before a new hotshot quarterback stole my glory.

"We should catch a game while you're home."

"We'll see."

It's hard to believe that it's been fourteen years since I donned a cap and gown and collected my diploma, as surprised as anyone that I'd graduated. Mama Libby instilled in me the value of hard work and encouraged me to be myself. Papa Frank came to all my games and coached me from the sidelines. His passion for football motivated me not only to play, but to excel on the field.

Annie turns right onto Birch Lane. Restored Victorian houses with manicured lawns and lush flower beds line the left side of the street. The Sisters of Mercy Catholic Church, with its Gothic steeple constructed from native bluestone, occupies half a block on the right. Past the church lies Turtle Park, with its colorful playground and kidney-shaped swimming pool. The Victorians give way to sprawling ranch-style houses on spacious lots interspersed with clapboard farmhouses. The dwellings grow more rustic and further apart.

We cross over the Esopus Creek bridge, drive past an overgrown field, and wind our way through a densely wooded area. Mama Libby's two-story farmhouse with its gabled porch appears atop the hill ahead. The siding has faded. The lawn needs mowing. I have my work cut out for me.

Annie pulls into the driveway and parks behind an older model Pontiac. "Wait until you meet Sparky."

"Who?"

Grabbing my bags, I follow Annie up the rickety porch steps and through the wobbly screen door. Aromas of lilac and cinnamon welcome me home. Faint crayon drawings left behind by the dozens of foster children who sought refuge in this house over the years linger on the walls.

An energetic dog that's built like a German shepherd but has the coat of a golden retriever and the alertness of a border collie leaps on me. I stagger backward and catch my balance on the door frame.

"Meet Sparky," Annie says. "She's your problem now."

I crouch and pet Sparky.

"Fair warning," Annie says, "Sparky is a runner. Never let her go outside off leash. Speaking of which, she probably needs to go p-o-t-t-y."

Sparky's ears perk up. She races in circles, wagging her tail.

I follow Annie into the kitchen. Two dog bowls lie upside-down on the floor, surrounded by soggy chunks of kibble.

"Sparky, you naughty girl," Annie says. "Look at this mess you've made."

Sparky gobbles down a soggy bite.

A leather dog harness and leash hang on a hook in the mudroom off the kitchen.

"I assume these belong to her?"

"I'll hold her steady," Annie says, "while you slip on her harness."

Sparky seems in perpetual motion. I slip the harness over her head and buckle the straps. She licks my fingers. I snap on her leash. She tugs me through the mudroom and scratches on the back door.

"Will you two be all right?"

"We'll be fine," I say, hoping I sound more confident than I feel.

"Mama Libby keeps the dog food in the pantry," Annie says. "I left a note on the counter. Be sure you water her prize orchids."

Sparky drags me down the back porch steps into the yard and pulls me toward the woods. The dog is stronger than she looks. Grabbing her leash with both hands, I redirect her toward the front yard.

Annie waves and drives away.

A rabbit hops across the lawn. Its cottony white tail flashes in the moonlight. Sparky barks. The rabbit freezes, eyes wide, and sniffs the air. Sparky howls and paws at the ground. I restrain the dog. The rabbit scampers away and disappears into the field next door.

Sparky sniffs her way around the lawn for a few minutes and does her business. I drag her inside the mudroom and wrestle off her harness. She scratches on the pantry door. I read Annie's note. After every walk, Sparky is supposed to get a treat. I find a jar of bone-shaped biscuits and tell her to sit. She cocks her head from side to side like she has no clue what I'm saying. I pass her a treat, which she gobbles down.

Annie left detailed instructions on when and how I'm to water Mama Libby's prize orchids in the kitchen window. They look fine to me.

Once I mop up Sparky's mess, I search for booze. I left the whiskey I bought earlier in the city. Papa Frank always kept a bottle of bourbon stashed in the cupboard above the refrigerator, but that's filled with jars of home-canned fruits and vegetables now. Mama Libby has been busy.

Someone knocks on the back door. I left gun case with my Beretta in the living room. I peek through the curtains. A lanky Black man with snow-white hair flashes a toothy grin. I crack open the door.

"Apologies for intruding, son, but I saw the light on. Thought after being in the hospital, Elizabeth might appreciate a home-cooked meal."

"Mama Libby isn't home. I'm her foster son, Cal."

"The lost boy."

This is why I don't come home more often. Everyone knows who I am and what I saw that awful night.

"I'm Moses. I'm sure Elizabeth told you about me. I rent the apartment above the garage."

I had no idea that Mama Libby had a tenant. The older model Pontiac in the driveway must belong to him. We shake hands. The old guy has a firm grip for his age.

Moses holds up a plastic margarine tub. "I cooked more ham hocks and beans than I can eat."

"Those sure smell good."

"Here you go." Moses shoves the warm tub into my hands.

"I wouldn't want to—"

"I'm glad Elizabeth has a young fella to look after her. I do what I can for the old gal, but I've got a bum knee. Took a bullet in Nam."

I sense Moses could talk all night, and I'm exhausted. "Thanks for dinner. I'll tell Mama Libby you dropped by."

"You need anything, son, you give me a shout."

I watch Moses hobble across the lawn and up the stairs. Once he gets inside his apartment, I lock the door.

Sparky stands on her hind legs and sniffs the plastic tub. I shove her snout aside. The savory aroma of the ham and beans makes my mouth water. In the city, I subsist on deli sandwiches, pizza slices, and hot dogs from food cart vendors. I plop down at the kitchen table and wolf down every bite. When I finish, I put my spoon and the empty tub in the dishwasher, a luxury my apartment in the city lacks.

Bags in hand, I trudge upstairs. Sparky trots along on my heels. The third step down from the second floor landing wobbles. I need to repair that while I'm home.

My old bedroom smells of lemon-scented furniture polish. I slept on the lower berth of the set of twin bunk beds throughout high school. The box springs creak even worse now. I set my gun case on the nightstand and put away my clothes, something I never do at home. I stash my duffle in the closet. My old letterman jacket hangs on a hook inside the door. I run my fingers over the stitches where Mama Libby mended the hole that Kit tore in the sleeve when he ripped off my varsity patch during our big fight.

Once I finish unpacking, I change into sweatpants, grab my toothbrush and toothpaste, and pad down the hallway into the bathroom. The sink faucet drips. So does the shower head. This old house is falling apart.

CHAPTER THREE

Sunlight streams through my bedroom window Saturday morning. I peer through the faded curtains. Billowy clouds roll over distant mountain peaks. Every shade of green imaginable blankets the ground, which is dotted with wildflower buds in a rainbow of colors. Having a few days off might not be so bad.

When I wash my face, the leaky bathroom sink faucet reminds me that I need to buy washers. I could use a haircut, too. I wonder if Earl still owns the barbershop.

Sparky scratches on the bathroom door. I forgot I'm dog sitting. I follow her downstairs and wrestle her into her harness. The instant I open the back door, she bolts outside. Perhaps I can teach the dog some basic commands while I'm home. I worked in the canine unit for six months after I graduated from the academy.

"Sit." I press Sparky's hindquarters toward the ground. She resists. I press harder. She yawns and plops her butt down. "Good girl." I pass her a treat.

Sparky tugs me toward the woods. I redirect her around to the front lawn. She does her business, and we go back inside. I fill her bowl with kibble and review Annie's note. I wasn't supposed to feed the dog that much food. Too late. She's wolfed down all but a few stray bits.

I brew a pot of coffee and rummage through the refrigerator. I'm no chef, but I can scramble eggs and fry bacon. After I finish cooking, I drain the grease from the skillet into the owl-shaped ceramic crock on the stove, the way Mama Libby taught me to do.

While I'm eating breakfast, Annie calls, and we make plans to visit Mama Libby in the hospital this afternoon. Annie mentions that some of our friends from high school are getting together for pizza and bowling tonight.

"You must come."

"I don't know..."

"Everyone wants to see you."

"I doubt that's true."

"I won't take no for an answer."

Annie hangs up before I can protest further. I rinse and put my dishes in the dishwasher and carry a load of laundry out to the garage. To reach the washer, I must squeeze past Papa Frank's Chevy Silverado. The summer after our sophomore year, Annie and I lost our mutual virginity in that pickup. A few months later, we froze our asses off in the middle of a blizzard, while I struggled to find the words to tell the girl I'd thought I was going to marry that I was gay. I didn't know what I was going to do if she rejected me. I needn't have worried. She kissed me on the cheek and whispered, "I'll always have your back."

I load and start the washing machine. Water streams across the floor. I pull the machine out from the wall. The cold-water hose has sprung a leak around the inlet valve. I attempt to tighten the connection. The hose splits. Water gushes out. I turn off the spigot.

Time to go to the hardware store. I check the fuel gauge on the lawn mower. Empty. I toss the gas can into the bed of the Silverado and find the keys hidden in their usual spot under a tray of fishing lures in Papa Frank's tackle box. The engine turns over. The warning light on the dashboard flashes. The pickup needs a tune-up.

Backing the Silverado out of the garage requires careful maneuvering, but once I'm on the road, I'm surprised by how well I find my way around the town. I follow Birch Lane to Main Street and turn left. Three blocks ahead on the right, I pull into the parking lot of the local hardware store.

As I step through the door, a bell overhead tinkles. I step around a carousel rack of seed packets and wander the cluttered aisles. Besides hardware and home improvement products, the store stocks firearms and ammunition, and hunting, fishing, and camping gear. I find and sort through their selection of hoses.

A fine Black man around my age—Demetrius, according to his name tag—asks if I need help. He stands a couple of inches shorter than me, perhaps six feet even, and wears his hair in a medium fade. His violet eyes and dazzling smile disarm me. I dig out the crumpled note with the model number of the hose I need from my pocket.

"I don't have that model in stock," Demetrius says. "But I can order one. In the meantime, this hose might do the trick." He shows me his suggestion.

"I'll give it a shot."

An adorable little Black girl runs up and tugs on Demetrius's pant leg. "Daddy, I'm thirsty."

"Let me finish helping this nice man, Cora, and I'll get you a juice box."

"Take care of your daughter," I say.

"Are you sure?"

"I'm in no rush."

I steal a surreptitious glance at the bulge in his crotch.

"I'll be right back."

Demetrius follows his skipping daughter through a door in in the rear of the store. He has a nice ass. And most likely, he's straight. I don't need to go down that road again. I sort through bins of rubber faucet washers until I locate the sizes I need.

"Sorry about that," Demetrius says. "Did you find everything okay?"

"Sure did."

I follow Demetrius to the cash register. He rings up my purchases. I hand him a twenty-dollar bill.

"You up from the city?"

"Is it that obvious?"

"I haven't seen you around town."

I share why I came home.

Demetrius's eyes widen. "You're the lost boy. I heard about your case when I was in middle school. Sorry about your mother."

I cringe inside.

"Tell Libby that Cora and I wish her a speedy recovery," Demetrius says. He must've noticed me checking out the dimple on his ring finger because he adds, "I'm divorced."

"I'm sorry."

"I'm not."

Demetrius hands me my change. That smile again. I can't tell if the guy's flirting or if I'm letting wishful thinking color my imagination. Not that it matters. He's out of my league.

When I leave the hardware store, I spot Kip across the street, arguing with a barefoot man wearing a stained tee shirt and dirty jeans. "Stay the hell away from me, you moron!" Kit shoves the homeless man to the ground. "My family bought your house fair and square."

That's no homeless man. That's Griffin Garfield. At a scrimmage game one afternoon in high school, Kit tackled Griffin so hard that he fell into a coma. When he woke up days later, he had the mental capacity of a child. To make matters worse, his medical bills bankrupted his family. The finance company foreclosed on their house, which Kit's parents purchased for a pittance at auction and gave to Kit and Annie as a wedding present. I rush across the street.

"What the hell do you think you're doing, Kit?"

"This doesn't concern you, Nowak."

I help Griffin onto his feet and ask if he's okay. From his furrowed brow, I gather he doesn't recognize me. I dust off his clothes. He shambles away, muttering under his breath.

"Put a uniform on white trash," Kit says, "and it still stinks."

"Take your best shot, golden boy." I stick out my chin. "It'll be your last."

A barrel-chested police officer with a salt-and-pepper crewcut approaches. Tattoos sleeve his powerful arms. "Is there a problem here, boys?"

"We're old high school buds," Kit says. "Ain't that right, Nowak?" He slaps me on the back and grins.

Too annoyed to speak, I nod.

"Nowak, huh? The lost boy. Heard you were in town."

Gossip travels fast.

"Chief Harris." He extends his hand, which I ignore. "Shame about your mother. I worked that case as a rookie."

"You boys let her killer get away."

"We might still close the case."

"I won't hold my breath."

Chief Harris lights a cigarette.

"You're with the NYPD now?"

I nod.

"What say we let bygones be bygones?"

Kit steps between us, sparing me from saying, or worse from doing something I might regret.

"I'm still waiting on that package you owe me, Chief," Kit says.

"Soon," Chief Harris says. He tips his cap. "You boys stay out of trouble."

CHAPTER FOUR

FOLLOWING an hour's drive through the mountains, Annie and I reach the hospital in Ellenville. Mama Libby looks smaller than the last time I saw her. I brush a stray wisp of gray hair off her face and kiss her cheek. "How're you feeling?"

"I'm lying in a hospital bed. How do you think I feel?"

"Can we get you anything, Mama Libby?" Annie asks. She straightens Mama Libby's pillows.

"Quit fussing over me like I'm an invalid."

"But you are an invalid," I say.

"Don't be a smart ass, boy." Mama Libby scrutinizes me. "You need a haircut."

"I know."

"How are you and Sparky getting along?"

"That dog needs obedience training."

"I spoil her rotten," Mama Libby says. "I can't help myself. After Frank passed away, that pup gave me a reason to get out of bed in the morning."

Despite being fiercely independent, Mama Libby married Papa Frank right out of high school. Unable to conceive, the newlyweds became foster parents and changed dozens of children's lives for the better. It's understandable that she would have a hard time coping with his loss. I should've been there for her. At least I'm here now.

"I borrowed Papa Frank's pickup."

"That Silverado was Frank's pride and joy," Mama Libby says. "Don't drink and drive."

"No, ma'am."

A baby-faced doctor who looks too young to have a medical degree strolls into the room.

"How are we feeling today, Elizabeth?"

"You and Nurse Ratched haven't killed me yet, Doogie Howser."

"I'd like to run another set of x-rays in the morning, Elizabeth." The doctor checks Mama Libby's vitals and scribbles notes on her chart. "If those look good, you can check out on Monday." He gets paged, and he excuses himself.

"We should get going," Annie says. "You need your rest."

"All I do here is rest."

A nurse pops her head into the room and announces in a singsong voice, "Time for your medications, Elizabeth."

"I've told these people a dozen times to call me Libby," Mama Libby says. "They don't listen. It's a miracle I'm not dead."

"Elizabeth, don't talk that way," the nurse says. "The medical personnel in this hospital are first-rate."

"Listen to the professionals, Mama Libby," Annie says. "So you can go home."

"I'll call you tomorrow," I say. I kiss Mama Libby on the cheek and follow Annie out the door.

WOODLAWN AVENUE RUNS ONE-WAY. I circle the block twice before I find a parking spot on Fox Hollow Road and walk two blocks to Maestro's Pizzeria. Annie waves from a large table in the rear of the restaurant.

"I'm meeting those losers," I tell the hostess.

Weaving my way through the bustling restaurant, I slide into the only open seat at the table. Kit slips his arm around Annie. I recognize Helena Potter with her wild curls piled atop her head by the spider tattoo crawling up her neck. She wears a loose black T-shirt cinched with a studded silver belt over black jeans. Next to her, Joe Farley, in his sports jacket and tie, sits with his arm around an Asian woman wearing a floral dress, whom I assume must be his wife.

Bo Satterlee sits sprawled back in his seat at the end of the table, wearing his signature flannel shirt and jeans. With his walnut-brown hair pulled back in a sleek ponytail, he looks even hotter than he did in high school, where he spent more time seducing cheerleaders under the bleachers than tackling opponents on the football field.

"Dude." Bo high-fives me. "Or should I say, Officer Dude?"

"Heard you have your own studio now, Bojangles."

"Guilty as charged."

Bo made passing grades, but he excelled in shop class. His furniture designs won statewide competitions.

"And Farley, the fisher cat. I can't believe you found a woman willing to put up with your shenanigans."

Joe Farley used to rally the crowds at our games, dressed as a fisher cat, our school mascot. The reclusive forest weasels reportedly inhabit the nearby woods, but I've never seen one.

"I'm a lucky fella, all right," Joe says.

"Farley the fisher cat." Kit scoffs. "More like Farley the fat cat."

Joe slouches in his seat. Kit can be such an asshole.

"I'm Suki," the Asian woman says.

Joe sits forward and grins. "Suki's an emergency services dispatcher."

I introduce myself.

"The lost boy," Suki says.

"I prefer Cal."

"I didn't mean—"

"I doubt you see much crime in Nyes Landing."

"A family of raccoons invaded the stockroom of the grocery store last month," Suki says. "It took our entire force of four officers and the chief an entire afternoon to bring the thieving fur balls to justice."

"I haven't had to fend off raccoons in the city . . . yet. But I once rescued an alligator from the sewer. I hope I never have to do that again."

The flustered young woman serving us asks if we're ready to order. We scan our menus.

"Let's get three large pies, a couple of pastas, and a salad," Kit says, "and share family style."

"I'm lactose-intolerant," Helena says. "I remind you every time we go out for dinner." She rolls her eyes. "I don't know how you do it, Annie." She smiles at the server. "I'll have the Italian wedding soup with no parmesan cheese."

"Bring us a pepperoni pie, a sausage and mushroom pie, and a fresh mozzarella and basil pie," Kit says, "the family-style spaghetti and meatballs, and a large house salad. And Helena's soup with no cheese . . . because she's lactose intolerant. But I'm sure you knew that."

No one else seems bothered that Kit ordered for us all.

"And three pitchers of beer," Kit says.

"A diet cola for me," Suki says. "I'm working the night shift."

"I've worked my share of those," I say. "They're rough."

"Speaking of rough, I can't imagine what you must've gone through when terrorists attacked the city last fall," Suki says.

Joe leans forward, eyes wide. "Were you working when . . . ?"

Every time I run into someone who wasn't in the city that dark day, I must relive the horror.

"My partner and I were patrolling the Lower East Side when the south tower fell." I take a deep breath. "We sped to the scene." The memories flood back. "It was like traversing a war zone. I could barely see through the debris. Then the north tower fell, and all hell broke loose."

"How awful," Suki says.

"Flyers with photographs of the missing plastered every spare wall space in the city. Most of them were never found."

"Did you lose anyone you knew?"

"No one from my precinct. But I attended enough officers's funerals to last me ten lifetimes. If I never hear 'Taps' played again, it'll be too soon."

An awkward silence falls over the table.

"Will there be anything else?" our server asks.

"I'll have a shot of Wild Turkey," Helena says. "And bring water for the table. We need hydration."

"And a round of tequila shots," Kit says. "So we can celebrate the second coming of the lost boy."

"A shot of Jameson's for me," I say. It's going to be a long night.

Our server scurries into the kitchen, scribbling on her pad.

A tan, blond guy escorts a striking woman with ebony hair and ruby lips through the door. The stylish couple look out of place in the rustic pizzeria. The woman smiles toward the rear of the restaurant where we sit. Her gaudy wedding ring glimmers. The man wears a wedding band as well. The hostess escorts the couple to a table by the window. The man takes a seat. The woman disappears down the hallway that leads to the restrooms.

"Nature calls," Bo Satterlee says. He goes to the men's room.

The tan, blond guy stares in our direction. Kit flips the guy the bird. The guy averts his eyes. Instinct, coupled with history, tells me Kit is having an affair with the guy's wife. Small-town drama. I feel bad for Annie.

Our server brings our tequila shots with a plate of lime wedges, rushes back to the bar, and returns with our pitchers of beer and other drinks. Given how busy she is, it's to her credit that she got our order correct.

"Bottoms up, Nowak," Kit says. He lifts his glass. "Your favorite position."

"You remembered," I say. "How sweet."

"Fuck you, asshole."

"I'm not into closet cases."

"Watch your step, Nowak—"

"Or what? I'll have to kick your ass again."

"Enough," Annie says. "Both of you." She pulls a prescription bottle from her purse and takes a pill with a sip of water.

A gaunt woman with hollow eyes and rotten teeth who could be anywhere from twenty to fifty stumbles through the door. A hush falls over the restaurant. The woman wears a stained halter top and faded jeans. Multiple earrings pierce her lobes. She shuffles over to our table.

"You and me need to talk, big bro."

"Not here, Jewel."

Kit takes Jewel by the arm and drags her through the restaurant, kicking and screaming expletives that would make a gangbanger blush. I recall Jewel being a precocious child who sold Girl Scout cookies in front of the grocery store. I ask what happened.

"Jewel met a boy who introduced her to crystal meth," Annie says. "We offered to pay for a drug treatment program, but she doesn't want our help."

Helena's soup and our house salad arrive. Suki passes around paper plates. I take a small portion. Annie serves Kit and herself and offers Helena the salad.

The woman with the ebony hair and ruby lips returns from the ladies's room, her face flushed, and her hair mussed. She smooths her skirt and takes her seat. Bo weaves his way through the crowd and slides into his chair. Lipstick blots his collar. If he's having sex with the woman, perhaps I'm wrong about Kit. But I don't think so.

Our pizzas and pasta arrive.

"They make the best meatballs here," Joe says.

"Leave a few for the rest of us," Kit says.

"I only took one."

"So far."

"How's the used car business, Joe?" I ask.

Joe launches into a story about an unstable woman who came into the dealership and demanded a free car. We laugh so hard at the way he describes her tantrum and mimics her shrill tone that other diners shoot us nasty looks.

"How long will you be in town, Nowak?" Kit asks.

"As long as Mama Libby needs me. You have a problem with that?"

"Yo, bitches!" Oakley Reeves shouts. He and Howie Clark swagger in our direction. The last time I saw those bullies they were gawky teenagers with bad acne and more brawn than brains. Led by Kit, they terrorized our high school. Anyone who stole their spotlight the way I did incurred their wrath.

"Heard you were in town, No Good," Oakley says. His sense of humor is as feeble as his intellect. He's aged well, though. Tall, lean, and with rugged yet boyish good looks.

"Who's bowling tonight?" Howie asks. Tall and husky, with broad shoulders, but weighed down by a flabby gut that overhangs his belt, the former tight end has gone to seed.

"Suki has to work," Joe says. "But I'll go."

"I can't bowl worth shit," Helena says. "But I'll tag along."

"Why not?" Bo says. "I don't have anything better to do."

"Are you going, Annie?" Howie asks.

"Hell yeah, we're going," Kit says. "I'm not about to miss the chance to kick Nowak's sorry ass."

"Bring it," I say. I haven't bowled in years, but I'm not about to let Kit best me.

Kit calculates how much we each owe, collects our money, and pays at the cash register up front. Annie, Helena, and Suki go to the ladies's room. Joe tells an off-color joke that reminds me of why we aren't closer. The woman with the ebony hair and ruby lips steps outside the diner and lights a cigarette. Kit follows her. They slip around the corner, out of sight.

Annie and Suki return.

"Helena is reading a woman's palm," Suki says.

"You don't buy into that mumbo-jumbo, do you?" Joe asks.

"It's harmless fun," Suki says.

I step outside the restaurant and overhear the woman with the ebony hair and ruby lips say, "Trevor doesn't understand why you're behaving this way."

"Your husband needs to leave me alone," Kit says. "Or he'll be sorry." The tan, blond guy steps outside. Kit shoves him. "Stay out of my face, Trevor."

The tan, blond guy, Trevor, climbs inside a blue SUV. "Let's go, Brandy."

"Fix this mess," Brandy says. She joins her husband in the SUV, and the couple drive away.

"What's going on, Kit?" I ask.

"None of your business."

"You better not hurt Annie."

"Says the man who broke my wife's heart."

CHAPTER FIVE

By the time I drag my ass out of bed Sunday morning, it's almost noon. My head pounds. I pad down the hallway to the bathroom and splash cold water on my face.

Sparky scratches on the door. I forgot about the dog again. I'm not used to taking care of anyone but myself, and I do a piss-poor job of that most of the time.

After I walk Sparky, I discover I'm out of coffee, so I drive into town and buy a fresh can from the grocery store. While I'm there, I order a loaded Italian sub from the deli counter for lunch and pick up a quart of the reddest strawberries I've ever seen.

On my way home, I stop at the liquor store and buy a bottle of Jameson. As I'm leaving, I spot Kit and Trevor arguing in the parking lot. Kit punches Trevor. Trevor stumbles backward into a red Mercedes coupe.

"You're pathetic," Kit says.

"Don't say that."

Kit hops behind the wheel of the Mercedes and burns rubber out of the parking lot. Trevor sinks onto his knees and wipes his bloody mouth on his sleeve. I consider asking if he's okay. But if I were him, I'd want to be left alone. So I take my whiskey and drive home.

After I walk and feed Sparky, I brew a pot of coffee. I pour a shot of the hair of the dog into my cup and call the hospital.

"About time," Mama Libby says. "My parole came through. I get released tomorrow afternoon." She rattles off a list of chores she needs me to do before she gets home. Her doctor interrupts our call. I assure her I'll take care of everything.

My Italian sub, which is loaded with layers of thin-sliced meats and cheeses and vegetables so fresh they crunch, might be one of the best sandwiches I've ever had, and the strawberries explode in my mouth. I save half of my lunch for later and review my list of chores. The first thing I should do is fix the washing machine and do my laundry.

Moses stops by the garage while I'm changing the inlet hose.

"Any word on when Elizabeth gets home, Carl?"

"Cal," I say. "She gets released tomorrow."

"What are you doing?"

I show Moses the split in the old hose I'm replacing.

"If I sat on the floor cross-legged the way you're doing," Moses says, "I wouldn't be able to get up."

Thunder rumbles in the distance.

"Storm's coming," Moses says. "When I was in Nam, it rained all the damn time."

I tighten the connection on the new hose and turn on the water. No more leaks.

"I should get going," Moses says. "Midnight will want her lunch."

"You have a dog?"

"Cat. And she's a cranky old cuss. I'll see you later, Carl."

"Cal."

I start the washing machine and return to the house, where I repair the leaky bathroom faucets and take a shower. By the time I'm dressed, Sparky needs to go for a walk again. While we're outside, we practice the sit command. After a few tries, the dog catches on that she'll earn a treat when she plops her butt on the ground.

Once I transfer my clothes from the washer into the dryer, I reward myself with a swig of whiskey and fill Sparky's bowl half-full of kibble. She wolfs down her lunch and curls up on her blanket. I take my bottle upstairs, climb into bed, and slip my hand down my pants.

Little paws that sound too heavy to be field mice scamper overhead. Probably squirrels. Pleasure will have to wait. I climb the rickety ladder into the attic, which is filled with boxes of toys and bags of clothing collected over three decades of caring for foster children; a steamer trunk full of quilts; a set of worn suitcases; a cracked globe piled atop a three-legged chair and a splintered headboard; a bent plastic Christmas tree stuffed inside a tattered cardboard carton; and several boxes marked "Christmas decorations." Forty years of junk collected over the course of a couple's lifetime.

A squirrel leaps out of a mountain of plush toys piled inside a faded blue crib. Another squirrel follows, and another. The chattering trio scampers up the wall and crawls outside through a hole in the rafters. Another repair I must make.

A familiar face smiles from atop the pile of plush toys— Chippy. Mama Libby kept my worn-out sock monkey all these years. My mom sewed him for me when I was a baby. He's sleeping with me tonight.

A stack of high school yearbooks catches my eye. I find mine —class of 1988. I only collected a handful of signatures. Annie wrote "Best friends forever" and dotted the *i* in her name with a little heart. I flip through the pages. A photograph of me atop the shoulders of my teammates after we won the game that earned us our berth at the state championships opens the athletics section. What a difference fourteen years makes!

The edge of a manilla envelope with my name scrawled on the

flap pokes out from under the stack of yearbooks. Inside, I find newspaper clippings with headlines like "Woman Stabbed to Death," "Mother of Two Assaulted in Own Trailer," and the most egregious, "Lost Boy Refuses to Talk." I didn't refuse. I couldn't speak for weeks after that awful night.

I stumble down the ladder, dash into the bathroom, and retch into the toilet bowl. Whiskey burns worse coming up than going down. Sinking to the floor, I hear the desperation in my mom's voice as she screams at me to run. See the glint of the knife that that monster butchered her with. The blood splattered white walls of the bedroom. So much blood.

CHAPTER SIX

ON MONDAY MORNING, I awake from a nightmare in which I'm lost in the woods and can't find my way home. My head pounds. My throat burns. I drink a pitcher of water from the fridge and call the hospital. Mama Libby answers on the first ring. "I get sprung from the joint this afternoon," she says. She shares the details of when and where I need to pick her up. I assure her I'll be on time.

After I walk and feed Sparky, I bring the quilts Mama Libby wants down from the attic and set them on her bed. With that done, I drive the Silverado to Clark's Automotive Repair. Howie stands beneath a car on a hydraulic lift, draining the oil pan.

"What the hell do you want, No Good?"

"The Silverado needs a tune-up."

"I'm booked solid."

"Your old man never turned Papa Frank away. But he was a professional."

"Give me a couple of hours, and I'll squeeze you in."

I figured if I intimated Howie's father was the better man, he'd change his tune. I toss him the keys and walk across Main Street at the light. Helena Potter sits hunched over a potter's wheel in the bay window of her gallery, shaping an unwieldy lump of wet clay with her fingers. She sees me and rushes outside.

"You have your own gallery, Helena. I'm impressed."

"I'm leasing while I save my pennies to buy the house," Helena says. "I live upstairs." She touches my cheek. "I'm worried about you," she says. "Your aura is so dark it's almost black. You may be in danger."

A self-professed psychic, Helena believes we all radiate colored energy fields, which most of us can't see. But you don't have to be psychic to predict danger surrounds a cop. I put my life on the line every day. I assure her I'll watch my back.

At the next corner, I turn right onto Warbler Lane and spot Earl's barber pole sandwiched between the pharmacy that's been on that corner for as long as I can remember and a discount furniture store. Upon entering the shop, I inhale the scent of menthol shaving cream and a citrusy aftershave.

Oakley Reeves occupies Earl's chair, dressed in his Nyes Landing cop uniform. Given what a delinquent the guy was in high school, I'm surprised he chose a career in law enforcement. Earl finishes shaving Oakley's neck and blows the loose hairs off his shoulders with a hand dryer. Oakley stands and admires his reflection in the mirror. He hands Earl a twenty dollar bill and tells him to keep the change. Spying me, he smirks.

"You find that badge in a box of Cracker Jacks, Reeves?"

"If you so much as jaywalk in this town, No Good," Oakley says, "I'll lock your smart ass up faster than you can say faggot. I don't care if you are a cop." He swaggers out the door.

"That asshole is going to push me too far one of these days—"

"Don't go stirring up trouble," Earl says.

"I won't if he won't."

"You boys need to grow up."

Earl's right. I know he's right. But that's easier said than done.

Earl brushes off his barber chair and tells me to have a seat. Once a legend on the football field, he's withered over the years.

Age spots mottle his trembling hands. I hope he doesn't nick my scalp.

"You're a good egg, Cal. I always thought you and Annabelle Leighton would get hitched."

"Yeah, well—"

"I know the score. You're a sissy boy. Ain't nothing wrong with that."

Earl means well, so I don't take offense.

"It was touch and go for a while as to which side of the law you'd end up on. What with that temper of yours."

Earl is not wrong about that.

"How're the mean streets of the Big Apple treating you?"

"Can't complain."

Of course, I could, but Earl respects cops. I wouldn't want to disappoint the old guy by sharing the shame of my administrative leave.

Earl clips and snips my thick, wavy brown hair into a squared-off crew cut and trims my beard. I pay and leave a generous tip for less than half of what a haircut in the city costs.

As I step outside, I run into Demetrius. In his tank top and running shorts, he looks even hotter than he did at the hardware store.

"How did that hose work out?" Demetrius asks.

"Like a charm. How's Cora?"

"Keisha picked her up last night."

I could drown in Demetrius's seductive violet eyes.

"Guess I'll see you around," I stammer.

"I hope so," he says.

By the time I reach the garage, Howie has the Silverado tuned up and ready to go. He even washed the exterior and vacuumed the cab. I ask how much I owe.

"I charge fifty bucks for a tune-up," Howie says. "But seeing as it's for Mama Libby, it's on the house. She and Papa Frank took good care of me and my brothers when our parents couldn't."

I slip three twenty-dollar bills into his fist. "Consider this a tip, then." I'm sure he could use the cash. And I saved more money working overtime after the terrorist attacks last year than I can spend on whiskey.

By the time I reach the hospital, Mama Libby is dressed and ready to go.

"I'll take that." I pry her suitcase from her fingers. "What about all these flowers?"

"Leave them for the next poor soul who gets stuck in this deathtrap they call a hospital."

"And the cards?"

"Trash."

An orderly arrives with a wheelchair.

"I can walk."

"The hospital won't allow you to do that," I say. "If you want to go home, sit."

"Fine." Mama Libby climbs into the wheelchair and smooths her skirt. "What are you waiting for, boy? An engraved invitation?"

The young orderly wheels Mama Libby down the hallway onto an elevator, ignoring her stream of gripes, and drops her off outside the hospital. I pull the pickup around and help her inside the cab.

On the drive home, Mama Libby wants to know if I'm taking care of myself. She thinks I look tired. She asks me if there's anyone special in my life. I tell her no. She doesn't like the thought of me being all alone in the world. I assure her I'm fine. She shares gossip like I know who she's talking about, which I don't, no matter how many times she insists I must recall so-and-so's cousin such-and-such. By the time we pull into the driveway, I'm in dire need of a shot of whiskey.

Sparky runs around the house, barking her head off. I lock the dog in the mudroom and help Mama Libby make her way upstairs. Of course, I brought down the wrong quilts from the attic. Mama Libby waits at the bottom of the ladder while I find the correct ones. She explains why she needs this particular pair, but I'm not listening. I'm obsessing over Demetrius. Even if I'm not imagining things, which I've done before, and the guy's gay or bisexual or whatever, he has a kid and an ex-wife, and that's messy.

Mama Libby announces she's hungry. I help her downstairs and toast her a bagel. While she eats, I take Sparky for a walk. When we return, I tell the dog to sit, and she does. I pass her a treat.

"You want to impress me," Mama Libby says, "teach that pup to feed and walk herself."

"If Sparky doesn't learn to behave, she's going to put you in the hospital again."

A petal falls off one of Mama Libby's orchid blossoms. She pokes her finger into the dirt in the pot and sighs. "Dry as a bone. It's lucky I got home when I did." She turns on the water and tests the temperature with her fingers. "Use lukewarm water. Never cold." She runs each orchid under the faucet for a few seconds and sets their pots in the sink to drain. "This beauty took first place at the flower show last fall." She holds up a plant with tall green stalks topped with candy-apple red flowers.

Someone knocks on the back door.

"Moses," Mama Libby says. "I haven't even been home for an hour."

"You want me to get rid of the old guy?"

"That would be rude. He worries about me."

I answer the door.

"Howdy, Carl," Moses says. "Is Elizabeth home?"

I don't bother correcting my name this time.

"Come in, Moses," Mama Libby says.

"I brought fried chicken and potato salad," Moses says. "I thought after spending a week in the hospital you might be hungry for some actual food."

"Bless you, Moses," Mama Libby says. "Have a seat. Cal, grab us some plates and forks."

Mama Libby says grace, and we dig in. Even cold, the chicken is crisp, and the potato salad bursts with flavor. I can't recall the last time I ate this good.

Moses and Mama Libby catch up on local gossip.

"There's this couple," I say. "Brandy and Trevor . . . I don't know their last name. Do you know who I'm talking about?"

"The Speedmans," Mama Libby says. "Snooty Californian winemakers. They bought a vineyard in the valley west of town."

I share my theory that Kit's having an affair with Brandy.

"That wouldn't surprise me," Mama Libby says. "Kit's a dog. And that Speedman woman is what my mama would've called a floozy."

"Now, Elizabeth," Moses says, "that's not nice."

"But it's the truth."

After we eat, Moses hobbles home to feed his cat and Mama Libby turns in for the night, saying she can't wait to sleep in her own bed. It's only nine o'clock, but I'm beat. I wash my face, brush my teeth, and gargle with a shot of whiskey.

Crawling under the sheets, I fantasize what Demetrius and me would do were he here.

CHAPTER SEVEN

A METALLIC CLANGING wakes me at the crack of dawn. I rush downstairs and find Mama Libby in the kitchen, clutching a skillet in her good hand. I pick up the pan's lid and a steel spatula off the floor and put them in the dishwasher.

"You like your eggs scrambled, right?" Mama Libby says.

"I should be waiting on you."

"I don't want you messing up my kitchen."

An egg slips from Mama Libby's grasp and breaks on the floor.

"Looks like you're doing a good job of that all by yourself."

I grab a paper towel and wipe up the gooey mess.

"Don't get smart with me, boy."

Mama Libby shoos me out of her way. Sparky whines and races in circles. I insist the dog sit while I slip on her harness. We step outside. Moses joins us on the lawn.

"Morning, Carl."

"Cal."

"How's Elizabeth?"

"Glad to be home."

"I'll bet." He glances up at the sky. "It's going to be a nice day."

"Looks like."

"Midnight would enjoy playing in the yard today, but I can't take the risk."

"What risk?"

"Last fall, she got bit by a tick and almost died from Lyme disease. She's better now. But it was touch and go for a while."

"I didn't realize cats got Lyme disease."

"It's rare, but it happens," Moses says. A whistle sounds. "Oh, shoot, I left the kettle boiling on the stove." He hustles upstairs as fast as his old legs can go.

Sparky does her business, and we go inside the house. I pass her a treat and pour myself a cup of coffee. Mama Libby passes me a plate of scrambled eggs and bacon with toast and tells me to have a seat. She joins me and says grace.

"The other night, I chased three squirrels out of your attic," I say. "There's a hole in the rafters."

"Maybe you can help me clean out the attic while you're home."

"I found an envelope filled with news articles."

"Oh, shoot. I forgot I left those up there."

"Why'd you save them?"

"You can't escape your past."

"Like I don't know that."

"There are facts in those articles you might not know . . . or remember."

"I doubt that."

"You're an adult now. Throw them away."

We finish eating in silence.

After I do the dishes, I help Mama Libby clear out the attic. She shouts at me to be careful from the bottom of the ladder. The floorboards might be rotten, and she doesn't want me stepping through the ceiling. I lug everything downstairs, so she can decide what she wants to keep and what she wants me to take to the dump. My yearbook, I set in my room, along with the manilla envelope. I take a swig of whiskey and eat a fistful of breath mints.

By the time I put everything Mama Libby wants to keep back in the attic and carry the junk she wants to get rid of out to the garage, it's midafternoon. I load the bed of the pickup and notice that I forgot to fill the gas can for the lawnmower. I'll do that while I'm out running errands.

A red AMC Pacer that must be at least twenty years old but looks brand new pulls into the driveway. A frazzled woman wearing cat-eye sunglasses tumbles out. An orange scarf covers her taupe curls. She strides across the front lawn in her lime-green tracksuit and bright white sneakers, cradling a little dog in her arms. I consider pretending I don't see the woman, but I do the right thing and go inside.

"Cal, come here, please."

I find Mama Libby seated in the living room with the woman from the Pacer.

"This is Gladys Crabtree. She and I went to school together when we were girls."

"We're still girls," Gladys says. She giggles. The little dog on her lap squirms. "This is Mr. Squiggles. He's a registered Pomeranian. His parents and grandparents were champions. He could've been a champion, too, but I didn't want to put my precious baby through the stress of competition."

Sparky sniffs Mr. Squiggles and wags her tail. Gladys shoos Sparky away. Sparky runs around the room barking.

"Did I ever have a scare the other night, Betty dear? I heard rustling in my backyard. So I peeked out the window, like any sane person would, and I caught this wild-eyed vagrant with shaggy hair and a bushy beard who looked like he hadn't bathed in years digging through my trash cans. I called the police—twice. That Mexican lady sergeant showed up at my door. Treated me like I was bonkers. Looked around the place for a few seconds, wrote a brief report, and left. If I get murdered in my sleep, it'll be her fault."

"Sergeant Jimenez is Puerto Rican," Mama Libby says. "Not Mexican."

"What's the difference?"

"Gladys, what you don't know could fill a book."

Sparky jumps on me. "Sit," I say. The dog plops her haunches down. I pat her head.

"I never thought I'd live to see that mongrel behave," Gladys says.

"Sparky is a smart dog," I say.

"If you say so," Gladys says. She turns to Mama Libby. "It's that Nye woman's fault. She leaves leftovers for the man on her back porch. Some people don't use the brains God gave them."

Oh no, she did not attack Annie. I'm about to go off on the woman.

"I hate to rush you, Gladys," Mama Libby says, "but my wrist hurts. I should lie down."

"What can I do to help?"

"Cal's here if I need anything."

"I suppose I should get going, then." Gladys doesn't move. "If you're sure there's nothing you need?"

"Run along now, Gladys."

"All right, Betty dear," Gladys says. She takes her time getting up. "Call me if there's anything I can do."

"Bye now." Mama Libby escorts Gladys out the door and locks the deadbolt. "That woman is living proof that there's no fool like an old fool."

———

IT TAKES me an hour to reach the waste management facility and thirty minutes to unload and sort all the junk into the appropriate bins. On my way home, an overturned tractor trailer on the two-lane state highway has traffic backed up for miles. I might as well be driving in the city.

By the time I return to Nyes Landing, dusk has fallen. Mama Libby asked me to pick up bread and milk on my way home. I turn into the grocery store parking lot and pull into a spot up front.

Mama Libby likes watermelon. Maybe I'll buy one for us to share. While I'm examining my choices, Demetrius rounds the corner and flashes his disarming smile. Why is the universe torturing me? He sorts through the bin and tosses me a melon. "This one will be juicy and sweet."

That's not the only thing that's juicy and sweet. I ask how he can tell.

"By that large patch of yellow rind."

Frozen pizzas, buffalo chicken wings from the fresh food section, and a six-pack of pale ale fill Demetrius's cart.

"Ever since the divorce, I've eaten like a teenage boy," Demetrius says. "As you can probably tell." He rubs his scant belly.

"That's nothing," I say. I lift my tee shirt. "I can pinch an inch. Guess I need the Special K diet."

Demetrius laughs at my lame sense of humor. We chat as we shop. He played football in high school, too.

"I remember when we faced off against you guys," Demetrius says. "You wiped the field with us."

"We rode a winning streak to the state finals that year."

He and I line up at the only cash register that's open.

"Do you like jazz?" he asks.

"Sure. Why?"

"There's a jazz festival in Woodstock this Saturday. I thought I might check it out." Demetrius unloads his cart onto the conveyor belt. The haggard cashier, who sounds like she's smoked three packs of cigarettes a day since she was twelve years old, rings up his items. He pays and smiles at me. "Maybe I'll see you there." I watch his ass stroll out the door.

What is Demetrius's deal? Was he inviting me to Woodstock? Should I go? Why do I care so much? I need to get laid.

Before going home, I stop at the gas station and fill the tank of the Silverado, and the gas can for the lawnmower. The Speedmans pull up to the pump behind me in their SUV.

Brandy steps out and slips her credit card into the payment slot. "You need to get over this," she tells Trevor, who sits slouched against the passenger door, his lip busted. His teary eyes look bloodshot. "Or get over me."

I am convinced Brandy and Kit are having an affair. And she and Bo Satterlee hooked up at the pizzeria. Mama Libby is right. The woman gets around. Not that I'm in any position to judge. But I'm not married. I suppose I am judging a little.

My cellular phone rings. Service is sporadic in and around Nyes Landing, but it works at the gas station. It's Annie. She sounds out of breath. "I baked a lasagna for Mama Libby's homecoming," she says. "I'd planned to bring it to her. But my mom and my monster-in-law are coming for dinner tonight. Is there any way you could stop by and pick up the dish?"

"Be there in a jiffy."

CHAPTER EIGHT

As I round the corner onto Hummingbird Lane, a gun shot rings out. I can't say for certain from which direction the sound came. Considering the town is surrounded by woodlands, someone is likely hunting who shouldn't be.

From the opposite end of the block, a woman screams. I floor the accelerator. A black SUV parked at the curb blocks my view of Annie's front door.

"She shot her husband!" a woman shouts.

I slam on the brakes and leap out, wishing I'd brought my Beretta. The heel of my boot snags on the curb. I tumble head-over-heels across the grass, scramble onto my feet, and rush up the porch steps. The front door isn't locked. I rush inside and find Annie sprawled on the floor, cradling Kit across her lap. Blood soaks her white bathrobe and pools on the blond hardwood floor. A wave of nausea washes over me.

"Help!" Annie cries. "Oh, God . . . do something!"

Pulling myself together, I take charge of the situation.

"Call nine-one-one!"

Annie scrambles for the phone. An engine on the street outside turns over. A dog barks. A vehicle speeds away.

Blood soaks Kit's pant leg. Images of the blood-splattered white walls of my mother's bedroom flash before my eyes. Willing myself to focus, I shuck off my tee shirt and press the garment over the wound. It looks like the bullet may've pierced the femoral artery. "Stay with me, Kit. Come on, man. You can't kick my ass if you're dead."

"An ambulance is on the way," Annie says. She paces the floor, wringing her hands and muttering, "This can't be happening."

Kit blanches. I fear I'm losing the guy.

"Help . . . the boy," Kit mutters, his voice a gurgled rasp.

"What boy, Kit?" I lean in closer. "Give me a name."

Kit's eyes roll back inside his head. He coughs up blood. Why are the paramedics taking so long? In the city, they'd be here by now.

Gladys Crabtree pokes her head through the door. "I warned everyone that she's unstable. But no one would listen."

Sirens wail in the distance. Dogs howl. The sirens draw closer. An ambulance speeds down the street. Tires screech to a stop. Lights flash through the open front door.

"In here officers!" Gladys Crabtree shouts from the porch. "She shot her husband!"

Kit tries to speak. I can't make out his words.

A stocky Latina officer with a buzz cut—Sergeant Jimenez, according to her name tag—charges through the door with her weapon drawn.

"Show me your hands!"

"He's bleeding out," I say. "I'm applying pressure to his wound."

"Do something, Sergeant." Annie sobs. "Please!"

"Everybody remain calm," Sergeant Jimenez says. "Paramedics will arrive at any second." She crouches beside Kit. "Hang in there, buddy. Help is on the way."

Kit's eyes glaze over.

"Stay with us, buddy." Sergeant Jimenez says. She cinches her belt around Kit's thigh.

A husky Black female police officer barges through the door with her weapon drawn. "Is there anyone else in the house?" Annie shakes her head. The officer advances upstairs.

"Are you armed?" Sergeant Jimenez asks.

I shake my head. The sergeant glances at Annie.

"We don't keep guns in the house," Annie says. "Kit owns a hunting rifle, which he leaves locked up in our cabin on the lake. We'd planned to go camping next—"

Kit emits an aborted snort and falls slack in my arms. The light leaves his eyes. Annie hugs her husband's limp body and begs him to wake up.

Oakley Reeves—Officer Reeves, rather—lopes through the door with his weapon drawn. His jaw drops. Officer D. Lecoq, according to his name tag, follows. The prematurely balding young cop with his bushy mustache holsters his weapon and pulls a pad and pen from his pocket. He scrutinizes the room through his thick black glasses.

"Reeves! Lecoq!" Sergeant Jimenez shouts. "Secure the perimeter." She radios for Harris. He doesn't respond. "Where the heck is the chief?"

Sirens shriek down the street. Brakes screech. Doors slam. Two paramedics rush inside the house. "Step back," the older paramedic says. He crouches over Kit and checks his vitals. The younger paramedic with the lazy eye looks on. The older paramedic shakes his head.

Annie releases a gut-wrenching wail. I enfold her in my arms. She sobs into my shoulder.

"You're with the NYPD?" Sergeant Jimenez asks.

"That's right."

"What happened here?"

As calmly as I can, considering that moments ago a guy I've known most of my life died in my arms, I share what I heard when I drove up, followed by what I witnessed upon entering the house. I take a deep breath and recount the facts of what happened in the moments after that to the best of my rather fuzzy recollection.

"Who is this boy he mentioned?" Sergeant Jimenez asks.

"I have no clue."

Sergeant Jimenez asks Annie the same question. She shrugs. The sergeant asks what happened before I arrived on the scene.

"I had a migraine," Annie says. "So, I took a pill and went upstairs to get dressed. While I was in the shower, I heard a loud bang. I thought a car had backfired. Then, the back door slammed, which alarmed me. I threw on my robe and ran downstairs, where I found . . . I'm going to be sick." She dry heaves.

Chief Harris arrives on the scene wearing a sweatsuit and sneakers. His hair is damp. "I came straight from the gym as soon as I heard."

Sergeant Jimenez catches the chief up to speed.

Officer Lecoq rushes through the door. "The woman next door says Mrs. Nye shot her husband."

"But when I pressed her further," Officer Reeves says, following his partner inside, "she admitted that she heard the gunshot, but did not see the shooter."

"The Crabtree woman was not on the scene when I arrived," I say.

"What are you doing here?" Chief Harris asks me. I explain. He grunts. "I'm detaining you until we figure out what went down tonight. Reeves, place NYPD in a squad car. Handcuffs won't be necessary . . . yet."

"With pleasure," Officer Reeves says. He shoves me out the door. Yellow crime scene tape surrounds the yard. I stride across the lawn and climb into the rear of the squad car when he opens the door. Although I have nothing to hide, I keep my mouth shut.

Gladys Crabtree watches from her porch swing. She has a

bowl of popcorn balanced on her lap. Mr. Squiggles prances around her feet.

Chief Harris steps outside onto Annie's porch. "If Mrs. Nye shot her husband, there must be a weapon on the premises."

"She murdered him all right!" Gladys hollers.

"Humor the old bat, Lecoq," Chief Harris says. "Take her statement."

Officer Lecoq approaches Gladys. She seems more than happy to share her opinions. He frantically scribbles on his pad.

"We searched the yard front and back," Officer Reeves says, "and combed the woods behind the residence."

"Search again," Chief Harris says. "Especially the woods."

Officer Reeves shrugs and shuffles off, fanning his flashlight across the grass and under the shrubbery that borders the house.

Sergeant Jimenez leads Annie outside wearing a tee shirt and jeans. The plastic trash bag the sergeant clutches in her fist likely contains Annie's blood-soaked robe. The sergeant tosses the bag into the trunk of her squad car and helps Annie into the back seat.

It makes sense that Annie and I would be prime suspects. We were found at the scene, covered in the victim's blood. But Kit had already been shot by the time I arrived, and I refuse to believe Annie pulled the trigger. So who did? And who is this mysterious boy Kit asked us to help?

"Where the hell is Washington?" Chief Harris shouts.

The husky Black female officer rushes outside. "The upstairs rooms are clear."

"Guard the front door, Washington," Chief Harris says. "No one goes in or out without my authorization."

"Yes, sir."

I've stood guard at many crime scenes, but I've never worked a murder investigation. I'm itching to assist, but this isn't my jurisdiction, and, like it or not, I'm incriminated.

A late-model Cadillac pulls up to the curb. A petite woman

with silver hair steps out and straightens the skirt of her navy-blue suit. "What on God's green earth is going on?" she asks in a calm, measured tone that commands attention. "Oakley?"

"Mrs. Nye," Officer Reeves stammers. "I'm afraid—"

"You should have a seat, Mrs. Nye," Chief Harris says.

"I don't want to sit down, Chief. Tell me what is going on. Where is my son?"

A Volkswagen Beetle rumbles up and parks across the street. A buxom blond woman in her fifties, wearing a floral sundress and sandals and carrying a shiny pink tote bag, steps out. I recognize Nadine Leighton, Annie's mom. She charges across the lawn.

Sergeant Jimenez intercepts Nadine. "You need to step back, ma'am. This is a crime scene."

"What did that man do to my daughter?" Nadine asks.

"Calm down, ma'am."

"Don't tell me to calm down. I demand to see my daughter."

"Your daughter is being detained for questioning, ma'am."

"Where's my son?" Mrs. Nye asks.

"I'm afraid he's been shot, ma'am," Chief Harris says.

"But he's all right?"

Chief Harris takes off his cap and lowers his eyes. The shriek that erupts from Mrs. Nye rips through me like a bullet. She collapses in Oakley's arms. No matter what I thought of Kit, he didn't deserve to die.

CHAPTER NINE

CHIEF HARRIS CLIMBS inside the squad car and tosses me a blanket. I had forgotten I'd taken off my shirt and am covered in blood. On the drive downtown, the chief attempts to engage me in banter, no doubt hoping I'll incriminate myself. I ignore his questions or answer I don't recall.

When we reach the Nyes Landing police station, officers lead Annie and me toward separate interview rooms. Before we part ways, I whisper in her ear not to say anything without her lawyer present.

"You're a cop, yet you advise Mrs. Nye not to cooperate with our investigation?"

"I didn't advise her not to cooperate. I told her to wait for her attorney. I know how these interviews go down."

The chief leads me inside a drab gray room. Three metal chairs surround a folding table that's shoved against the wall.

"Have a seat," Harris says. "I'll be back." He shuts the door on his way out.

The acrid scent of blood stimulates a bitter tang on my tongue. I need a shower. I take a seat and stare at the walls, wondering who could've shot Kit. Perhaps Trevor Speedman pulled the trigger in a fit of jealous rage, or one of the Garfields sought revenge for losing their home. And Gladys Crabtree spotted a homeless man lurking around the neighborhood and claims Annie leaves food out for the guy. Perhaps he bit the hand that feeds him.

Chief Harris returns. "Sorry to keep you waiting. We don't catch many violent crimes in Nyes Landing. An occasional hunting accident, but nothing serious. Not since—" He stops short of mentioning my mother's case, but we both know what he's thinking. He takes a seat across from me. "Walk me through everything that happened after you arrived at the Nye residence."

I recount the same facts that I told Sergeant Jimenez. The chief asks several questions that sound worded to trip me up. I stick to the truth. After several failed attempts to get me to contradict myself, he moves on.

"You didn't see Mrs. Nye shoot her husband?"

"Annie didn't shoot Kit."

"Were you there?"

"No."

"So you don't know if she shot her husband or not."

"I know Annie."

"That's not how this works." Chief Harris glances over his notes. "You were a dinner guest of the Nyes?"

"Annie asked me to pick up a lasagna she baked for Mama Libby."

"How is Mrs. Goodman?"

"Glad to be home."

"I'll bet." Chief Harris studies me for a moment. "You and Mr. Nye have butted heads in the past."

"Kit had already been shot by the time I arrived on the scene."

"So you say."

"I attempted to save Kit's life, but he'd lost too much blood."

"Were you armed?"

"I left my Beretta locked up in my room at Mama Libby's house."

"When was the last time you discharged your weapon?"

"A little over a week ago, at the firing range."

"Mind if I swab your hands for residue?"

"Be my guest."

Chief Harris opens a testing kit and slips on a pair of plastic gloves. "You must've seen some shit when those rag heads attacked the city."

"All in a day's work."

"You boys are heroes in my book."

Chief Harris swabs the sides of and webbing between my fingers and places the samples in labeled vials he seals inside an envelope. "I'll send your samples to the laboratory."

"Do what you have to do, but you're wasting time."

Chief Harris leans back in his chair and studies me. "I'm not so sure about that."

"Am I being detained?"

"You're free to go. I know where to find you if I have follow-up questions. Which I'm sure I will."

I emerge from the interview room and find Nadine speaking with a slight gentleman with wavy salt-and-pepper hair, wearing a navy-blue suit and tie. She rushes over and hugs me.

"Cal! Am I ever glad to see you. Annie's a wreck. Who would do this?"

Half the county despised Kit, and the other half feared him, but I keep those thoughts to myself.

"Daniel Fields," the gentleman in the suit says. He extends his hand. "I'm Annie's attorney." We shake.

Sergeant Jimenez rushes through the door and charges down the hallway. Chief Harris steps out of his office. Sergeant Jimenez shares an update on the crime scene. I sidle closer and eavesdrop on their conversation.

"No sign of the murder weapon," Sergeant Jimenez says.

"You searched the woods behind the residence?"

"Twice."

"It must be there."

"Two detectives and an investigator from Kingston are working the crime scene now."

"This is our case. Make that clear."

"Yes, sir."

"Anything else?"

"The shot passed through the victim's thigh and lodged in the wall. Detectives recovered a .45 caliber bullet and shell casing."

"That narrows our search."

"Not by much."

"My money's on the wife or the lost boy. NYPD has a short fuse."

"Looks like the Nyes were getting ready for dinner. We found two pans of lasagna in the oven."

"That tracks with NYPD's story."

Annie emerges from the ladies's room. She looks ghostly pale. I fear she might faint. She hugs me and cries on my shoulder. I wrap my arms around her and pat her back.

Daniel leads us outside. "Don't talk to anyone about the case," he tells Annie. "Especially not the media."

Annie nods.

"Should you find yourself in need of my services, Officer Nowak." Daniel passes me his business card.

"Come on, sweetheart," Nadine says. "Let Mommy take you home." She passes me her realtor business card. "Annie is staying with me in Kingston."

Daniel Fields offers me a ride to the Silverado. His SUV smells brand-new. He lays a plastic trash bag across the seat, so I don't get blood on the fabric. I draw my blanket around my shoulders and climb inside. Daniel agrees that Annie is innocent, but he doesn't have a clue who shot Kit. Nor can he imagine how anyone fled the scene of the crime without being noticed. Gladys

Crabtree strikes us both as the sort of neighbor who doesn't miss a trick.

When I get home, I find Mama Libby pacing the floor. "I can't believe Annie shot Christopher," she says.

"Annie didn't shoot Kit. But someone did."

"You're covered in blood."

"After I take a shower, I'll share what I know."

"Hold on." Mama Libby retrieves a plastic bag from the kitchen. "Put your clothes in this."

She leaves me alone. I strip down to my underwear and bag my clothes. Trudging upstairs, I knock back a swig of whiskey and climb into the shower. Blood streams off me and swirls down the drain. It's like I'm watching that monster plunge a knife into my mother's chest all over again. I lean against the tiles and breathe until the darkness passes. I'll get lectured for wasting hot water, but I don't mind. Being scolded by Mama Libby feels like home. I get dressed and join her in the kitchen.

"I brewed us a pot of chamomile tea," Mama Libby says. "If I drink coffee this late, I'll be up all night."

I doubt I'll sleep, no matter what I drink. I've witnessed my share of violence, my mother's murder being the most egregious example. But before tonight, I've never held anyone in my arms while the light left their eyes. I replay those frantic final moments over and over in my mind, wondering what I could've done differently.

"How're you holding up?" Mama Libby asks.

I shrug and share the facts.

"Are you sure he said, 'help the boy'?"

"That's what I heard."

"I wonder who he could've meant."

"Who knows if he even knew what he was saying?"

"Poor Annabelle. She's such a gentle soul."

"Annie is tougher than she appears."

"Between you and me," Mama Libby says, "I'm surprised someone didn't shoot that little snot before now."

Moses knocks and enters. "I hope I'm not intruding," he says. "I heard there was a shooting tonight."

On autopilot by this point, I share what I know.

"A member of my platoon died in my arms in Nam," Moses says. "You never get over an experience like that."

"We were about to turn in, Moses," Mama Libby says. "You should run along now."

Mama Libby shoos Moses out the back door. He apologizes for bothering us. Mama Libby locks the door and goes upstairs to bed. I rinse our cups, turn out the lights, and follow her.

Alone in my room, I knock back a swig of whiskey and savor the burn, chug another and another, and tumble into bed, hoping I don't have nightmares.

CHAPTER TEN

Wednesday morning, I wake up from a restless sleep to the phone ringing and scramble to answer before my voicemail picks up.

"I'm sorry to bother you so early."

"That's okay, Nadine." I sit up and rub my eyes. "Is everything okay?"

"Annie needs her medications. I would get them myself, but I don't want to leave her alone."

"I'm on it."

"You're the best."

Pans clang in the kitchen. Mama Libby must be awake. I hustle downstairs.

"You're up early," Mama Libby says.

"Annie needs her medications."

"Eat your breakfast first."

"I'm fine with coffee."

"Annie's waited this long." Mama Libby passes me a plate of scrambled eggs and sausage links. "Toast is coming."

There's no point in arguing, and I am hungry, so I take a seat.

Mama Libby says grace, and we dig in. I tell her about the confrontation I witnessed in the parking lot of the liquor store.

"I'll bet you're right," Mama Libby says. "Kit's having an affair with that Speedman woman. But I can't imagine Trevor pulling the trigger."

"Me either," I say. "And if he did, how did he flee the scene without anyone noticing?"

"If Gladys saw anything suspicious, the whole town would've heard about it by now."

After breakfast, Mama Libby asks me to stop by the grocery store and pick up a dozen eggs while I'm out. "White is fine. Don't pay an extra dollar for the brown ones. They come from the same place."

When I pull up before Annie's house, two detectives from the sheriff's department are rummaging through the front hedges. Officer Washington intercepts me before I reach the yellow crime scene tape. I identify myself. She hands me a brown paper bag. "I was told to give you this."

"How's the investigation going?" I ask.

"I'm not at liberty to discuss the details of the case," Officer Washington explains by rote. She glances over her shoulder before whispering, "They haven't found shit." She smiles. "You didn't hear that from me."

"Hear what?"

Officer Washington laughs. "I like you." She slaps me on the back, so hard that she knocks me off balance.

I climb inside the pickup and sift through the contents of the bag. Librium—10 mg four times daily for anxiety; Maxalt—10 mg as needed for migraines; Ambien—10 mg as needed for sleep; birth control pills; several herbal supplements—valerian root, passionflower, and St. John's wort; a bottle of lavender aromatherapy extract. That's a lot of medications.

An uneventful half-hour's drive later, I pull up before Nadine's two-story cottage in Kingston, with its pink wood siding trimmed in green. Evening primroses border the porch. Hydrangea bushes encroach on the steps.

Nadine answers the door before I ring the bell. "You're a saint, Cal."

"I don't know about that."

Nadine invites me inside. Throws and pillows in a myriad shades of pink from bubblegum to fuchsia accent floral-printed furnishings. China ballerinas pirouette atop the mantel.

"How is Annie?"

"She's a mess, but that's understandable. Right now, she's resting. Would you like coffee?"

"If it's not too much trouble."

"No trouble at all," Nadine says. I follow her into the kitchen. "Annie did not shoot Kit," she says. "I know my daughter."

I'm inclined to agree. But if I've learned anything from working in law enforcement, it's to never make assumptions. Wait until all the facts are in before you draw conclusions.

"Annie sure does take a lot of medications."

"She's been struggling with mood swings for some time now," Nadine says. She pours water into the tank of the coffeemaker and scoops ground coffee into the filter. "Her doctor put her on Librium, which makes her nauseous. But after what she's been through, I'm not about to—"

"Mom?" Annie hollers.

"Coming, sweetheart," Nadine says. "Excuse me." She goes upstairs.

If Annie didn't shoot Kit, who did? And how did they flee the scene unnoticed? I need an inside source on the local force. Oakley Reeves won't do me any favors. Officer Washington confided in me earlier, but I'm unsure of her level of involvement in the case. Same with Officer Lecoq. Sergeant Jimenez seems to be the most on the ball. If only I could draw her out.

Wandering into the living room, I settle into an overstuffed armchair and, while I have cellular service, I check in with my partner.

"I convinced our suspect not to press assault charges," Tran says.

"Assault, my ass. That prick got what he deserved."

"Do you want to lose your badge, Nowak?"

Tran's right. I let my anger get the best of me that day. "It won't happen again," I say. I'll try to keep that promise, but it won't be easy.

"How's small-town life?"

I tell Tran about Kit dying in my arms and the fallout since.

"You're shitting me."

I hear footsteps on the stairs. "Listen, I need to go. Stay safe."

"You, too."

Nadine and Annie shuffle into the room, arm in arm, and sink onto the sofa. Annie's bloodshot eyes appear dull. Her hair hangs limp. She does not look well.

"Let me fix you a cup of tea, sweetheart," Nadine says. She leaves the room.

"I feel like I'm living inside a nightmare and can't wake up," Annie says. "I spoke to my best girlfriend, Zelda, last night. You remember her?"

"Who could forget Zelda with her neon hair and eclectic fashion sense? Whatever became of her?"

"She moved to San Diego and became a travel writer. She's in Thailand right now, so she won't make it back for Kit's funeral."

"I have to ask you—"

"I didn't ... I wouldn't ... I hate guns."

"Can you think of anyone who have a vendetta against Kit? Have you seen or heard anything suspicious? Received any threatening letters or calls? Think hard."

"I don't know anyone who would—" Annie covers her mouth with her hand. Tears spill down her cheeks.

Nadine sails into the room, balancing three cups and saucers on a silver tray, which she sets on the coffee table. "Here we go." She passes Annie her cup of tea and a box of facial tissues. I help myself to a cup of coffee.

"I spoke with the medical examiner's office," Nadine says. "The bullet pierced his femoral artery."

"That explains why he bled out so fast."

"The coroner ruled it a homicide," Nadine says. "As soon as he signs the death certificate, they'll release the body."

Annie bursts into tears and rushes out of the room.

"I should go." I set down my cup.

"Thanks for bringing Annie her medications."

"If the police don't catch the killer, I will," I say with more certainty than I feel. I've never even guarded a murder scene before, much less solved a case. But I scored in the top percentile of applicants on my detective's exam, so I must have some skills.

———

ON THE DRIVE back to Nyes Landing, I pull over and halt traffic while a mallard and her ducklings waddle across the highway. When I reach town, I buy eggs from the grocery store and drive home. As I pass Turtle Park, I spot Demetrius walking a chubby black-and-white puppy who looks like a pit bull mix. I pull over.

"Cute puppy," I say. "What's his name?"

"Flower. Cora named him after the skunk in *Bambi*."

"Hello, Flower." The puppy licks my face.

"I heard you had a rough night," Demetrius says.

"That's an understatement."

"Any idea who shot Christopher Nye?"

"Only vague hunches."

Flower runs in circles around us. Our legs become tangled in his leash. We laugh and extricate ourselves.

"Flower starts obedience classes tomorrow," Demetrius says. "Here in the park. Don't you, buddy?" Flower barks.

"Mama Libby's dog needs obedience training."

"I've met Sparky and you're right. You should bring her."

"I might do that."

Demetrius shares the details.

Griffin Garfield cheers for a group of young boys playing soccer nearby. The ball rolls in his direction. He kicks the ball back and joins in the game.

"Hey!" Chief Harris leaps up from the bleachers. "What do you think you're doing, huh? Step back."

"I was only—"

"You're making these boys uncomfortable," Chief Harris says. "Move along. Or I'll arrest you for disorderly conduct."

"I want to play," Griffin says.

Chief Harris charges toward Griffin. "Get lost."

Griffin turns and shuffles away, muttering under his breath.

Chief Harris tosses the ball to a little boy with ginger hair and freckles and sends the kid back onto the field with a pat on the rump.

"I need to get back to the store," Demetrius says. "Maybe I'll see you and Sparky at class tomorrow." He smiles, and I forget where I am for a moment. What is my problem?

I join Chief Harris on the bleachers. He offers me a cigarette. I decline. He lights up, takes a puff, and exhales smoke rings. "Did Frank Goodman own any firearms?"

"He did," I say. "But I haven't noticed any guns around the house. Mama Libby may have sold or given them away."

"Ask her, would you?"

"Why?"

Chief Harris receives a page. "Don't skip town," he says, and he gets in his squad car and drives away.

———

When I get home, I find Mama Libby planting tomato seedlings with her good hand. I plop down and help. She replants the seedling I put in the ground. Taking the hint, I sit back and watch her work.

Mama Libby plants the last of the seedlings and says, "I don't know about you, but I could use a cold drink." I help her onto her feet. She shuffles inside the house.

The lawn needs mowing. I peel off my tee shirt so I can get some sun while I work and crank-start the mower. Leveling row after row of the tall grass imbues me a sense of accomplishment. By the time I'm finished, it's late afternoon.

When I step inside the kitchen, Mama Libby passes me a glass of cold lemonade, which I chug in one gulp. "I'll fix you a sandwich," she says

"You don't need to wait on me."

After I wash the grass and dust off my hands and forearms, I slather mustard onto two thick slices of bread, and pile on slices of ham and cheese. To avoid a lecture about the importance of eating my vegetables, I add a crisp lettuce leaf and a slice of ripe tomato. Grabbing a bag of chips from the counter, I take a seat at the table.

"Annie didn't kill Kit," Mama Libby says. "I'm as sure of that as I am that the sky is blue."

"Finding the murder weapon will exonerate her."

"Lord knows, plenty of folks have issues with the Nyes."

"Perhaps Brandy Speedman shot Kit."

"Brandy may be a tramp, but I don't think she's a killer."

"Me either. How about the Garfields?"

"The Garfields are not the only family the Nyes have screwed over. Lots of folks bear grudges."

"What about Jewel Nye?"

"That poor, lost soul. She's strung out, but I've never known her to get violent."

"We're speculating. We need facts."

"You're on vacation," Mama Libby says. "Let the police do their job."

"Time is running out."

"Chief Harris is a good man and Sergeant Jimenez is sharp as a tack. They'll catch whoever pulled the trigger."

"Do you still have Papa Frank's guns?"

"Why?"

"Chief Harris asked me to find out."

"I gave the rifles to Howie Clark and his brothers. Those boys had so much fun going hunting with Frank."

Fearing the woods, I never hunted with Papa Frank, and he never pressed the issue.

"But I keep Frank's revolver in my nightstand drawer."

CHAPTER ELEVEN

A SHRILL YELP, followed by a loud thud, interrupts my shower on Thursday morning. I tug on a pair of sweatpants and rush downstairs. Mama Libby sits in the middle of the kitchen floor, holding her injured wrist over her head. "I'm fine," she says, dismissing my concern. I help her onto her feet.

"What happened?" I ask.

"I wasn't looking where I was going and tripped over Sparky."

"Demetrius from the hardware store told me there's an obedience class that starts this afternoon in the park."

"If you think you can teach that pup to mind," Mama Libby says, "be my guest."

I help Mama Libby into a chair. "What would you like for breakfast?"

"A bowl of cornflakes."

"You don't want eggs and bacon?"

"I'm not that hungry."

"Suit yourself. But that's what I'm having." I set the skillet on the stove, turn on the burner, and take the carton of eggs and the slab of bacon out of the refrigerator.

"If you're going to make a mess of my kitchen, you might as well fry me an egg while you're at it."

"Yes, ma'am."

As I suspected, Mama Libby only asked for cereal because she didn't want me cooking. I take care not to spill anything. When I finish, I wipe down the stove and counter and wash the skillet.

After breakfast, Mama Libby asks me to drive her to the farmers market. Knowing there's a killer on the loose, I strap on my Beretta, which I conceal beneath a bulky sweatshirt. I help Mama Libby climb into the Silverado. She directs me to the Kiwanis Club on the north side of town. Two dozen stalls selling local vegetables, fruits, meats, cheeses, and other foodstuffs line the perimeter of the parking lot.

Mama Libby leads me over to a stall that sells honey with and without the comb. Bees swarm around a crude wooden hive, which rests atop a table that's stacked with jars of canned goods. I swat one of the pesky insects away from my face. The rangy woman behind the counter with the white bob wears a bib apron over a red tracksuit; the squat woman beside her with the messy gray curls wears a faded Save the Whales tee shirt with khaki shorts. From the way they're finishing one another's sentences, I assume they're a couple. They offer the young couple ahead of us in line tastes of their various jam flavors. They also sell several varieties of pickles. Mama Libby introduces me when our turn comes. The taller woman is Trixie, and the shorter is Rose.

"Have you heard?" Trixie says. "Someone shot Christopher Nye.

"Kit died in Cal's arms," Mama Libby says.

"Oh dear," Rose says. "Have they caught the killer?"

"No," I say, swatting another bee away from my face. "But they will."

"I won't rest easy until they do."

"I'll take a pint of honey with the comb," Mama Libby says.

"Our jams are on sale," Trixie says. "We harvested a bountiful crop of berries last season."

"I put up more jam last fall than I can eat," Mama Libby says. She hands Rose a ten-dollar bill and takes her change.

Trixie passes me the jar of honey in a paper bag. "Nice to meet you, Cal."

"It was a pleasure meeting you ladies," I say, thankful they didn't bring up my mother.

Mama Libby inspects the tomatoes from several vendors's stalls before she finds one that meets her standards. She buys onions and potatoes as well.

"Shot him in cold blood," a familiar voice says. I turn around. Gladys Crabtree stands before a captive audience. "I witnessed the whole affair."

"For heaven's sake." Mama Libby strides before the crowd. "Gladys heard the shot, but she did not see who pulled the trigger. No one did. But it wasn't Annie Nye. I'm certain of that."

"You weren't there, Becky Goodman."

"Cal witnessed more than you did," Mama Libby says.

"I live next door to the Nyes."

"Kit died in Cal's arms."

"I know what I know."

"Don't listen to this old fool," Mama Libby says.

"What did you call me?"

"You heard me, Gladys. I didn't stutter." Mama Libby turns to me. "Let's get out of here."

"She may not have pulled the trigger, but mark my words," Gladys shouts after us, "The Nye woman killed her husband."

Mama Libby takes a deep breath and continues walking. "That old fool is lucky that I have a broken wrist."

———

When Mama Libby and I get home, we follow a trail of fabric scraps into the kitchen. Sparky lies curled up on one of Mama Libby's quilts, which she has chewed holes through.

"That's it, pup," Mama Libby says. "You're going to school. God help your poor teacher."

After I shower and brush my teeth, I rub hair wax on my fingers and comb them through my crewcut and put on a clean tee shirt and jeans. I hustle Sparky into the Silverado and drive to the park.

Demetrius stands chatting with a swarthy man in his fifties who's struggling to control a miniature schnauzer. Flower bounds around their feet. Three women wearing sundresses and sandals fuss over their pets.

Sparky tugs on her leash and barks her head off. I tell her to sit. She ignores me. I massage her ears. She yawns and calms down.

"You came," Demetrius says. He smiles and crouches. "Hello, Sparky." Sparky gives Demetrius kisses—lucky dog.

Flower chases Sparky's tail. The two dogs tumble around on the ground, growling and nipping at one another. Flower rolls onto his back. Sparky licks the wiggling puppy's belly.

A pale woman with ginger hair and freckles introduces herself as Penny Miller. She collects our payments in cash and suggests we share our names and the names of our pets. Going around the circle, we meet Raj and Pongo the schnauzer, Linda and her floppy-eared mutt, Biscuit, Sally and Ollie the wiener dog, and Miranda and her toy poodle, Coco. I pet Sparky to keep her calm, while Penny explains what we can expect from the classes.

For the next thirty minutes, I tug Sparky around the lawn in a figure eight formation, telling her to heel, while she ignores my commands. The rest of the class struggles too. But they didn't work in the canine unit. I should be better at this. I find a couple of dog biscuits in my pocket, which I show to Sparky. She trots around the course with her shoulder aligned with my knee, and we end class on a high note.

Demetrius walks Sparky and me to the Silverado. Flower plops down on the grass and closes his eyes.

"Somebody's sleepy," I say.

"It's past his nap time," Demetrius says. "Sparky caught on fast."

"She's a whore for treats."

I open the passenger door. Sparky leaps inside the pickup.

"I should get going," Demetrius says. He scoops up Flower. "Perhaps I'll see you in Woodstock Saturday night." He smiles and walks away. What is his deal? Maybe I should go to the concert and find out.

While I have cellular service, I call Mama Libby. She's been working in her garden and hasn't had time to cook. I suggest takeout. She agrees.

Turning right onto Main Street, I drive a few blocks and pull into the parking lot of the Jukebox Junction. The landmark burger joint maintains its original 1950s vibe—red vinyl booths and chairs, a white Formica counter lined with red vinyl stools, and a black-and-white checkered linoleum floor. The jukebox spins 45-rpm records like Buddy Holly's "Peggy Sue," which is playing now. Servers dressed like kids in the movie *Grease* rush around. Blenders whir, burgers crackle on the grill, and fries sizzle in the deep fryer.

Straddling the only open stool at the counter, I study the menu. My family couldn't afford to eat here when I was a child, so this is a treat.

Seated next to me, Sergeant Jimenez devours a cheeseburger with a chocolate shake that looks delicious. If I can win her trust, she might confide in me what she knows about the case.

A scrawny young man with braces on his teeth slaps a menu on the counter and asks if I'd like something to drink.

"I'll have a chocolate shake."

"You want that made with chocolate or vanilla ice cream?"

"Chocolate."

"Sure thing, man."

Once the kid leaves, I ask Sergeant Jimenez if they've found the murder weapon yet.

"I can't talk about the case . . . but no."

"Any good leads?"

"We'll know more once the county processes the evidence they've collected."

"Did crime scene investigators find anything other than a .45 caliber bullet and shell casing?"

"How did you—?"

The young man returns with my shake. "Are you ready to order?"

"Two cheeseburgers with the works, an order of fries, an order of onion rings, a vanilla shake, and another one of these," I say, holding up my glass. "To go."

"And I thought I was hungry."

"It's not all for me," I say. "I'm picking up dinner for Mama Libby too."

"My girlfriend, Marta, does Mrs. Goodman's hair."

"Is that so?"

"How about you?"

"I got a haircut from Earl the other day."

"No, doofus," Sergeant Jimenez says. "I'm asking if there's anyone special in your life."

"I'm still kissing frogs."

"Bullfrogs?"

"How'd you guess?"

"Word gets around. Me and some friends are going to the Roadhouse tonight."

"What's the Roadhouse?"

"Local queer bar."

"In Nyes Landing?"

"Right outside of town."

"You're shitting me."

"You grew up around here, right?"

I nod.

"Remember that old barn they renovated into a steak restaurant?"

"The Chop House?"

"It's a queer bar now," Sergeant Jimenez says. "You should come. I'll introduce you to the gang."

This could be my chance to ingratiate myself into the investigation.

"Maybe I'll do that."

"Hope so," Sergeant Jimenez says. She tosses a twenty-dollar bill onto the counter. "Hate to eat and run, but duty calls."

CHAPTER TWELVE

By the time I reach the Roadhouse, cars and pickups crowd the cramped parking lot. I can't believe there are this many queers in the area. How times have changed. I pull into a space behind the dumpster and venture inside the rustic bar, which lacks the pretentiousness of most of the gay bars in the city. From the jukebox, Tim McGraw laments that he's his own worst enemy. I can relate to that sentiment.

Sergeant Jimenez sits in a corner booth with her arm around a young woman who has dark-brown braids and a tawny complexion. A slight Black woman with curly gray hair and a heavyset white woman with blue hair who has a pierced lip, nose, and eyebrow sit with the couple. The latter looks familiar, but I can't place where I might know her from.

"Scoot over, gals," Sergeant Jimenez says. "This is that cute cop I told you about."

Cute is not how I'd describe my goofy mug.

Sergeant Jimenez introduces her girlfriend, Marta, with the braids, Opal, the slight Black woman with the curly gray hair, and the heavyset white woman, Megan, with the blue hair and piercings.

"We went to high school together," Megan says. "I'm Griffin Garfield's sister. I was a sophomore when you and my brother were seniors."

That's why Megan looks familiar.

"How is Griffin?" I ask.

"He has his good days and his bad days."

I mention that I saw Griffin and Kit arguing.

"Christopher Nye is a bully," Megan says. "Was, rather."

"Should Griffin be wandering around town alone?" I ask.

"Griffin likes to go for walks. Especially when the weather's nice."

"Is that wise? I mean—"

"He may have the mind of a child, Cal, but my brother is an adult. We can't force him to stay home." Megan takes a swig of her beer. "Unless we have him declared incompetent, and we're not about to do that."

"Of course not."

"Griffin believes Christopher stole our house," Megan says. "And there's no getting around the fact that the Nyes did my family dirty." She swigs her beer and bangs her glass down on the table. "I am not sorry Christopher is dead. That's a terrible thing to say. But it's the truth."

"Could Griffin have—?"

"My brother did not shoot Christopher Nye. Guns terrify him."

"Do you have any idea who pulled the trigger?"

"The Nyes have made a lot of enemies."

"Can we change the subject?" Sergeant Jimenez says. "I've worked on the investigation all day. I came out tonight to blow off some steam."

Perhaps Megan shot Kit. She makes no bones about the fact that she loathes the Nyes for what they did to her family.

A husky country boy wearing a brown suede shirt, blue jeans, and cowboy boots asks what I'd like to drink. I order my usual pint of Guinness with a shot of Jameson.

"Not that anyone asked my opinion," Opal says, "but if Annie Nye shot her husband, I don't blame her."

"The Nyes are vultures," Megan says. She glances my way. "Not Annie, of course. Her only crime is having terrible taste in men."

Annie went from dating me to marrying Kit, so I can't argue with that assessment.

The husky guy in the suede shirt brings my beer and shot.

"Gunner," Sergeant Jimenez says. "This is Callum Nowak."

"The Touchdown Titan," Gunner says.

Nobody has called me the Touchdown Titan since my days on the football field. Gunner wasn't in my class, though. I would've remembered. Perhaps he attended a rival high school, and we played against one another.

"Cal is visiting from the city," Sergeant Jimenez says. "He's an NYPD officer."

"Is that so? I have a question for you," Gunner says. "What happens when a cop goes to bed?"

I've heard this groaner many times but don't wish to hurt Gunner's feelings, so I shrug.

Gunner grins. "He goes undercover."

"Don't quit your day job, Gunner," Opal says.

"Let's Get This Party Started" blasts from the jukebox. "I love Pink!" Marta shouts. She drags Sergeant Jimenez onto the dance floor.

"How's Libby doing?" Opal asks.

"She's not about to let a broken wrist slow her down, that's for sure."

"Do me a favor and give her this flyer. My thrift store is having a sale this weekend. In case she feels like getting out of the house."

"I bought this jacket at Second Chance Threads," Megan says.

She stands and models her white blazer, which is splattered in colorful paint drops, rather like the Jackson Pollack paintings I viewed when I worked security for an event at the Museum of Modern Art in the city.

Over two rounds of drinks, I learn Opal used to be a foster parent. She met Mama Libby through social services. Megan works at a convenience store and plays guitar in an all-girl band.

"Like the Spice Girls only edgier," Megan says. "We're playing at the Memorial Day picnic in Turtle Park. If you're still in town, you should come."

At eleven o'clock, Sergeant Jimenez announces that she's had enough. "I'm on patrol at six in the morning and need my beauty rest." She and Marta pay their portion of the tab and leave.

"I should get going too," Opal says. "I have to do inventory tomorrow." She contributes two twenty-dollar bills to the tab,

"I'm going your way," Megan says. "I'll give you a lift." She pays her share. "Take care, Cal."

"You do the same."

"Nice to meet you," Opal says.

"I'll see that Mama Libby gets your flyer."

Abandoned in a booth for six, I move to the bar.

Gunner pours me another round. He leans over the bar. His bloodshot eyes droop. "You don't remember me, do you?"

If he's asking, I suppose I should. I hope we haven't slept together. That would be awkward. I may get around, but I remember my tricks.

"We went to high school together," Gunner says, saving me from having to admit that I don't recognize his face. "I was a year behind you." He grins sheepishly. "After you came out, I used to watch you practice. You looked so hot in your uniform."

I'm flattered. Gunner is my type. Big and simple. No complications.

"I fantasized you and I—" Gunner blushes. "I'm sorry. It's my birthday. I've knocked back a few tequila shots."

"Have another on me," I say.

Gunner pours two shots and sets one before me. He raises his glass. "May we never go to hell but always be on our way." We toss back our shots and bite down on salty lime wedges. I need to get laid, and a husky country boy could be just the ticket.

Around midnight, the bar empties. I settle my tab. Gunner pours me another beer, which I sip while he does his closing paperwork. He keeps eying me.

"What's your deal, Nowak?"

"How so?"

"Are you a top or a bottom?"

"Why don't you bend my ass over that pool table and find out?"

In a flash, I'm facedown over the corner pocket with my pants around my ankles. Gunner must've been a Boy Scout, because he comes prepared with a condom and a packet of lubricant. I close my eyes. He's big, but I've taken bigger. I relax into his rhythm and, caught up in the moment, lose all sense of time. We finish together, drenched in sweat.

"Happy birthday," I say. I tug up my pants and swagger out the door.

CHAPTER THIRTEEN

FRIDAY MORNING, I wake up sprawled across my bed, fully dressed except for my boots. I shuffle down the hallway into the bathroom. The taste of stale whiskey lingers on my breath. I brush my teeth and take a hot shower. By the time I make it downstairs, it's noon.

Mama Libby left a note on the refrigerator.

> *Somebody had a late night. There better not be a scratch on Frank's pickup. Coffeemaker is ready. Just press the start button. Gone to town to help Moses sort out some business.*

I promised Mama Libby I wouldn't drink and drive. I've disappointed her. I need to be more careful. Had I gotten pulled over, I could've lost my badge. I press the start button on the coffeemaker and call my sergeant.

"Are you getting your act together, Nowak?"

"Trying, sir."

I tell Sarge about Kit's murder.

"Take all the time you need."

"I appreciate that, sir."

"I don't want you back on duty until you've worked through your shit."

A commotion erupts on Sarge's end of the line. He hangs up.

Sparky bounds through the kitchen and scratches on the back door. I tell the dog to sit. She does. I pass her a treat and buckle on her harness. She rushes outside and wanders around the yard, sniffing every blade of grass for the perfect spot to do her business. After she finishes, we sit on the front porch while I sip my coffee. It's peaceful here in the mountains. The afternoon breeze smells of honeysuckle and wild strawberries. I wish I didn't have so many awful memories of the place.

The phone rings. It's Annie. "I have a two o'clock appointment at the funeral home," she says, "and I could use your support."

"Tell me where, and I'll be there."

INSIDE THE OLD colonial house that had been converted into a funeral home, the scent of bitter roses cloys the air. A too-cheerful mortician with an adenoidal voice, wearing thick glasses and an ill-fitting black suit with white crew socks, introduces himself as Irving and expresses his condolences as he shows us around.

Annie narrows the casket choices down to either the solid mahogany with the ivory velvet lining or the eighteen-gauge gunmetal steel with the silver velvet lining.

"Kit would admire the classic mahogany," Annie says, running her fingers over the casket's sleek surface, "but he'd appreciate the durability of the steel."

"Which one do you prefer, sweetheart?" Nadine asks.

"I can't do this," Annie says. She bursts into tears.

Nadine hugs her daughter. I ask Irving to give us a minute.

"That's okay," Annie says, pulling herself together. "Let's get this over with."

"Why don't we take care of your paperwork?" Irving says. "And then you can choose the model."

Irving walks Annie through the process. Annie decides on the mahogany casket, changes her mind to the steel, and hands Irving her credit card. The bank declines the charge.

"Must be a glitch," Annie says. "Run the card again."

Irving gets the same result. Nadine hands Irving her debit card, and he processes the charge.

After Annie and Nadine use the ladies's room, we step outside.

"Christopher's office is up the street," Nadine says. "Walk with us." She leans in and whispers in my ear, "I called the bank. They declined Annie's card because Christopher hasn't paid the bills for months. We need his laptop and bank statements."

Nadine leads us past a garden center. She stops to smell the pink roses. When the salesclerk looks away, she plucks a bud, which she slips inside her shiny pink tote.

Annie steps into the street. A passing motorist honks and veers around her. I pull her back onto the sidewalk. Nadine leads us across the street at the crosswalk. We stroll another block.

Using Annie's key, Nadine unlocks the door of a restored nineteenth-century schoolhouse, and we step inside a sunny office with mint-green walls and polished hardwood floors. An open laptop rests atop a wood-and-steel desk. Nadine slips the laptop into her tote and rifles through the file cabinets behind the desk. "Bingo!" She pulls a bundle of unopened bank statements out of the bottom drawer and stuffs them into her tote.

"I need to get out of here, Mom."

"Just a sec, sweetie," Nadine says. "You have got to be kidding me." She shows me a stack of unpaid bills, which she tucks inside her tote.

We say our goodbyes on the sidewalk outside and I drive away more determined than ever to clear Annie's name. I can't believe that between the chief and his team and the sheriff's department, they haven't found the murder weapon. I'll do some snooping on the down-low, seeing as I have no official jurisdiction.

Before going home, I drive down Hummingbird Lane. The crime scene tape around Annie's house has blown loose. I park and stroll around the property, wishing I could see the crime scene reports. I spot what looks like the bloody partial print of a boot sole on the back deck. Smaller than my foot. I'd guess a size ten or eleven.

Chief Harris lumbers out of the woods. "What are you doing here, NYPD?"

"Annie asked me to check on the place."

"Did she?"

"You boys haven't found the murder weapon yet?"

"We will."

"Have you got any leads?"

"I couldn't tell you if we did."

"I hope you do a better job of catching Kit's killer than you did of finding the monster who butchered my mother."

"You little shit," Harris says. "Keep your nose out of my investigation."

"Or what?"

"Your sergeant said you were a loose cannon." Harris smirks. "That's right. Me and him spoke this afternoon. You've got quite the temper, which is why you're on administrative leave. I'd watch my step if I were you."

Chief Harris trudges into the woods and searches through the underbrush. My phone rings. I'm surprised that I have cellular service.

"Callum Nowak?" a gruff male voice asks.

"Who is this?"

"Detective Moore, with the county sheriff's office. My partner and I would like to speak with you."

SEATED ACROSS FROM DETECTIVE MOORE, a muscular Black guy with a shaved scalp and a stern demeanor, and his partner, Detective Davis, a stocky white guy who smiles too much, I share what I saw and heard.

Detective Moore leans back and clasps his fingers behind his head. "Tell me again why you were at the Nye residence that night."

"Like I said, Annie Nye asked me to pick up a lasagna for Mama Libby."

"You say this Elizabeth Goodman you're staying with was recently released from the hospital?"

"That's right."

"Is Annabelle Nye addicted to prescription medications?"

"I wouldn't know."

"We can subpoena her medical records."

"You should do that."

"What size shoe do you wear?" Detective Davis asks.

"Twelve. Why? Is this about the bloody footprint you found on the Nye's back deck?"

"Who told you about that?"

"I have eyes."

Detective Moore leans forward. "Don't be a smart ass."

"Am I being detained?"

"Not yet."

"You're free to go," Detective Davis says with a smile. He rises and passes me his card. "If you think of anything that might help bring your friend's killer to justice, let us know."

CHAPTER FOURTEEN

While I am trimming Mama Libby's roses Saturday morning under her watchful eye, she asks me what happened. I update her on the case.

"That's not what I'm talking about. How did you get this many days off?"

"I've accrued more vacation time than I can ever use."

"I suspect there's more to the story than that," she says. She points at the rose bush. "You missed some dead leaves there."

I snip off the dried stem.

"I want the truth, Cal."

I focus on clipping the roses, hoping she'll drop the subject.

"Whatever it is, it can't be that bad."

"I'm on administrative leave."

"Why is that?"

"If you must know, I lost my temper and punched a suspect."

"You did what, young man?"

"You don't understand. He was a real scumbag. Beat up his girlfriend. Assaulted me."

"Look me in the eye."

I lift my head.

"Do you send every suspect you apprehend to the hospital?"

"No."

"Then why did you beat up this guy?"

"I don't know."

"I think you do."

I can never lie to Mama Libby.

"I'd found out that I didn't make detective that morning," I say. "I wanted to prove myself."

"How did that work out?"

"I'm here, aren't I?"

"The world isn't out to get you, son."

"Are you sure about that?"

Mama Libby sighs. "Of all the children I've fostered over the years, you were my toughest nut to crack. But underneath that hard shell lies a kind and generous heart."

My cellular phone rings. It's Nadine. "I need to take this," I say, and I step away.

"The police released the crime scene," Nadine says. "Annie wants to go home."

"I'm surprised she'd want to return so soon after—"

"I think it's a terrible idea," Nadine says. "But she feels the longer she stays here, the harder it will get."

"I suppose that makes sense."

"The medical examiner's office gave me the phone number for a crime scene cleaner. But I don't have the foggiest clue what to ask the woman."

"Give me her number."

———

WHEN I REACH Annie's house, a rangy woman wearing coveralls and work boots is pacing the front lawn. She introduces herself as Molly. We go inside the house, and she inspects the crime scene.

"Looks like a pretty straightforward job. When do you need the place cleaned up by?"

"As soon as possible."

"I can start tomorrow. I charge time-and-a-half for weekends. I'll need a day to clean and a day to disinfect."

Molly quotes me an estimate. I call Nadine and share the figure. She agrees and pays Molly over the phone. Molly passes me a receipt and assures me she'll get started first thing in the morning. I show her where Annie hides the spare key.

After Molly drives away in her rusty van, the cop in me can't help but take a walk around the house, hoping I might find something the detectives missed. As I round the corner into the backyard, a filthy ape of a guy with shaggy hair and a bushy beard retreats into the woods bordering the rear of the property. This may not be my jurisdiction, but I took an oath to protect and serve. As much as I dread following, I must.

Fleeting glimpses of the fleeing homeless man's red flannel shirt guide me through the dense trees. Sweat soaks my armpits and trickles down my spine. I lose track of where I came from and wander in circles, disoriented, on the verge of hyperventilating. I should never have ventured into the woods alone.

Water rushes in the distance—Esopus Creek must be nearby. A car horn honks. I stagger in that direction, hoping I'm heading toward the street and not wandering further into the woods. After fighting my way through the tangled underbrush for some ways, I stumble out into Annie's backyard and sink onto my knees.

Gladys Crabtree was telling the truth when she said there was a homeless man loitering around the neighborhood. I wonder what else she may have witnessed.

As I pull away from Annie's house, a black cat runs across the street. I slam on the brakes and miss hitting the daredevil feline by a whisker. No doubt, Helena Potter would interpret a black cat crossing my path as a bad omen. I'm just grateful the cat's alive and I'm out of the woods.

AROMAS OF BASIL and oregano greet me when I walk through the door. Mama Libby has made minestrone soup using vegetables and herbs from her garden.

"You're supposed to be resting," I say.

"I'm taking regular breaks like Doogie Howser said to do."

I grab a spoon and taste the soup. "Yum." I scoop up another bite.

Mama Libby shoos me out of the kitchen. I hustle upstairs and scrub my face and hands. I might as well have a nip of whiskey while I'm here.

Over dinner, I tell Mama Libby about the homeless man.

"Let me get this straight," Mama Libby says. "You pursued a potential murder suspect into the woods without backup. You could've gotten yourself killed."

"I had my Beretta on me."

"Armed and panicked. There's a lethal combination."

Arguing with Mama Libby is a fool's pursuit.

"I need a ride to church in the morning," Mama Libby says before she turns in for the night.

By now, it's after nine o'clock. Too late to drive to Woodstock. The jazz festival would be over by the time I arrived. That's likely for the best. I'm probably misreading Demetrius's signals and would've made a fool of myself.

After I rinse and put the dishes in the dishwasher, I take my whiskey bottle outside and sip on the back stoop. Moses emerges from his apartment and shuffles downstairs.

"Evening, Carl."

"If we're going to be drinking buddies, Moses, you need to learn my name. It's Callum. But everybody calls me Cal."

"Sorry, son. Half the time, I can't remember my own name."

I hand Moses the whiskey. He takes a swig and passes back the bottle. We sit and sip in silence. Stars twinkle in the night sky, a sight I never see in the city. I tell Moses about chasing the homeless man into the woods and panicking.

"After I came home from Nam, it took me a long while to come to grips with the fact that, if I didn't face my demons, they'd defeat me."

"It's been a long day," I say before Mose launches into another war story. "Time to turn in."

CHAPTER FIFTEEN

MAMA LIBBY KNOCKS on my bedroom door Sunday morning. "Out of bed, sleepyhead," she says. "Don't make me late for Mass."

"I'm awake," I say. I sit up and stretch. Sweat soaks my sheets from racing through the woods all night in my dreams. I pad down the hallway and take a hot shower. Aromas of bacon frying and of biscuits baking entice me downstairs.

"I should be taking care of you, Mama Libby."

"You want to be helpful? Set the table."

"Yes, ma'am."

After breakfast, I wash the dishes and take Sparky for a walk. A gentle rain falls. By the time we get back inside, Mama Libby stands by the door, wearing a loose-fitting floral dress. She asks me to zip her up and turns around so I can do so.

On the drive into town, Mama Libby explains where I should drop her off and what time to pick her up. I sense she'd like me to join her for Mass, but she knows better than to ask. We pull up before the Sisters of Perpetual Mercy Catholic Church. I help her climb out of the pickup. She ties a scarf over her head with her good hand and strides up the walkway.

With an hour to spare, I drive by the hardware store. The open sign on the door faces out. I pull into the lot and park. The bell tinkles as I enter. That must get annoying.

Demetrius emerges from the back room, all smiles. I explain I need to patch a hole in the rafters and share the dimensions.

"I have some plywood leftover from another order that should do the trick."

Demetrius disappears into the back room. Moments later, a saw blade whirs. I pick up a box of nails and a can of rubberized sealant. Demetrius returns with a half dozen cuts of wood, which should more than do the job.

"You missed a cool jazz concert last night."

Demetrius's smile makes me regret not driving to Woodstock. I explain about the crime scene cleaner and the homeless man I chased into the woods, but I don't mention my panic attack.

"Any clue who the guy is?" Demetrius asks.

"I didn't get a good look at his face."

Brandy Speedman sails through the door, clutching several fabric swatches in her fist. "I need paint samples," she says. "I'm renovating my kitchen."

"Let me see if I have these colors in stock," Demetrius says. He takes the swatches and steps into the back room.

"You're that cop from the city, aren't you?" Brandy says. "You were there the night that someone shot Christopher Nye."

"Kit bled out in my arms."

She shudders.

"Were you and Kit close?" I ask.

"No."

"That's a nice color," I say, pointing toward the deep blue in one of her swatches, so she'll think I'm interested and keep talking.

"That's my husband's favorite. I prefer the green with the orange."

"Your husband's Trevor, right?"

She nods.

"What is his beef with Kit?"

"I don't know what you mean."

I mention the fight I witnessed outside the liquor store and ask if she and Kit were having an affair.

Brandy Speedman throws back her head and laughs. "Not that it's any of your business, but no. I was not having an affair with that jerk."

"What were he and Trevor fighting about?"

"Ask my husband."

Demetrius returns with three sample-size paint cans. "I have the cobalt blue, the emerald green, and the blood orange in stock. I'll have to order the metallic gold."

"You're a sweetheart, Demetrius," Brandy says. "Your wife was a fool to let you get away." She turns to me. "I was sorry to hear about your mother."

Surprised by her offhandedness, I get tongue-tied. She struts out the door. I can't help but feel the woman is hiding something. But I can't imagine her husband killing anyone.

"How much do I owe?" I ask.

"Two dollars and sixty-seven cents for the nails," Demetrius says. "You can have the plywood. I had planned to toss those scraps in the trash."

"I appreciate that." I pay and leave, wondering if Demetrius is this nice to everyone.

Mama Libby stands on the chapel steps when I drive up, wagging her finger in the priest's face. She throws up her arms and walks away, shaking her head. The priest looks flabbergasted. I leap out, open her door, and support Mama Libby's arm while she climbs inside.

"Is everything okay?" I ask.

"There's no reasoning with that old fool when he proselytizes about the gays."

"He's a priest. He must toe the papal line."

"We're not living in the Dark Ages," Mama Libby says. "The Church should grow with the times."

Mama Libby and I will never agree on our views of the Catholic Church.

"Most Sundays, I have brunch at the diner after Mass," Mama Libby says. "But if you're not hungry, we don't have to go."

"I can always eat."

When Mama Libby and I arrive at the Nyes Landing Diner, the parking lot is full. We circle the block. A late-model Cadillac backs out of a space in front of the restaurant. I recognize Bonnie Nye behind the wheel. As she drives away, I pull into her spot.

"Bonnie Nye is a nasty woman," Mama Libby says, "but no mother should have to bury her own child."

The hostess informs us there's a thirty-minute wait for a table. I give her my name, which she scrawls on a clipboard. A sign on the cash register advertises their Mother's Day special in two weeks.

Nadine leads Annie out of the ladies's room. Annie's eyes appear red and puffy. I rush over and ask what's wrong.

"Bonnie Nye accused Annie of being a murderer in front of the whole diner," Nadine says.

"I don't know why I let that woman get under my skin," Annie says.

"The Nyes are living proof that money can't buy happiness," Mama Libby says. She hugs Annie.

Nadine and Annie invite Mama Libby and me to join them at their table by the window.

"How is your wrist doing, Libby?" Nadine asks.

"Better now that I'm home."

A sweet young woman brings us menus and asks if we'd like coffee.

"I'll have a blackberry iced tea, Kiki," Mama Libby says. "That sounds refreshing."

I'd like a shot of whiskey, but I settle for black coffee.

A gregarious woman with cinnamon red hair, dressed in a forest-green suit, approaches our table. She offers Annie her condolences and asks Mama Libby how her recovery is going.

"It'll take more than a broken wrist to keep me down."

"Lucille Miller," the woman says. She extends her hand. I introduce myself. We shake.

"Lucille is the mayor of Nyes Landing," Mama Libby says. "Frank and I fostered Cal when he was in high school. He's like a son to me."

Hearing Mama Libby say those words out loud means more to me than she will ever know.

"The lost boy," Lucille says. "I heard you were in town."

In the city, I'm anonymous. Here, even people I've never met know my story.

Lucille excuses herself and strolls around the diner, shaking hands and kissing babies, of which there are too many for comfort.

Kiki brings Annie and Nadine their food and Mama Libby and me our drinks. She asks us if we're ready to place our order. I study the menu.

"I'll have the Smoked Trout Benedict, Kiki," Mama Libby says. "With the hollandaise sauce on the side and some extra lemons. And extra napkins. I'm eating one-handed."

I order the pot roast special with mashed potatoes and gravy.

Helena Potter and Bo Satterlee stumble through the door wearing rumpled clothes more appropriate for a Saturday night on the town than a Sunday morning. Their eyes look bloodshot. Bo whispers in Helena's ear. Helena giggles. I would've thought she had better sense. Bo flits from woman to woman like a honeybee pollinating flowers. The couple make their way over to our table, reeking of cannabis, an illegal substance. But as I've been told multiple times, this isn't my jurisdiction.

"If you need anything, anything at all," Helena says, "you call me." She hugs Annie.

Bo slaps me on the back and says, "Crazy times, dude."

"How's your wrist, Mama Libby?" Helena asks.

"I'll be in a cast for a few weeks," Mama Libby says, "but I'll live." She pats Annie's hand. "I'm sorry, sweetheart. I didn't mean . . . ."

The hostess shows Helena and Bo to a booth in the rear of the restaurant.

Kiki brings our food and refills my coffee cup. She removes Annie's and Nadine's plates and asks if they'd like dessert.

"I'll have a cappuccino," Nadine says.

"Me too," Annie says. "I need to wash my hands. That barbecued chicken was messy." She goes to the ladies's room.

Nadine leans in and whispers, "Annie is broke. Worse than broke. Kit racked up thousands of dollars in debt. Took frequent trips to Atlantic City. Told Annie he had business there, but I suspect he was gambling. And who knows what else?"

"What a mess!" Mama Libby says. "I never trusted that boy."

"Me either," Nadine says. "But Annie wouldn't listen to reason."

Kiki brings the cappuccinos.

"Those look good," Mama Libby says. "I'll have one too."

Annie returns. She stirs a packet of sweetener into her cappuccino. Her eyes look heavy. I wonder what she's taken.

Kiki brings Mama Libby her cappuccino and asks if we would like dessert.

"I couldn't eat another bite," Mama Libby says.

I decline as well. Kiki brings our checks. I pay both. Nadine insists on leaving the tip. We say goodbye on the sidewalk outside and go our separate ways.

On the drive home, the sky darkens. By the time we get inside the house, it's raining hard, but Sparky needs to go for a walk. I borrow a raincoat from Mama Libby and take the dog outside. She does her business faster than I've ever seen her go.

Taking the plywood scraps, nails, sealant, and tools upstairs into the attic, I patch the hole in the rafters before too much rain leaks inside.

My mind churns. Is Brandy Speedman telling the truth about her and Kit? Or is she covering for her husband? There was tension between Trevor and Kit. That's certain. The question is, over what? Perhaps I'll take Brandy's advice and ask her husband. And who is the homeless man I chased into the woods? I need to pay Gladys Crabtree a visit. And see what I can find out about Kit's dealings in Atlantic City. I'm going to be busy.

CHAPTER SIXTEEN

Monday morning, Molly calls and tells me that she can't find Annie's house key. She swears that she left the key under the flowerpot when she finished work on Sunday. I drive over and search for myself with no luck.

"I left the key under here," Molly says, lifting the flowerpot by the door where Annie hides her spare key. "I'm sure I did." She paces the porch, chewing on her fingernails, while I call Nadine, who offers to bring us a spare key.

"I'm sorry," Molly says. She checks under every flowerpot on the porch again. "I can't imagine where the darn thing could've gone."

While we wait, Molly takes a seat on the porch swing and I plop down on the steps. I learn that she got divorced last year and her son has been acting out.

"In what way?" I ask.

"Skipping school. Telling lies. Taking money from my purse without my knowledge."

Her son might be the boy Kit asked me to help.

"Did you ever meet the Nyes?" I ask.

"Never had the pleasure."

Chief Harris pulls up in his squad car and leaps out, clutching a machete. He swaggers up the sidewalk and tips his cap.

"I thought they released the crime scene," I say.

"They did," Chief Harris says. "I'm here to clean up the underbrush in the woods behind the property. See if I can locate the gun she used."

"Annie didn't shoot her husband."

"Maybe you did," Chief Harris says. "I heard that you and Mr. Nye had a long-standing feud."

"You think I shot Kit because we were rivals in high school?" I shake my head. "If that's your best theory, you're about to let another killer go free."

"You're a smart ass."

"Am I a suspect?"

"Not officially."

"Then I'm done talking."

"Suit yourself."

"Bass are biting downstream of the old paper mill, chief," Molly says. "Caught me a seven-pound Walleye last week. Scrappy fish put up quite a fight."

"I don't have time to go fishing. I'm investigating a murder," Chief Harris says. "Speaking of which, I should get busy." He strides around the house and hacks his way into the woods.

Nadine arrives with Annie's key and unlocks the house. Molly goes to work.

Nadine and I venture upstairs. Detectives have stripped the beds, rifled through drawers, and scattered clothes and personal items everywhere. We tidy up as best we can without knowing where Annie keeps her things. Nadine offers to buy me lunch, but I need to get home.

"Another time," Nadine says.

"I'll lock up when I leave," Molly says. "But you should change the locks."

"I know a locksmith in Kingston," Nadine says. "But I imagine there's someone closer."

"I met the guy who owns the local hardware store," I say. "I can ask him."

"If you don't mind."

Any excuse to see Demetrius.

I STRIDE through the door of the hardware store. A blond woman wearing a halter top that barely contains her more-than-ample cleavage leans over the counter and bats her false eyelashes at Demetrius. "Now that you're divorced, Demi, you and I should get together for drinks."

Demetrius steps back from the counter. "I'm not sure—"

"When you're ready," the blond woman says. She takes Demetrius's hand and writes her phone number on his wrist. "Call me." She blows Demetrius a kiss and struts out the door. But not before giving me the once-over.

"She's friendly," I say.

"Not my type."

"Who is your type?"

"Not her," Demetrius says, dodging my question. I need to quit fantasizing about the guy and focus on finding Kit's killer. Anytime I need my libido stroked, I can pay Gunner a visit.

"What brings you by?" Demetrius asks.

"Can you recommend a locksmith in the area?"

Demetrius shares a guy's name and number.

"Bye, Demi," I say on my way out the door.

WHEN I GET HOME, I find Mama Libby seated in the living room, chatting with Sergeant Jimenez.

"The sergeant asked to see Frank's revolver," Mama Libby says. "It's missing from my nightstand drawer."

"Have you seen the weapon?" Sergeant Jimenez asks.

"No. I never go into her room."

"But she told you she kept the revolver in her nightstand drawer?"

"That's right."

"You didn't check to make sure?"

"I had no cause to doubt her word."

Sergeant Jimenez doesn't look satisfied, but she thanks us both for our time. I walk her outside.

"The Roadhouse has happy hour from five to eight on Mondays," Sergeant Jimenez says.

"Is that so?"

"I ran into Gunner at the grocery store yesterday," Sergeant Jimenez says. "He asked about you."

"Did he now?"

"You should stop by the bar."

"Another time," I say. "Mama Libby needs me."

"When you find that Colt, give me a shout."

"Don't mind me," Mama Libby says when I step back inside. "Go have fun with your friends."

"Are you sure? If you need me, I don't have to go."

"For heaven's sake, young man. You're driving me nuts. Go out. Stay home. Makes me no never mind. I'm going to watch reruns of *Highway to Heaven*."

Spending the night watching Michael Landon play an angel fighting crime with an ex-cop sounds like torture.

"In that case," I say, grabbing the keys the Silverado, "I'll see you later."

"Don't stay out all night."

Mama Libby expects me to behave like an adult, but treats me like I'm still a teenager.

VEHICLES CROWD the Roadhouse parking lot, many squeezed into spaces never intended for such use. If I were on duty, I'd ticket the more egregious violations. I pull up behind a row of cars that are parked on the shoulder of the road.

Inside the bar, I don't see Sergeant Jimenez anywhere. Opal crouches over the buffet, piling boiled shrimp onto a plate. I order my usual pint with a shot and join her.

"How are you doing, handsome?" Opal asks.

"What's up?"

"Grabbing a bite to eat after work."

I check out the buffet of boiled shrimp, cocktail wieners in barbecue sauce, fried chicken tenders, a platter of fresh vegetables with ranch dip, and chips and salsa. Basic fare, but the food is fresh and the portions generous. I prepare a plate.

The bartender brings my beer and shot.

"Is Gunner working tonight?" I ask.

"Afraid you're stuck with me," the bartender says. He extends his hand. "Name's Tanner."

"Cal."

"The lost boy," Tanner says. He strokes his goatee. "Gunner mentioned he ran into you."

"If you see Gunner, tell him I said hello."

Two guys at the opposite end of the bar call Tanner over and order another round of drinks.

"How's Annie holding up?" Opal asks.

"She's returning home tomorrow."

"That's fast."

"I agree."

"If she didn't shoot her husband, who did?"

"I'm at a loss," I say. "Many people hold grudges against the Nyes." I take a sip of beer. "But I can't tie anyone to the scene of the crime." I knock back my shot. "It baffles me how anyone could've pulled the trigger and fled the scene that fast. I rushed through the door seconds after I heard the shot fired."

"Perhaps the shooter escaped into the woods behind the house."

"That's possible, I suppose. I can confirm the homeless man who Gladys Crabtree claims to have seen exists. I chased him into the woods on Saturday, but he evaded me."

"You've had quite the ride since you came home."

"That's for sure."

"Are you glad you're here?"

"Feels weird."

"I'll bet." Opal chugs her beer and orders another. "I knew your mother."

I'm taken aback.

"She deserves justice." Opal shakes her head. "But I doubt they'll ever catch her killer."

"How did you know my mom?"

"I fostered her for a few months when she was twelve."

"What was she like as a little girl?"

"Bright, precocious, but moody. One minute she would be bouncing off the walls." Opal peels a shrimp and dips it into cocktail sauce. "The next minute, I couldn't drag her out of bed." She pops the shrimp into her mouth.

"That sounds like my mom."

"I tried to get her help." Opal calls Tanner over and orders a shot of tequila. "The county refused to cover the counseling services she needed. I appealed to the state. They did nothing." Tanner brings Opal her shot, which she knocks back with salt and lime. Her face puckers. "The system failed that child."

That children's services placed Mary Catherine and me with Mama Libby and Papa Frank after we lost our mother is nothing short of a miracle. Siblings in foster care—tweens and teens in particular—often get split up. And thirteen-year-old boys with behavioral issues get placed in group homes.

"When your mother met your father, I thought she'd found her prince," Opal says. "But her mood swings drove that poor man away." She finishes eating her last shrimp and pushes her plate aside.

After Dad left, Mom brought home strange men like some women rescue stray cats. She took pills to wake herself up, pills to dull the pain, and pills to help her sleep. Washed down with a swig of rotgut vodka from the bottle she kept on her bedside table.

"When I heard what'd happened to her," Opal says, "I wept for the troubled little girl I couldn't help."

I don't recall the last time I discussed my mom with a person who knew her. It hurts when I think about why she's not here. But it's comforting to know that she hasn't been forgotten.

Sergeant Jimenez strolls through the door a little before seven o'clock and joins Opal and me at the bar.

"Long day?" I ask.

Sergeant Jimenez nods and orders a Don Q with pineapple juice. "I'm starving," she says. She fills a plate at the buffet. I finish my last few bites.

"Any new leads?"

Sergeant Jimenez shakes her head while she chews.

"I know. You can't talk about the case."

"There's nothing to talk about," Sergeant Jimenez says between bites. I'm not sure if Sergeant Jimenez is shooting straight with me, but nothing in her demeanor suggests otherwise. She isn't in a talkative mood, so I pay my tab and say goodnight.

Outside the bar, I spy Trevor Speedman sitting in his black SUV. Our eyes lock. He speeds away. Something's off about that guy.

CHAPTER SEVENTEEN

After breakfast on Tuesday morning, I drive to Annie's house and meet the locksmith. A wiry Black man sits waiting in his van when I pull up. He leaps out and introduces himself as Lamonte, which he pronounces La-MON-tay. I show him the front and back doors of the house.

"Give me a few minutes," Lamonte says, and he goes to work.

I wander around behind the house. Chief Harris has chopped down several yards of underbrush on the edge of the woods. He seems certain the killer ditched the murder weapon there. Given the tight timeframe of their escape, he may be right.

Gladys Crabtree stumbles out of her back door wearing a sky-blue tracksuit with bright white sneakers. A blue-and-white scarf covers her hair. She lowers her sunglasses and looks me over. "Can I help you, young man?"

"Maybe," I say.

"I remember you."

Her breath smells of gin and it's not even ten o'clock in the morning. I share that I chased the homeless man into the woods.

"See! Nobody listens to me." Gladys Crabtree wobbles my way. "You're tall." She hiccups. "Tall, dark, and handsome."

"You heard the shot that killed Christopher Nye, right?"

"Loud as day. After the chief left, I fixed dinner for Mr. Squiggles. I prepare all his meals fresh."

"The chief was here that day?"

"I caught that vagrant digging through my trash can again and called the police. By the time the chief arrived and looked around, he'd retreated into the woods."

"How long does it take you to feed your dog?"

"I cook Mr. Squiggles's food in batches and freeze individual portions in plastic bags. At mealtime, I thaw a bag in a pot of simmering water on the stove, which takes about five to seven minutes. Then I mix in his protein powder and vitamins and let the food cool before pouring it into his bowl. The entire process takes me about thirty minutes."

Her dog eats better than many children in the world.

"Did you see anyone come and go from the Nye residence during that time?"

"I was busy in the kitchen."

"You rushed outside when you heard the shot?"

"I didn't realize it was a gunshot until she screamed."

"Mrs. Nye, you mean."

"I figured she would snap one day."

I stifle the urge to defend Annie and ask Gladys why she feels that way.

"Just a hunch. I get those. And I'm seldom wrong."

Lamonte shouts from the back door of Annie's house, "All done!"

"I should go," I say. "Nice to see you again."

"Likewise, I'm sure."

I don't know what to make of Gladys Crabtree. I pay Lamonte in cash and take the new keys.

As Lamonte drives away, Annie and Nadine arrive. Annie appears jittery. I wonder what drug she's on. I take her suitcase and hand her the keys. I worry about how she's going to react. She only hesitates for a second before entering the house.

"I'm afraid the police made a mess of the place," Nadine says.

"I'll put everything back where it belongs," Annie says. "I need to keep busy." She straightens the cushions on the sofa and rearranges the occasional pillows.

"I'll brew a pot of coffee," Nadine says, and she goes into the kitchen. "Goodness, what a mess! Cal, did you not see these lasagnas sitting on the stove?"

"I didn't go into the kitchen," I say, following her.

"The crime scene cleaner must've used the sink because it's spic and span. But the rest of the kitchen is filthy. For as much as I paid that woman, she should've cleaned up in here as well. I'll take care of this mess. You go see if Annie needs anything."

Annie isn't in the dining or living room. I venture upstairs. She lies curled up on her bed, sobbing into her pillow. I take a seat beside her and hold her hand. We sit in silence for a few minutes before she says, "I can't do this."

"I can't imagine what you're going through. But I'm here for you."

"You'll be going home in a few days."

She's right.

"I've never lived alone," Annie says. "I moved from my parent's house into my husband's house."

I can't imagine what that must be like. I've been on my own since I aged out of foster care when I turned eighteen.

"I need to pick out a suit for Kit to get buried in," Annie says. "His funeral is tomorrow."

"I'll help you." I stuff clothes back inside the overflowing drawers and straighten the bureau. An expensive looking 35mm camera in a leather case that smells brand new sets atop a box of watches. "I didn't realize you were into photography."

"Kit bought that camera a few months ago. He took it with him when he went hiking with the boys last month, but I never saw any pictures from their trip. I'll bet he never even took it out of its case."

I sort through Kit's suits. He may have been an asshole, but he was a handsome asshole, and he would look good in any of these.

"Perhaps the tan double-breasted," I say. "Or the navy-blue three-piece might be more appropriate."

"You choose."

"We'll take both suits to the funeral home, and you can decide there."

"I've cleaned the kitchen and taken out the trash!" Nadine hollers from the bottom of the stairs. "How're things going up there?"

"We'll be right down, Mom."

Annie sits up and pops a pill from the bottle on the nightstand. We make our way downstairs. Nadine offers to buy us lunch at the diner.

"I don't know, Mom."

"We'll see how you feel after we drop off Kit's suits at the funeral home."

Nadine offers to drive. On our way to the car, Gladys Crabtree shouts from her porch, "Stop leaving food out for that vagrant! You're going to get us all killed."

"Ignore that woman," Nadine says.

Annie climbs into the back seat and lies down. I ride shotgun. When we reach the funeral home, I take Kit's suits inside. Irving assures me he'll have both garments dry cleaned and ready for tomorrow. He needs to know by nine o'clock in the morning which one Annie would like Kit laid to rest in.

Nadine drives to the elementary school, so Annie can discuss her schedule with principal Elena Martinez. The school bell rings while Annie is inside. A shrieking horde of munchkins scramble out the double doors and rush into the arms of their waiting parents.

A haggard woman with frizzy blond hair, wearing a faded

sundress with flip-flops, gets into a shouting match with a scrawny guy with stringy brown hair who's wearing a worn-out tee shirt and jeans with scuffed work boots. A frail boy with dark circles under his eyes trudges along behind the couple.

Annie stops and speaks to the little boy. She smiles and musses his hair. He smiles back. She gives the bickering couple a withering glance and climbs into the back seat.

"Cal, remember I told you about Evan? The little boy who wandered off the school grounds? That's him. And those are his parents."

I don't know which is worse. Losing your parents like I did or living with parents who fight all the time.

———

When we reach the diner, Nadine requests a quiet booth in the rear. While I have cellular service, I call Mama Libby and check in.

"The diner makes the best turkey meatloaf," Mama Libby says. "Better than my own recipe, if you can believe that. Bring me an order with mashed potatoes and the vegetable of the day."

"Yes, ma'am."

Kiki takes our order and goes into the kitchen.

"I can't believe I'm burying my husband tomorrow," Annie says. "I thought we would have children one day. Grow old together. Spoil a bunch of grand babies. Excuse me."

Annie rushes off to the ladies's room. Nadine follows her daughter. Kiki brings our drinks and asks if everything is all right. I explain that Kit's funeral is tomorrow.

Jewel Nye weaves her way through the parking lot. I step outside and shout her name. She side-eyes me and says, "I ain't got nothing to say to the pigs."

Even out of uniform, I get made for a cop.

"I'm not on duty."

"Then why're you harassing me, huh?"

"I knew your brother."

"I'm sorry."

"Do you have any idea who might've shot him?"

Jewel shrugs. "My brother made a lot of enemies."

"What about Trevor Speedman?"

"Who the hell is that?"

It's clear from Jewel's perplexed expression that she doesn't know who I'm talking about.

"I'm sorry for bothering you."

I hold out a five-dollar bill. Jewel snatches the cash and staggers away. I return to my seat. Kiki brings our lunch and refills my iced tea. The sky darkens outside.

"The weatherman said there's a seventy percent chance of rain today," Nadine says. "Good thing I brought an umbrella." She tastes her sandwich. "This bread is so fresh. Would you like a bite, Annie?"

"I'll be lucky if I finish my salad. It's huge."

"How about you, Cal?"

With my mouth full of cheeseburger, I shake my head.

"I think the tan suit will complement Kit's complexion best," Nadine says. "But the navy-blue suit might be more appropriate for the occasion. What do you think, sweetheart?"

"You decide, Mom."

"Are you sure?"

Annie nods.

"Which suit would you choose, Cal?"

"I'd go with the tan double-breasted."

"Not the navy-blue three-piece?"

"Kit would look good in either suit."

"You're no help," Nadine says.

Griffin Garfield shuffles past the window of the diner. He presses his nose against the glass and stares at Annie. His lips move. I wish I could hear what he's saying.

Nadine pays the check. I leave a ten-dollar bill on the table for Kiki and grab the shopping bag with Mama Libby's meatloaf. We part ways on the sidewalk outside.

Griffin disappears around the corner. I feel sorry for the poor guy, but I can't help but wonder if he ever gets violent. I've dealt with homeless people in the city who've snapped and attacked innocent bystanders.

CHAPTER EIGHTEEN

ON WEDNESDAY MORNING, Mama Libby announces she wants to bake muffins and asks me to get the pans and bowls she needs out of the cupboard. While she cooks, I go upstairs, shower, and dress for Kit's funeral. I didn't bring any dress shirts or slacks with me. A tee shirt and jeans will have to do. At least, they're black. I borrow a black sports jacket from Papa Frank's closet and find a flask in the pocket, which I fill with whiskey.

When I come downstairs, Mama Libby is standing by the door, clutching her purse. She asks me to zip up her dress. I do so. "Bring the muffins off the kitchen counter," she says. I grab the bag and follow her out to the pickup.

I drive us to Annie's house. Howie Clark sits on the front porch when we arrive. He rushes over and helps Mama Libby out of the pickup. I find Nadine in the kitchen, surrounded by casserole dishes covered in aluminum foil, and pass her the muffins.

"Good lord," Nadine says. "We have enough food here to feed the whole county."

"Don't shoot the delivery boy," I say.

Someone brought deviled eggs. I stuff one into my mouth.

"Help yourself to coffee."

I pour myself a cup, turn my back, and add a splash of whiskey from my flask.

Mama Libby joins us in the kitchen. "What can I do to help?"

"I need to check on Annie," Nadine says. "See if you can find a place for all this food." She goes upstairs.

"Take this trash out, Cal," Mama Libby says. "I'll see if I can make space for some of these casserole dishes in the refrigerator."

I carry the trash out to the garage and dump the bag into the garbage can. When I return, I help Mama Libby organize the food in the kitchen.

The doorbell rings.

"I'll get that," Howie says. He returns with Officer Reeves.

"Nowak," Reeves says. He tips his cap. He didn't call me No Good. Perhaps he'll stay off my case today.

Gladys Crabtree bursts through the back door without knocking and sets a bowl of wilted salad greens on the kitchen table. "I hope none of this food gets left outside."

"Give it a rest, Gladys," Mama Libby says.

"Becky Goodman, don't start with me."

"This is neither the time nor the place."

"Well, I never—"

"Do everyone a favor, Gladys, and go home."

"You're not the boss of me, Becky."

Officer Reeves steps in. "Ma'am, if you don't leave, I can have you trespassed."

"I understand everyone is upset today," Gladys says, "but that's no cause to be rude." She storms out the door in a huff.

"One of these days—" Mama Libby says.

"Is that horrid woman gone?" Nadine shouts.

"For now," Mama Libby says.

Nadine leads Annie downstairs, and they take seats on the sofa. Howie sits beside Annie and asks if she's okay. Annie shakes her head and sobs.

"Stupid question," Howie says. "I'm such an idiot. If there's anything you need—"

The doorbell rings. Howie leaps up and answers. Helena Potter steps inside, followed by Bo Satterlee.

"I brought vegan chili," Helena says. She passes Howie a plastic tub, which he carries into the kitchen.

"Would you like coffee?" Nadine asks.

"We can't stay," Helena says.

"We'll see everyone at the church," Bo says.

"If she needs anything," Helena whispers to Nadine, "call me."

Shortly after Helena and Bo leave, the doorbell rings.

"It's like Grand Central Station around here," Nadine says on her way to answer.

"I'm sorry for your loss," Sergeant Jimenez says. She wipes her boots on the doormat before stepping inside.

"Would you like coffee, Sergeant?" Nadine asks.

"If it's no trouble."

"Cream and sugar?"

"Black is fine."

Mama Libby follows Nadine into the kitchen and returns with a muffin, which she sets before Annie. "You need to eat something."

"I'm not hungry."

Nadine returns with a cup of coffee for the sergeant and takes a seat on the sofa beside Annie. "You have to keep your strength up, sweetheart."

Annie nibbles crumbs off the top of her muffin.

"You should eat more than that."

Annie leaps off the sofa and shouts, "Stop telling me what to do!" She runs upstairs.

"I better—" Nadine says.

"Allow me," I say.

I find Annie seated on her bed, gazing at a framed photograph of her and Kit on their wedding day. I wrap my arm around her. She sinks against me and mutters, "Why did you have to be gay?"

I shrug.

"After we broke up, I didn't think I would ever date again." She smiles. "That's being sixteen for you."

"Would you go back?" I ask. "If you could?"

"No way."

"Me either."

"Kit made me feel special."

"Unlike me."

"You know what I mean."

Every girl in the school had a crush on Christopher Nye, but he wanted Annie. And whatever Kit wanted, he got.

"Kit flirted with other women. He may even have had affairs. But I thought he'd never leave me." Annie sobs. "Yet he did."

"Kit did not leave you. He was shot at point-blank range. And if the police don't find his killer, I will."

I hope I don't regret making that promise.

"I miss Zelda."

"Why don't you call her?"

"She's traipsing through the jungle right now."

"Sounds exotic."

"Hold me, Cal."

I enfold Annie in my arms. Nothing I can say will bring Kit back. But finding his killer might bring his family some peace.

BY THE TIME we depart for the funeral, dark clouds loom over the mountain peaks northwest of town. Annie insists that Mama Libby and I ride in the limousine with her and Nadine. By the time we pull into the parking lot of the First United Methodist Church, it's drizzling. Officers Washington and Lecoq flank the entrance.

"Did you bring an umbrella?" Mama Libby asks. I shake my head. "It's a good thing I brought two." She passes me a portable umbrella that's much nicer than the flimsy models vendors hawk on street corners in the city when it rains.

We rush inside the foyer, collapse our umbrellas, and sign the guest book. Organ music invites us into the church. Up front, sprays of roses and carnations flank the blue-gray steel casket.

Bo Satterlee and Helena Potter sit in the back pew. In her long black dress and veiled hat, Helena could pass for Morticia Addams's sister. Bo wears a black leather sports jacket over a tee shirt with jeans and boots, so I don't feel out of place.

Joe Farley greets us dressed in a black suit and tie. He ushers Annie and Nadine down the aisle to the right front pew.

Mama Libby walks up to the open casket and pays her last respects. When she finishes, I step up. Kit looks like he's asleep. Irving did a nice job. Kit and I had our differences, but he didn't deserve to die. I promise I'll catch his killer and take my seat.

Bonnie Nye sits stiff as a gargoyle on the left front pew, wearing a black lace dress with a pill box hat. She turns her head and glares at Annie through her veil.

Horace Nye sits hunched forward beside his wife, with his head cradled in his hands. Under his rumpled suit jacket, his massive shoulders quake. A giant of a man, dwarfed by grief.

Further down the aisle, Jewel Nye slouches against the back of the pew with her arms folded across her chest. She wears a ripped black tee shirt with a red plaid skirt and a studded black leather belt. Her stringy hair hangs limp, like she hasn't shampooed in days. She coughs hard and blows her pierced nose into a crumpled tissue.

Mourners fill the church. The Nyes hold sway over many local lives.

Demetrius stands at the rear of the church, looking more handsome than ever in a gray suit and tie. I undress him with my eyes and like what I see. He smiles when he catches me staring. My cheeks warm. I avert my gaze.

Gunner and Tanner, the bartenders from the Roadhouse, arrive together and squeeze into the back row beside Helena and Bo. I haven't seen Gunner since our moment of passion over the pool table.

Brandy Speedman strolls into the church wearing a daffodil yellow dress that's cut too low for a funeral and spiked heels that add three inches to her already impressive height. Whispers ripple through the crowd. Trevor follows his wife down the aisle wearing a rumpled brown suit and tie. The disheveled guy looks like he hasn't shaved or bathed in days. The mourners seated in the row behind us scoot over to make room for the couple.

A pudgy man climbs on top of a stool so he can see over the pulpit and introduces himself as Reverend Proctor. He wears a stole over his robes. I believe that's what that shawl is called. A crown of bushy gray curls surrounds his shiny bald scalp. After acknowledging everyone's grief, he assures us that Christopher is with his father in heaven now. He slips on his glasses, reads us a passage from the Bible about mercy for the merciful, and sermonizes about forgiving our enemies.

A small choir of men and women of various ages sings about Christ rising and washing us in the blood of the lamb. They harmonize well, I'll give them that.

Officer Reeves steps behind the pulpit and rubs his bloodshot eyes. He pulls a piece of paper from his pocket and reads a heartfelt eulogy. While sharing the details of a prank he and Kit pulled on the school bus their senior year, he chokes up and returns to his seat.

Reverend Proctor prays for Kit's immortal soul. The choir praise the lord in song. Officer Reeves, Howie Clark, Bo Jenkins, and three other guys I don't recognize hoist the casket onto their shoulders and solemnly proceed outside, and they slide the casket inside the hearse that will transport Kit to his final resting place.

Mama Libby and I follow Annie and Nadine out the door into the rain.

Mayor Lucille Miller hugs Annie. "If you need anything, dear, just ask." I'm sure she hopes Annie will remember her come election time.

Trixie and Rose, the honey and jam ladies from the farmers market, offer their condolences. In their matching navy-blue suits, they make a handsome couple.

Elena Martinez catches up with us. In her chic black dress and pearls, she looks like a model. She hugs Annie and tells her to take as much time off as she needs.

Nadine leads Annie away. Mama Libby and I follow the grieving mother and daughter. The limousine driver opens their door and then ours. We slide inside. None of us says a word.

CHAPTER NINETEEN

WITH THE LIGHTS flashing atop their squad car, Sergeant Jimenez and Officer Washington lead the procession of vehicles with their headlights on in the middle of the afternoon from the church to the cemetery. The pall bearers carry the steel casket to the gravesite, and everyone gathers around with our umbrellas raised, while Reverend Proctor says kind things about Kit and ignores his shortcomings, which is to be expected at a funeral.

Horace Nye leans against his stolid wife, Bonnie. A fidgeting Jewel stands off to the side, sniffling and scratching her arms.

Annie weeps into her mother's shoulder. Nadine strokes her daughter's back. Howie hovers around the grieving mother and daughter like a loyal guard dog.

Sergeant Jimenez studies the crowd. A misty-eyed Officer Reeves paces around the perimeter. Chief Harris leans against his SUV, smoking a cigarette. Detectives Davis and Moore from the sheriff's office stand behind the mourners, with their arms folded across their chests. Mirrored shades obscure their expressions.

When Reverend Proctor concludes his sermon, Annie pulls away from her mother. She plucks a rose from an elaborate floral spray and places the flower atop the casket. Running her fingers over the sleek blue-gray steel, she tells her husband goodbye.

Bonnie Nye approaches the gravesite. "My beautiful boy." She kisses the casket. "I won't rest until they catch your killer." She whispers in Annie's ear. Annie bursts into tears. Howie leads her away.

Nadine rushes over. "My heart breaks for you, Bonnie. But if you harass my daughter again, we will take out a restraining order against you."

"I demand justice for my son," Bonnie Nye says.

"We all want that," says Sergeant Jimenez. "Let us do our job."

"You should've arrested her by now," Bonnie Nye says, "It's been over a week."

"There's not enough evidence—"

"Kit was my best friend, Mrs. Nye," Officer Reeves says, interrupting the sergeant. "Believe me, we won't rest until we find his killer."

"That woman shot my baby in cold blood."

"Enough, Bonnie," Horace Nye says. "Let's go." He takes his wife by the arm and leads her away. Jewel follows her parents to their limousine.

―――

BACK AT ANNIE'S HOUSE, Nadine goes into the kitchen and pours herself a glass of wine. "We need ice," she says, "and paper plates."

"Anything else?" Howie asks. "I'll make a store run."

"More sauvignon blanc," Nadine says.

"Be right back."

Howie rushes out the door.

"Cal, put the kettle on," Mama Libby says. "I'll brew a pitcher of iced tea."

I sneak a sip of whiskey and do as Mama Libby asks. She shoos me out of the kitchen afterward.

Officer Reeves pats me on the back. "Mind if I have a nip?" I pass him my flask. "Are you doing all right?" he asks. I'm not sure why he's being nice, but I welcome the change of pace from his usual snark. He shakes his head and says, "I can't believe he's dead."

"I know what you mean."

"You heard the shot?"

I nod.

"But you didn't see who pulled the trigger?"

I shake my head.

"That makes no sense," Officer Reeves says. "It couldn't have taken you more than a couple of minutes to reach the house."

"If that."

"Someone must've seen something."

I offer Reeves my flask. He shakes his head.

"One is my limit when I'm on duty."

A slender woman with platinum-blond curls, whose cat-eye eyeglasses rest low on her button nose, approaches. "Forgive me for intruding," she says, extending her gloved hand. "Ernestine Middleton, editor of the *Nyes Landing Gazette*. I'm covering the murder of Christopher Nye and would like to hear your side of the story." She passes me her business card. "Call me."

Helena Potter and Bo Satterlee arrive, reeking of patchouli. Bo passes Nadine a crushed white pastry box. "We brought donuts."

"Nobody is going to starve today, that's for sure," Nadine says. She sets the box on the counter and refills her wine glass.

Elena Martinez and Annie's attorney, Daniel Fields, arrive arm in arm. Elena fixes a plate of food, which the couple share.

Joe and Suki bring stir-fried Udon noodles, which Suki heats in the microwave, while she helps Nadine and Mama Libby arrange the buffet.

"It was a nice service," Joe says.

"A real blast," Officer Reeves says. He steps outside onto the back deck.

"I didn't mean—"

"Don't take it personally, Joe," I say. "Oakley buried his best friend today."

Howie returns juggling two bags of ice, a grocery sack containing paper plates and napkins, and a box from the liquor store. I grab the ice to lighten his load and follow him into the kitchen.

Elena Martinez laughs at something Daniel Fields says. Howie blanches and steps outside onto the back deck. He rubs his eyes. I can't believe he and Elena were ever married.

Several guests I don't recognize arrive and swarm the kitchen table. I suspect they only came for the food.

Gladys Crabtree drops by, clutching Mr. Squiggles in her arms. "I'm sorry I missed the funeral," she says. "I wasn't sure I'd be welcome."

"Nobody touched your salad, Gladys," Mama Libby says. "Do you want to take this wilted mess home?"

"Cover the bowl with plastic wrap. I'll take it with me when I leave."

"What a cute doggie," Helena Potter says. She lets Mr. Squiggles sniff her fingers and scratches under his chin.

"He's a pedigreed Pomeranian," Gladys Crabtree says. She launches into a long-winded boast about the dog's championship bloodline. Helena Potter listens and nods while she shovels vegan chili into her mouth.

Sergeant Jimenez stops by and fixes herself a plate of food. She steps outside onto the back deck. I follow her. Officer Reeves stubs out his cigarette and goes inside the house. Howie follows him.

"How was the funeral?" Sergeant Jimenez asks.

"What can I say?" I take a swig of whiskey from my flask. "It was a funeral."

"Are you okay?"

"Nothing I can't handle."

"What size shoe do you wear?"

"The sheriff's detectives asked me the same question."

"Crime scene investigators found a print."

"I know." I nod toward the spot where the stain had been. "I had the crime scene cleaner scrub the deck." I smile. "But to answer your question, I wear a size twelve."

"That rules you out."

"I figured as much."

"That doesn't mean you didn't shoot Christopher Nye."

"I did not shoot Kit. Neither did Annie. If those are the only theories you're chasing, you have no case."

"I should go," Sergeant Jimenez says. She finishes her last bite of casserole and goes inside the house. I follow her. She grabs a donut from the box on the counter and says, "Let me know when you find that Colt."

Annie announces that she has a migraine. She thanks everyone for coming and retires upstairs. Most of the guests take the hint and leave.

Nadine and Mama Libby put away the leftovers and clean up the kitchen, while Howie and I gather the dirty paper and plastic goods that everyone left lying around the house. I toss the trash bag into the garage can in the garage.

"I should go home and rest," Mama Libby says, "so I can get this darn cast off."

"You do more with one hand than most people do with two," Nadine says. She pats Mama Libby on the back. "I can't thank you enough. And you too, Cal." She hugs me.

Gladys Crabtree sits on the sofa, feeding her little dog bites off her plate.

"Time to go home, Gladys," Mama Libby says. She hands Gladys the plastic shopping bag that contains her salad.

"Let Mr. Squiggles finish eating."

Gladys Crabtree sets her plate on the sofa. Mr. Squiggles laps up the last few crumbs. Mama Libby snatches the plate.

"You don't have to go home, Mr. Squiggles, but you can't stay here."

"Sometimes I wonder why we're friends, Becky Goodman."

"When you figure that out, Gladys, you let me know."

Gladys Crabtree scoops up Mr. Squiggles and strides out the door.

"Tell Annie I'll call her tomorrow," I say. I take Mama Libby's arm.

"I'm not—"

"An invalid. I know." I release her arm. "Sorry."

I follow Mama Libby across the lawn.

"Give me your hand," Mama Libby says. I assist her inside the pickup.

On the ride home, Mama Libby asks if I think they'll ever catch Kit's killer. Rather than giving her some bullshit answer about how slowly the wheels of justice turn, I tell her the truth.

"I'm not sure."

CHAPTER TWENTY

As soon as we get home from Kit's funeral, I change into a tee shirt and sweatpants and take Sparky for a walk. A red fox bounds across the lawn. Sparky howls and gives chase.

"Sparky, sit!"

Rather than obey my command, Sparky drags me into the woods. Towering hemlock trees form a tight canopy overhead, which blocks out the sunlight and cools the surrounding air. Fallen branches, pine needles, and dried twigs blanket the ground. Sparky yanks the leash out of my hand and runs away. I chase after her. She stops and peers over her shoulder. I dive for her leash. She darts ahead. I trudge after her. The trees all look the same. I wander in circles for several minutes. My throat constricts. I gasp for breath and will myself to calm down.

Water rushes up ahead. I stagger toward the sound and stumble out onto the shores of Esopus Creek. The rushing current from the melting snow off the mountain slopes swells the bank. Across the creek looms the abandoned paper mill, where I spent five of the worst days and nights of my life. I collapse to my knees and fight the urge to puke.

Sparky licks my face. I hug the dog close. She wiggles loose and laps up water from the creek. I gather my bearings. Esopus Creek flows northeast of Mama Libby's house. The sun sets low in the sky behind us. I snatch the dog's leash and trudge off in the direction we came from.

I spy Mama Libby's house through the trees. Relief washes over me. I dash across the lawn and up the porch steps into the house.

Mama Libby eyes me up and down. "You look like you've seen a ghost." I tell her about stumbling upon the abandoned paper mill. She pours me a glass of lemonade, but I need something stronger.

"I'm going to lie down."

Shutting myself inside my room, I take a long pull on my whiskey bottle and fall into bed. I hug Chippy against my chest, not sure what I should feel. Rage? Shame? Grief? Despair?

Mama Libby knocks and enters. "Booze may numb the pain for the moment, son." She takes a seat on the bed. "But until you forgive yourself, you'll never find peace."

I roll over, facing away from the door, and stare out the window.

Mama Libby rubs my back. "You were thirteen. Your mother told you to run, and you did what you were told. If you'd stayed behind and fought, there's not a doubt in my mind you'd be dead now."

She's right, but that's a small comfort. I set the bottle on the nightstand.

"Are you hungry?"

I shake my head.

"There's sandwich fixings in the fridge if you change your mind." Mama Libby rises. "I wish you would give yourself a break." She shuts the door on her way out.

I drift off into a restless sleep. Memories of my mother swirl in my dreams. I awake with tears in my eyes and realize what I must do.

Upon reaching the overgrown cemetery, I wander around for several minutes before finding the faded stake that marks my mother's gravesite. I haven't visited since her funeral when I was thirteen years old. I have sketchy memories from that day. The veiled black hat that my social worker, Moira Brighton, wore, and my sister, Mary Catherine, crying. I kneel and brush the dirt aside so I can read my mother's name.

"I'm sorry, Mommy," I say, wiping aside a tear. I take a seat. Crickets hum in the grass, which needs mowing. I should find out who the caretaker is and lodge a complaint. My mom deserves a proper headstone, too. I promise her one. And flowers.

On my way home, guilt-ridden from having been too numb at my mother's funeral to cry, I burst into tears. Unable to see where I'm driving, I pull over to the shoulder and knock back a swig whiskey from my flask. I don't know what has come over me. I'm a yeller, not a crier.

Officer Reeves taps on my window. I almost jump out of my skin and glance in my rearview mirror. Lights flash atop the squad car parked behind me. Officer Lecoq sits in the passenger seat.

"Is everything all right, Nowak?" Officer Reeves asks.

"Fine," I say. "I pulled over to make a phone call." I hold up my cellular phone as proof.

"Have you been drinking?"

"Not since Annie's house after the funeral."

"Are you sure?"

"Yep."

"Get home safe."

Officer Reeves walks back to his squad car. I roll up my window and pull out onto the road. Reeves and Lecoq follow several car lengths behind me. I watch my speed and make sure I don't drift across the center line or weave onto the shoulder. I'm sure Reeves would like nothing more than to arrest me for driving under the influence.

Turning right onto Birch Lane, I cross over the Esopus Creek bridge. Officers Reeves and Lecoq turn left toward town. I pull into the driveway and breathe a sigh of relief.

"Demetrius called," Mama Libby says when I walk in the door. "He left his number."

"Thanks."

"Where did you go?"

"To the cemetery."

"We just got back from the cemetery."

"Not that cemetery. I visited my mom's gravesite."

"Are you okay?"

"I promised I'd buy her a headstone."

"That would be a nice gesture."

I stretch out the kinks in my shoulders and neck. "This was quite a day."

"I'm worn out," Mama Libby says. "Time to brush my teeth and turn in."

After taking Sparky for a walk, I retreat to my room and call Demetrius. He answers on the first ring.

"Cal, I was hoping you'd call."

"What's going on?"

"How are you holding up?"

"It's been a long day," I say. "I visited my mom's grave tonight."

"That—wow. Are you okay?"

"I'm not sure how I feel." Hearing the television in the background, I change the subject. "What're you watching?"

"*Weird Nature*."

"I've never heard of that show."

"It's a British series about the strange behaviors of animals."

"You're really into nature, aren't you?"

"I enjoy hiking and practicing my survival skills, yeah. How about you?"

"The woods are for bears."

"You don't know what you're missing."

"Maybe you can show me."

We make small talk until the conversation reaches an awkward lull.

"Guess I'll see you and Sparky at class tomorrow," Demetrius says.

We linger on the line a moment longer before hanging up. I chug a swig of whiskey and crawl under the covers.

CHAPTER TWENTY-ONE

MAMA LIBBY and I are eating breakfast on Thursday morning when the phone rings. Annie whispers into the mouthpiece. I can't understand a word she's saying. I ask her to speak up.

"Someone's breaking into my house."

"Can you see who?"

"I'm hiding upstairs."

"Where's your mom?"

"Showing a house." Annie shrieks. "They're opening the kitchen door!"

"I'm on my way. Call nine-one-one."

I explain the situation to Mama Libby while I tug on my boots and buckle on my gun belt.

"Be careful," Mama Libby says.

"I'll call you as soon as I know more."

I rush out the door, leap inside the Silverado, and speed through town, screeching to a halt before Annie's house. There's no sign of the police. Jurisdiction be damned. I leap out, unsnap the retention strap on my holster, and dart across the lawn in a crouch. Sidling up against the side of the house, I creep forward.

As I near the backyard, I hear rattling. I draw my Beretta and whip around the corner. "Freeze!"

Griffin Garfield stands on the back deck, fumbling with the door handle. When he sees me, he says, "I can't get inside my house."

"You don't live here anymore, Griffin."

"Let me in!"

Griffin bangs his fists against the door.

"Calm down, buddy, and I'll help you." I advance with caution. "Keep your hands where I can see them." Leaping onto the deck, I holster my weapon. "Take a seat." Griffin squats. I crouch and look him in the eye. "Everything is going to be all right."

Tires screech. Doors slam.

"Hang tight, buddy." I back down the steps without taking my eyes off Griffin. "I'll be right back."

Intercepting Chief Harris and Sergeant Jimenez with their weapons drawn, I explain the situation.

"Stand down, NYPD. We'll handle this."

"I'll call Megan," Sergeant Jimenez says.

"If the Garfields can't manage Griffin," Chief Harris says, holstering his Sig P220, "they should lock that boy up somewhere safe."

Griffin recoils when Chief Harris approaches.

"Let the officers help you, Griffin," I say. He slips me a house key, which I'll bet he stole from under the flowerpot on Annie's front porch last weekend.

"Your sister is on her way, Griffin," Sergeant Jimenez says. "Let's take a walk out front and wait for her." She takes Griffin by the hand and leads him away.

Chief Harris knocks on the back door and identifies himself. Annie peeks out. Harris explains the situation.

"I should've known," Annie says. "As you know, Griffin grew up in this house. He gets confused sometimes."

"All the same, he's now a person of interest," Chief Harris says.

"Surely you don't think he could've—"

"Better safe than sorry."

Annie thanks Chief Harris. He leaves. She invites me inside and swallows a pill with a sip of wine. I set her key on the counter.

"I guess we know who stole your spare key now."

"That poor man," Annie says. "There's beer in the fridge. Help yourself."

"I came prepared." I pull out my flask and take a sip.

"When I heard the door rattle," Annie says, "I thought, 'Kit's home early.' But of course, that's crazy. He's—" Her eyes well with tears. I wrap my arms around her. She pulls away and checks the time. "I need to take my pill."

"Didn't you just take a pill?"

"That was for my migraine. I need my Librium."

Annie swallows a green pill with her last sip of wine.

"Should you be drinking when you're taking those?"

"Should you be drinking and driving?"

"I took a sip of whiskey."

"And I'm taking my prescription medications."

"I'm worried about you."

"Annie, take your pills. Annie, don't take your pills. I wish everybody would stop telling me what to do."

"I should go."

"That's right. Run away. It's what you do best."

"I can't do this right now."

I leave before one of us says something we'll regret.

INSTEAD OF TURNING left and driving home, I turn right, and another right onto Main Street. It's time I find out where Demetrius is coming from. I pull into the parking lot of the hardware store and find Demetrius standing behind the cash register when I enter, sorting through a stack of receipts. I want my hands on his body and his on mine. He looks up and smiles. "What brings you by?"

"Am I nuts to think . . .?"

"Think what?"

That annoying bell over the door rings. I peer over my shoulder. "Hey, buddy," Gunner says. He smiles. "I haven't seen you at the Roadhouse since—"

"I've been a little busy," I say. "What with . . . um . . . you know . . . everything that's going on."

Gunner asks where he can find paint rollers and drop cloths.

"Aisle five," Demetrius says.

Gunner leans in and whispers. "If you ever need to blow off some steam again, you know where to find me." He walks away.

"I should go."

"What did you want to ask me?"

"It can wait," I say.

I rush out the door. That was awkward.

———

"Annie called," Mama Libby says when I get home. "The poor girl was sobbing so hard I couldn't make out a word she was saying."

"I shouldn't have asked about her medications. But I'm worried about her."

"I'm worried about you both," Mama Libby says. "You're wound so tight that I'm afraid you're going to explode."

"I can't imagine why."

"You've had a rough few days, but you can't let that—"

"Kit died in my arms. I should've—"

"What? You should've what?"

"I don't know—something." My chest tightens. I choke back tears. "He bled out so fast."

"There you go again, beating yourself up over something you had no control over."

"I will be damned if I'm going to let another killer in this town go free."

"Finding the person who shot Kit won't bring your mother back."

"Why would you say that? I'm not—. You wouldn't understand."

I take my flask and retreat outside onto the back porch. The rhythmic buzzing of cicadas in the woods behind the house drowns out the twitter of birds and chatter of squirrels.

Moses hobbles downstairs from his apartment and shambles across the lawn. "Afternoon, Cal. It is Cal, right?"

I nod and pass Moses my flask.

"Don't mind if I do." Moses takes a sip. "Any news on the case?"

"Still no murder weapon."

"That reminds me. I need to return Elizabeth's Colt."

"You have Papa Frank's . . . why?"

"I offered to clean the revolver for her."

"She must've forgotten."

"This was around the time she broke her wrist."

Moses forgetting doesn't surprise me in the least, but that's not like Mama Libby to misplace something as significant as a gun. I suppose in the chaos surrounding her fall, though, it's understandable.

"I'll need to get that back," I say, "Sooner rather than later."

CHAPTER TWENTY-TWO

AFTER THE WAY I behaved at the hardware store earlier, I dread facing Demetrius at obedience class. When I arrive at the park, he's chatting with the instructor. Gripping Sparky's leash tightly in my fist, I step out of the pickup. Sparky tugs me across the lawn toward where the other dogs and their owners have gathered.

"You wanted to ask me something?" Demetrius says.

"It's not important."

Penny calls class to order and demonstrates our next lesson, which is stay, a command I suspect Sparky will balk over. I tell the dog to sit. She does so. I pass her a treat, which she gobbles down. Following Penny's instructions, I hold my palm out and tell Sparky to stay. I release her leash and step backward. A gray-tiger-striped cat rushes between us. Sparky gives chase. I pursue her down the block. The cat ducks between two houses. The dog follows. The cat leaps over a fence into someone's backyard. The dog races past the fence and disappears into the woods beyond. I grab my knees and gasp for breath.

Demetrius rushes up. "Which way did she go?"

"Woods," I say, between breaths.

A woman wearing an apron and oven mitts crack open her back door and shouts, "What's going on out here?"

"His dog ran away," Demetrius replies.

The woman wishes us luck and shuts her door.

Demetrius runs into the woods. I follow him. White pine and maple trees encroach on all sides. My chest tightens. I take a deep breath and remind myself that I'm not alone this time.

"This way!" Demetrius shouts. He leads us through a tangled thicket of vine-covered trees.

Sparky whimpers up ahead. I rush uphill past Demetrius and discover the dog has snagged her leash on a blackberry bush. I free her. She leaps on me and licks my face. A scrap of red flannel clings to her paw. The homeless man I chased wore a red flannel shirt.

"Where did you get this?" I hold the scrap under Sparky's nose. She snatches the scrap in her teeth. "No, Sparky!" I yank on the scrap. She tugs back. I rip the scrap out of her mouth and spot a buttonhole.

Another scrap of red flannel hangs off a nearby shrub. Further ahead, I spot another scrap. I scramble through the dense woods, following a trail of red scraps, and emerge into a small clearing that's littered with old clothes and bedding, broken appliances, and other junk. I snatch a dried branch off the ground and poke through the clutter.

"Wonder what's in here?" Demetrius picks up a tattered notebook and flips through the pages. "Holy crap!" He reads out loud. "'The angels have abandoned me. The demon's voice grows louder. He tells me to—'" He shakes his head. "I can't make out the rest of the words."

A glint of silver catches my eye. I lift the corner of a stained pillow with my stick. "Don't touch anything else."

"Why?"

"I may have found the murder weapon."

Demetrius's eyes grow wide when he sees the Smith & Wesson. He guides us back to the street, where I have cellular service. I dial 9-1-1, while Demetrius jogs to the park and retrieves Flower.

Within minutes, Sergeant Jimenez and Officer Washington arrive on the scene. Demetrius leads us back to the campsite.

Sergeant Jimenez crouches. "Smith & Wesson 1911 E-Series, .45 caliber. Could be the murder weapon all right." She slips on gloves and bags the firearm for evidence.

"I'll bet this is where that bum the Crabtree woman reported seeing around her place lives," Officer Washington says. "He probably dug this crap out of people's trash cans."

"Secure the scene," Sergeant Jimenez says.

Officer Washington produces a roll of yellow crime scene tape and cordons off the area around the campsite.

"We'll take things from here," Sergeant Jimenez says.

Demetrius leads me out of the woods, and we walk back to the park. Flower falls asleep in Demetrius's arms. Sparky climbs into the pickup and lies down. I've never seen her look so tired.

"That was exciting," Demetrius says.

"I should call—" I say at the same time as Demetrius says, "Would you like—?"

"You go ahead," I say.

"I was wondering if you were hungry. I thought we might want to grab a bite to eat."

Is Demetrius asking me on a date?

"I need to take Sparky home," I say. "And let Annie know what we found."

"Another time, then."

"I could meet you in a couple of hours."

"Oh . . . okay . . . great! Have you been to the Waterside Bar & Grille?"

I shake my head.

"It's at the marina," he says. He shares directions. "Say eight o'clock?"

"Sounds like a plan."

"Sparky, you're going to flunk out of obedience class," Mama Libby says when I tell her what happened at the park. "Do you think the homeless man shot Kit with the gun you found?"

"It's the right caliber."

"If he did, Gladys will never let the town forget that she warned us."

"I have plans tonight," I say. "I hope that's okay?"

"You don't need my permission."

"I don't have to go out."

"Don't be ridiculous."

"Demetrius asked me to dinner."

"Is there something going on between you two?"

I shrug.

"His little girl, Cora, is a clever child."

"I met her at the hardware store," I say. "She's adorable."

"Demetrius is a sweetheart," Mama Libby says. "But does he bat for your team?"

"I can't tell if he's flirting with me or just being nice."

"I guess you'll find out."

"What do you think?"

"I haven't given what Demetrius does between the sheets a second's thought."

I go upstairs, knock back a swig of whiskey, and call Annie.

"Did they catch Kit's killer?" Annie asks. Her voice sounds far away.

"I found a gun. It may be the murder weapon. I haven't heard if the police have apprehended the homeless man yet or not, though, so keep your doors locked."

Annie mumbles. I ask her to repeat herself. She does. I still can't understand her.

"Are you okay?" I ask.

"No, I'm not okay," Annie says. "My husband is dead."

Annie needs me. Demetrius will have to wait.

"I'm coming over."

"Don't," Annie says. "I'm going to finish my wine and go to bed."

"Are you sure? I can be there in ten minutes."

"Mom wants to talk to you."

"Cal?" Nadine says. "Did I hear right? They caught Christopher's killer?"

I fill Nadine in on what went down this afternoon. She promises she'll lock the doors and windows.

"How is Annie holding up?" I ask.

"She's sleeping a lot. But under the circumstances, that's understandable."

"I'm worried that she's taking too many pills."

"She has an appointment with her doctor tomorrow."

"That's good."

"I had better let you go," Nadine says.

I shower and brush my teeth, put on a clean tee shirt and jeans, and tug on and spit-polish my boots. Should I take my Beretta? Better not.

"Don't drink and drive," Mama Libby says.

"I won't," I say, even though I know there's a good chance I will.

———

THE WATERSIDE BAR & Grille sports a nautical theme. A wooden canoe and paddles swing from the ceiling, surrounded by swagged fishnets. Oars and ship wheels decorate the walls, interspersed with mounted bass and trout caught by local fishermen. The hostess shows Demetrius and me to a table by a large bay window that overlooks Esopus Creek.

"They purchase their meats and vegetables from local farmers," Demetrius says.

"Our dairy products, too," a young woman who wears her brunette hair tied back in a ponytail says. In her polo shirt and chinos, she looks like a college student. "I'm Chrissy. I'll be your server. Would you like something from the bar?"

Demetrius orders a local IPA. I do the same. We admire the view of the rushing creek, while we peruse our menus. Our beers arrive.

"Are you ready to order?" Chrissy asks.

Demetrius defers to me. I order the smothered pork chops with mashed potatoes and gravy. He considers several menu items before selecting the fried chicken and waffles.

"How's your little girl?" I ask.

"Cora is growing like a weed. She's with her mom this week."

"Does your wife live in Nyes Landing?"

"Keisha moved to New Paltz after we separated. She works for one of the colleges there."

"How long were you married?"

"All of Cora's life," Demetrius says. "Keisha was six months pregnant when we tied the knot."

I can't imagine getting married that young, much less having a baby.

"You like being a cop?" Demetrius asks.

"It's challenging work. But I can't imagine doing anything else."

"This afternoon gave me a thrill. Do you think we found the murder weapon?"

"It's possible."

Demetrius and I speculate about who could've shot Kit for a few minutes and don't come up with any new potential suspects.

Chrissy brings us our entrees. She asks if we want another round. We do.

"Where did you meet Keisha?"

"We hooked up at a party our senior year of college. Got shitfaced. Made a baby."

"Sounds like one hell of a party."

"We were stupid kids. But for Cora's sake, we grew up fast."

"I'll bet."

"Keisha has her issues, but she's a great mom."

Chrissy brings us our beers. Demetrius orders a brandy as well, so I request a whiskey.

"What about you?" Demetrius asks. "Is there a special someone in your life?"

"I'm not sure," I say.

I catch his eye and smile. He smiles back. Is he flirting? Am I?

Demetrius and I make small talk about the food. He offers me a bite of his fried chicken. I decline. He accepts a taste of my pork chops when I offer. I ask when his divorce became final.

"Today."

"I didn't realize—are you okay?"

"Better than okay."

Demetrius swirls and swallows his last sip of brandy. I knock back my whiskey and swig my beer. Chrissy brings our check.

"Dinner is on me," Demetrius says. "This is cheaper than a therapy session."

"I'm the last person anyone should turn to for advice."

Chrissy thanks us on our way out the door. I'm parked next to Demetrius.

"Thanks for dinner," I say. "Well . . . um . . . get home safe." I extend my hand for a shake.

Demetrius draws me in and kisses me hard. He grabs my hair

in a firm but playful grip. I kiss back. He pulls away and mutters, "Sorry."

Before I can say I'm not, he hops behind the wheel of his car and speeds away. I watch his taillights disappear into the night. My impulse is to chase after the guy. But a tiny voice of reason inside me whispers I should go home. And for once in my life, I listen.

CHAPTER TWENTY-THREE

Mama Libby wants a roll of film from the orchid show developed, so I drive into town on Saturday afternoon. Dark clouds loom over the surrounding mountaintops. I stop by Annie's house on the way. Nadine answers the door and invites me inside. I smell smoke and say as much.

"Helena lit a bundle of sage on fire this morning and waved the darn thing all over the house to 'cleanse the bad juju,'" Nadine says. "The smoke made Annie nauseous. She's lying down. Would you like a cup of coffee?"

"Sure." I follow Nadine into the kitchen, which looks spotless and smells like an orange grove. "Someone has been cleaning."

"If I don't keep busy, I'll scream. After you leave, I'll mow the lawn."

"Let me do that. I could use the exercise."

"You don't need to . . ."

"You have your hands full with Annie."

"I'm sorry that I'm such a burden," Annie says. I didn't realize she had come downstairs. She appears lethargic but more alert than the last time I saw her. "My pill, Mom."

"Sit down, sweetheart," Nadine says. She pulls out a chair for Annie at the kitchen table. "I'll brew you a cup of tea."

"Mom, please. My head feels about to explode," Annie says. "I need my pill."

"Coming right up, sweetheart."

Nadine passes Annie her pill with a glass of water. Annie swallows her medication. I rub her shoulders. She leans forward. I knead the knots from her neck with my thumb, backing off whenever she winces. Her eyes well with tears.

"Here's your tea," Nadine says, setting the cup and saucer on the table.

"Thank you, Mom," Annie says. "I'm glad you're here."

"My baby needs me."

"I should mow the lawn now," I say, "before the rain starts."

Kit sure kept his garage organized. A variety of shiny tools dangle on hooks above a tidy workbench. Snow skis and fishing rods lean against the wall. Tents and camping equipment stuff the shelves overhead. I raise the garage door and straddle the seat of the shiny red Craftsman. I've never driven a lawnmower before. How hard can it be? Finding the keys in the ignition, I turn over the engine and ride outside.

The sun shines through the clouds. I shuck off my tee shirt and soak up some rays while I mow the lawn, wondering if I should call Demetrius or wait for him to call me.

Sergeant Jimenez and Officer Washington hustle a shackled gorilla of a man with shaggy hair out of the woods by his elbows. I suspect that's the homeless man they've apprehended.

Gladys Crabtree rushes out of her back door. "What did I tell you?" She staggers down the porch steps.

"Calm down, ma'am," Sergeant Jimenez says.

"Don't tell me to calm down." Gladys Crabtree wags her finger in the homeless man's face. "You're an evil man. An evil, evil man."

"Step back, ma'am," Officer Washington says. The husky

officer shields the homeless man with her body. "Go back inside your house."

"I can stand in my own yard if I want. I know my rights."

"Mrs. Crabtree," Sergeant Jimenez says, "we want to hear your side of the story."

"Now you care about what I have to say?"

"If it's not too much trouble, perhaps you could come down to the station this afternoon and give us a statement."

"I suppose I could do that."

"I appreciate your cooperation. Now, please, for your own safety, go inside."

"Fine."

Sergeant Jimenez and Officer Washington place the homeless man in the rear of their squad car and drive away. I wonder if they've received a report on that Smith & Wesson yet. Being out of the loop sucks.

Once I finish mowing the lawn, I grab the weed eater and trim the edges of the driveway and curb. I wash off and put away the tools, and I shuck off my boots before stepping inside the house.

"I hung fresh towels in the downstairs bathroom," Nadine says. "Would you like a cold beer?"

"After I wash up. Where's Annie?"

"Lying down. Migraine."

"That sucks."

To reach the downstairs bathroom, I walk through Kit's home office, which I suspect was a parlor in the original house. I spot his ThinkPad on the desk. I'm surprised the police haven't confiscated the laptop yet.

After I wash up, I join Nadine in the office. She sits behind Kit's desk, studying the ThinkPad's screen. "Here you go." She passes me a cold beer.

"What are you working on?"

"I'm doing my best to sort out Annie's finances. If my figures are correct, Kit left her buried in debt."

"How can I help?"

"Are you any good with computers?"

"I type with two fingers, if that tells you anything."

"Kit had an email account we need to access, but we can't figure out his password."

"I may know someone who can help."

I pull out a crinkled list of phone numbers from my wallet and call the NYPD Information Technology Bureau. The operator transfers me.

"Dooley Mayes. How can I save your ass today?"

"By tracing an email for me," I say.

"Nowak!" Dooley exclaims. "When did you get back?"

"I haven't."

I catch Dooley up to speed.

"I'll need some information off the computer," Dooley says. "The IP address, for starters."

"Speak English."

"I'll talk you through what I need."

"Hold on." I place my hand over the receiver. "Do you know what an IP address is?"

"I believe so," Nadine says. "Why?"

"Dooley, I'm going to pass you over to someone who knows more about computers than me."

Nadine chats with Dooley and types on the keyboard. If anyone can hack into an email account, it's him. He helped me trace a suspect in a big case my first year on the force, which got me noticed by the captain. Knowing he's a Mets fan, I bought him season tickets as thanks.

What is Kit hiding? An affair with Brandy Speedman? Not according to her. Gambling debts? Those seem obvious. There's something we're missing here.

Nadine passes me the receiver.

"Did you get what you need?" I ask.

"Yeppers," Dooley says. "Let me see what I can dig up."

By the time I reach the print shop, it's almost six o'clock. "I'm about to close up shop," the clerk says. I set the roll of film from the orchid show on the counter. She glances up and blanches. "You don't remember me, do you?"

Late fifties, early sixties. Short and stout. Dark, curly hair with a dramatic wisp of silver sweeping off her brow. Kind eyes that look familiar, but I can't say where I've seen them before. I shake my head.

"I'm not surprised." She passes me Mama Libby's receipt. "I'm Moira Brighton. I was your social worker after—"

My chest tightens. I rush out of the print shop. I haven't seen Moira Brighton since she placed me with Mama Libby and Papa Frank, and I have no desire to revisit those days. I climb behind the wheel and speed away.

As I pass the hardware store, I make a sharp U-turn and pull into the parking lot. Demetrius stands behind the cash register when I enter, counting bills. "I'm closed," he says. He glances up. His eyes widen. He dashes past me, flips the open sign over, and locks the door. He turns around and stammers, "I owe you an explanation. I shouldn't have—"

"Stop talking," I say, kissing him perhaps a bit more aggressively than I'd intended. He stumbles backward into a carousel rack filled with seed packets. We fall on our asses. Seed packets rain down around us. We roll aside before the rack crushes us and burst out laughing. He kisses me, and we make out on the floor for a moment before composing ourselves.

"Kissing a man is so different," Demetrius says.

"You've never . . ."

"I came close once. After my divorce."

"What happened?"

"I went to a party. Got a little drunk. Ended up naked in a hot tub with the host. He got handsy. I freaked out and ran away."

Perhaps I should've expected that, but I didn't. I gather up and sort the seed packets into stacks by kind.

"You don't need to do that," Demetrius says.

"I should get going."

Standing the rack upright, I slip the packets into their slots and rush out the door. I fell hard for the first guy I had sex with. This was after I moved to the city when I was eighteen. He was an arrogant jerk, but I still recall with longing how he tasted and smelled. First times are a big deal. I mustn't start something with Demetrius that I can't finish. He deserves better.

———

WHEN I ARRIVE HOME, the delicious aromas from Mama Libby's kitchen make my mouth water before I step through the door. Mama Libby tells me to take Sparky for a walk while she finishes cooking dinner. Moses greets me on the lawn, carrying a bottle of red wine.

"Elizabeth invited me to dinner."

"Sure smells good in there."

"I can't cook that well with two hands."

"I think you underestimate your culinary skills, Moses."

Over dinner, Mama Libby reminds me she needs a ride to church in the morning. "Don't let me forget to take those baby clothes from the attic. I set the bag by the front door."

"Elizabeth," Moses says, "I haven't had pork this succulent since I ate Cantonese pork belly from a street vendor while I was on leave in Hong Kong."

If Moses launches into another Nam anecdote, I'm going to need my flask. I should call Demetrius and explain my behavior. Or would that be weird? I'm obsessing again. We're not in high school. We're grown men. He knows the score.

"Earth to Cal," Mama Libby says.

"I'm sorry, did you say something?"

"I asked if you'd like dessert."

"No, thanks." I pat my belly. "I need to get in shape."

"For Demetrius?" Mama Libby grins.

"Who's Demeter?" Moses asks.

"Demetrius," Mama Libby says. "Cal's friend. You need to get your hearing checked, old man."

I excuse myself from the table and go upstairs to my room. Reclining on my bed, I sip whiskey and contemplate what a roller coaster the past few weeks have been. I didn't make detective. Sarge placed me on administrative leave. Mama Libby broke her wrist, so I came home. Kit died in my arms. Annie seems lost. And I'm obsessing over a guy, which is so unlike me.

Meeting Demetrius has thrown me for a loop. I pick up the phone and dial his number. Uncertain of what I want to say, I hang up before our lines connect.

CHAPTER TWENTY-FOUR

Dragging my hungover ass out in the rain on Sunday morning takes every ounce of resolve I can muster. I drive Mama Libby to the church early, so she can drop off clothing before Mass. Or rather so I can, because I'm the one who gets drenched lugging the bag up the sidewalk. The effusive graciousness of the nun who accepts the donation makes me feel guilty for complaining, if only in my mind.

Finding myself with an hour to kill, I pick up two coffees from the diner and drive by the hardware store.

Demetrius stands behind the cash register, ringing up several cans of ceramic glazes for Helena Potter. I smile. He ignores me.

"Morning, Cal," Helena says. "Have you met Demetrius?"

Demetrius extends his hand for a shake. I don't wish to embarrass him, so I play along with his ruse, but I don't appreciate being shoved back inside the closet I fought so hard to escape.

"How's Bo?" I ask.

"I haven't talked to Bo since Kit's funeral," Helena says.

"I'm sorry."

"Don't be. I'm too much of a woman for that boy."

Helena pays Demetrius and leaves.

I set a cup of coffee on the counter. "I thought you might appreciate a little midmorning pick-me-up."

"Listen, I'm sorry about—"

"Call me when you figure out what you want."

CONGREGANTS SWARM OUT of the church following Mass. I help Mama Libby climb into the Silverado and drive her to the Nyes Landing Diner for brunch. The hostess seats us at a table by the window seconds before hordes of Methodists stream through the door. We invite Annie and Nadine to join us.

"From the way Father O'Reilly rushed through Mass," Mama Libby says, "I assume the Red Sox must have a game this afternoon."

"They're facing off with the Yankees," I say.

"That rivalry always makes for an interesting matchup," Nadine adds.

"Any word from the police?" I ask.

Annie shakes her head.

"No news is good news," Nadine says. "Isn't that right, sweetheart?"

Kiki takes our drink order. Mimosas for Nadine and Annie. Orange juice for Mama Libby. A cup of coffee for me, which I spike with whiskey from my flask when no one is watching.

"Today's special is a Mexican breakfast skillet with chorizo and fresh salsa," Kiki says. "And we're out of the Bananas Foster French Toast."

Annie orders a poached egg on dry wheat toast.

"You need to eat more than that," Nadine says.

"I need to lose weight," Annie says. "Kit was right."

"That's ridiculous." Nadine hands Kiki her menu. "Bring us the special with an extra plate and we'll share."

"Blackberry pancakes with a side of turkey bacon for me," Mama Libby says. "I should eat turkey more often."

"It's healthier than pork," Nadine says.

Pancakes sure sound good, but I can't afford the calories. I order an egg white omelet with turkey bacon and spinach and a fruit cup rather than home fries. I never eat this healthy, but I must get in shape.

Sergeant Jimenez and Officer Washington amble through the door and place an order at the counter. I excuse myself and join the duo.

"All I can tell you, Nowak, is that the man we apprehended for questioning claims he found the firearm we recovered in the woods behind the Nye house on the night of the shooting," Sergeant Jimenez says. "We're hoping to receive a report from the lab in Kingston as early as tomorrow."

"What about his diary? Those weird ramblings?"

"The subjects mental state is questionable. The hospital admitted him for observation."

"Excuse me, son." I pass the young man behind the counter my debit card. "I'd like to buy these officers lunch."

"You don't need to do that," Sergeant Jimenez says.

"No disrespect, Sarge, but speak for yourself," Officer Washington says. "Add a slice of blackberry pie with a scoop of vanilla ice cream to my order."

"Yes, ma'am," the young man says. He processes my charge. I add a tip and sign the receipt.

"I'm glad you two are on the case," I say. "Enjoy your lunch."

I return to my table and share what I found out.

"If the homeless man has a screw loose," Nadine says, "are we safe?"

"He's in the hospital," I say. "But keep your doors locked. Even when you're at home."

"Especially when you're at home," Mama Libby says.

Megan Garfield picks up a takeout order from the counter.

She's dyed her blue hair a drab brown color. On her way out, she stops by our table. "I'm sorry Griffin tried to break into your house," she says. "He gets confused."

"My heart breaks for your brother," Annie says. "And for your family."

"We've placed Griffin in a facility in Albany." Megan's eyes tear. "Where he can get the help that he needs."

"You're doing the right thing," Mama Libby says.

"I hope so," Megan says. "Excuse me."

Jewel approaches Megan on the sidewalk outside. Megan gives the strung-out young woman a dollar bill.

"If the Nyes didn't own half the county," Mama Libby says, "Child Protective Services would've intervened. And that poor soul might've stood a chance."

Joe Farley and his wife, Suki, bustle through the door, beaming from ear to ear. The couple make their way over to our table.

"What are you two grinning about?" Nadine asks. "Did you close on your house?"

"Even better," Suki says.

"We're pregnant," Joe says. "I mean, Suki's pregnant." He pats his wife's stomach. "But I helped."

"This town could use some good news," Mama Libby says.

"Congratulations," Nadine says. "How far along are you?"

"Eight weeks," Suki says. "I'm due in November."

"Fall babies often come early," Nadine says. She turns to Annie. "You were supposed to be a fall baby, but you couldn't wait to enter the world. That's what Patrick used to say. Your daddy doted on you, sweetheart."

"I miss him, Mom."

"Me too."

Weeks after Annie and I started dating our sophomore year, Patrick Leighton keeled over from a heart attack. He'd appeared in perfect health, so his death shocked us. But he didn't leave. He died. My old man abandoned me and never looked back.

"You're smart not to wait," Annie says. "You never know—" She shakes her head. "Kit and I wanted a family. Now he's gone." She chokes back a sob. "And I'm left to pick up the pieces. Excuse me—" She flees to the ladies's room.

"I'd better—"

"Nadine, sit," Mama Libby says. "Give her a minute."

"I'm sorry," Joe says. "We shouldn't have—"

"You're going to be parents," Mama Libby says. "That's wonderful news. Don't let Annie's grief spoil your joy."

I can't imagine being a parent. I can barely take care of myself. But I congratulate Joe and Suki.

Kiki clears away our plates. I ask for the check and pay in cash. She thanks me.

"Let me leave the tip," Nadine asks.

"It's taken care of."

Annie returns. "I'm sorry I made a scene."

"I don't know how you're holding up as well as you are," Mama Libby says. "After Frank's funeral, I took to my bed for weeks."

We step outside and say our goodbyes.

"I need to pick up my prescriptions on the way home," Mama Libby says. She directs me to the drugstore.

While Mama Libby waits for her medications, I search the aisles for toothpaste. I squeezed the last drop out of my tube this morning. A heavyset clerk directs me toward oral care on aisle seven.

A woman shouts obscenities. Her voice rises in volume and pitch. A child sobs. I rush around the corner. The mother of the boy Annie expressed concern about is holding her son by the arm and spanking his butt. Other shoppers gather to gawk. The woman drags her son out of the store, bawling that he's sorry.

"I should call Child Protective Services," Mama Libby says, "and ask for someone to perform a wellness check."

Mama Libby and Moses clean out their respective refrigerators and warm up leftovers for dinner. While we eat, I mention I might go out tonight.

"By all means," Mama Libby says. "Moses and I have plans to watch the new Reba McEntire special tonight."

"That woman is a national treasure," Moses says. "But Dolly is the queen of country."

"I wouldn't have pegged you for a country music fan, Moses," I say.

"I enjoy all kinds of music, son."

I rinse and put my plate and fork in the dishwasher and take Sparky for a walk. When I get back, I shower and get dressed. I have limited wardrobe options. A black tee shirt with black jeans and boots will have to do.

"Don't drink and drive," Mama Libby says.

"I made that mistake once," Moses says. "Right after I got back to the States, I had—"

I duck out the door before I get stuck listening to another one of Moses's war stories and drive into town. It's not even nine o'clock yet and the only business that's open is the gas station. If I were in the city, the night would be young.

At the Roadhouse, I belly up to an empty bar. Gunner sets me up with a pint of stout and a shot of whiskey.

A young Black woman with a pierced eyebrow sings a karaoke rendition of Tammy Wynette's "Stand by Your Man" that strikes me as incongruous with her tough chick fashion sense. Two women wearing plaid shirts, jeans, and cowboy boots shoot pool. Four guys sit around a circular booth in the bar's rear, shouting over one another and laughing. The only other patron in the joint sits slouched over a table behind the jukebox with his back turned to the bar.

"Is it always this exciting around here?" I ask.

"You should've stopped by last night," Gunner says. "A rowdy bunch of city queens livened up the joint." He grins. "And spent a butt load of cash."

A burly guy with a bushy beard and a saggy gut takes the microphone from the Black chick when her smattering of applause dies and drowns out conversations with a screeching rendition of "I'd Do Anything for Love (But I Won't Do That)." His buddies join in from their seats. The Black chick dances by herself.

A muscular Black guy covered in tattoos swaggers into the bar. "Let's go, Laila!"

"Sam!" The Black woman throws her arms around the Black man and kisses his lips.

"You know I don't like you hanging out in no fag bar," Sam says. "Why do you always got to be testing me, huh?"

"I like to sing," Laila says. "Is that a crime?"

Sam takes a step toward the guys in the booth. "What are you faggots looking at?"

"All right, buddy," Gunner says on his way out from behind the bar. "Time to go."

"Touch me, faggot, and I'll kick your ass."

Sam's eyes look wild. He's on drugs.

"You heard the man." I stand, prepared to back up Gunner. "Get lost."

Sam sizes us up and says," Where's your purse, woman?"

Laila staggers in a circle. Her face lights up. "Here it is!" As she grabs her bag, she knocks over a chair.

"Move your ass, Laila."

"Don't rush me, Sam. You're always bossing me around."

Sam hustles Laila out the door.

"I wasn't sure how that was going to go down," I say.

"Me either," Gunner says. "But it's not the first time and it won't be the last."

The phone behind the bar rings. Gunner answers. "Roadhouse." He smiles. "Hey, baby." Holding the receiver against his ear, he pours me another shot of whiskey. "Sure, I'll pick up cigarettes on the way home." He hangs up.

"You have a boyfriend?" I ask.

"You've met Tanner, haven't you?"

"I didn't realize you two were a couple."

"Ten years next month," Gunner says. "We have an open relationship."

"Does Tanner know that?"

The guys in the corner booth call Gunner over and order more drinks. Gunner was under no obligation to tell me about Tanner. All the same, I feel foolish for not knowing.

My bladder is about to burst. I find the men's room. I'm in mid-piss at the urinal when Trevor Speedman staggers through the door. He must be the guy who was sitting behind the jukebox. What is he doing in a gay bar? He dashes inside the first stall and pukes into the toilet. Stumbling out, he hugs his stomach and groans.

"Are you okay, man?" I ask.

"I've ruined my life."

"I'm sure that's not true."

"Brandy and I should've stayed in California."

"Let's clean you up." I haul Trevor onto his feet and lead him over to the sink. He blubbers into my shoulder. I wipe off his mouth with paper towels, clean up the front of his shirt and mine as best I can, and lead him out to the bar. Gunner passes me a glass of water. I insist Trevor drink every drop and ask if he drove here tonight. He nods. I offer the guy a ride home.

"You should take Cal up on that," Gunner says.

I pay my tab and help Trevor outside and into the Silverado. I ask where he lives. He hands me his driver's license and slouches against the door.

I'm driving northwest on the two-lane state highway toward the affluent hamlet of New Maastricht where Trevor lives when he sits up and says, "You're gay, right?"

"Yeah." Where is this leading, I wonder? "Why?"

"I blew a guy and wrecked everything."

I'm confused but intrigued.

"What are you talking about?"

"He's dead."

"A guy died because you . . . what?"

"No. But he's dead, all the same. I never should've . . ." Trevor leans his head against the passenger window. Tears streak his scruffy cheeks.

"I have no idea what you're talking about."

"Christopher's gone."

"Christopher Nye?"

"That's right."

"You gave Kit a blowjob?"

"In Atlantic City."

"You and Kit hooked up?"

"And my wife, Brandy. We took some blue mystic that I'd scored in Miami and partied hard."

Of course, illegal drugs were involved.

"Brandy went to get ice. Christopher couldn't get it up. I helped him out."

"Your wife knows about this?"

"We tell each other everything."

"Is that why you shot him?"

"I would never hurt Christopher. I—oh, what difference does it make now? I've destroyed everything."

If Trevor is telling the truth, that explains a lot. And I can't think of a reason he would lie. I take the next exit and drive the guy home.

CHAPTER TWENTY-FIVE

I'M HELPING Mama Libby weed her garden Monday morning when Gladys Crabtree pulls into the driveway in her red AMC Pacer. She leaps out and charges in our direction. "I said all along that woman shot her husband and I was right."

"What are you babbling about, Gladys?" Mama Libby asks. I help her onto her feet.

"The police arrested Annabelle Nye this morning."

"Good Lord," Mama Libby says.

"Took her away in handcuffs."

"On what grounds," I ask.

"How should I know? I don't pry into other people's business."

"Where did they take her?" Mama Libby asks.

Gladys shrugs her shoulders. "The police station, I suppose."

"If she's not there," I say, "I'll drive to Kingston."

"I'm coming with you," Mama Libby says.

"Should I follow you?" Gladys asks.

"Go home, Gladys," Mama Libby says. "And keep your mouth shut."

OFFICER REEVES IS SMOKING on the sidewalk in front of the police station when we pull up. "Guess you heard," he says. He stubs out his cigarette beneath the toe of his boot. "They're charging Annie with Kit's murder."

"Based on what evidence?"

"I shouldn't say, but that Smith & Wesson you found?"

"What about it?"

"It's registered to Kit."

"No shit. Did they recover prints?"

"Several. Including the chief's prints because he made the rookie mistake of handling the weapon without gloves."

"Were Annie's prints found on the gun?"

"No, but her gunpowder residue test came back positive. The chief seems convinced that she's the shooter. He wants this case closed."

"I can't believe they're pinning this on Annie."

"Without her prints or witnesses," Officer Reeves says, "they're a long way from a conviction."

I spot Nadine through the window, speaking with Annie's attorney, Daniel Fields.

"Excuse me," I say. Sidestepping around Officer Reeves, I enter the station and ask, "Where is she?"

"They're transporting her to Kingston for arraignment this afternoon," Daniel Fields says.

Sergeant Jimenez enters the station. I intercept her.

"I know what you're going to say," Sergeant Jimenez says. "But someone shot Christopher Nye with his own gun. No one else was in the house. She had residue on her hands. We'd be remiss if we didn't charge her."

"What about the homeless man? Weren't his prints found on the gun?"

"Staff at the shelter confirmed that Ray Toulouse had dinner in their cafeteria that night. He signed in at eighteen-thirty and didn't check out until they closed their doors at twenty-two hundred hours. Claims he found the gun in a patch of ferns behind the Nye residence."

"Why would Annie—?"

"I've said more than I should," Sergeant Jimenez says. "Excuse me." She disappears around the corner.

"Should I drive to Kingston?" Nadine asks. "Or will Annie need clothes from the house? Should I go there first? They won't lock her up, will they?"

"She'll get released on bail," Daniel says. "I'll drive. I can explain the process in the car."

"We'll follow in the Silverado," Mama Libby says.

"Ride with us," Daniel says.

"I wouldn't want to put you out," Mama Libby says.

"We have plenty of room."

I help Mama Libby into the back seat of Daniel's SUV and climb in beside her. Nadine slides the passenger seat forward, so I have more legroom, which I appreciate. Before we pull away from the curb, Nadine barrages Daniel with questions regarding what she can expect at the arraignment. He does his best to calm her fears and explain the process while he drives.

"Annie did not shoot Christopher," Mama Libby says. "We can all agree on that, right?"

"It doesn't matter what we think," Daniel says. "We have to convince a judge."

I cannot conceive of a world in which Annie pulled the trigger. But someone shot Kit with his own gun.

"If Annie needs a character witness, I've never testified in criminal court," Mama Libby says, "but I've taken the stand in family cases many times."

"She might have transferred gun residue onto her hands when she held the body," I say.

"Good point," Daniel Fields says. "If this case goes to trial, I'll retain an expert witness who'll corroborate that fact."

We drive over a dead skunk in the middle of the road. A

pungent musk infiltrates the car. We cover our noses and collectively groan. Aside from that unpleasantness, the drive is uneventful, and we arrive at the courthouse with time to spare. Daniel drops us off at the entrance and parks the car. We wait for him to join us and venture inside.

All these old Federalist buildings, with their drab gray plaster walls trimmed in walnut wainscoting and terrazzo tile floors, look the same. Stoic police officers stand watch at regular intervals along the corridor. Harried legal aides rush around. We pass through the security checkpoint with no issues and take the elevator to the second floor. Daniel Fields shows us the courtroom where Annie's arraignment will take place.

"Judge Miller?" Mama Libby says.

A statuesque woman who wears her steel-gray hair pulled back in a tight bun turns around. A black robe covers all but the collar of her navy-blue suit. She smiles. Her piercing gray eyes sparkle. "Libby Goodman, I haven't seen you since my days adjudicating in family court. I'm an Adams again. I took my name back after the divorce. What happened to your wrist?"

Mama Libby shares her harrowing adventures in that deathtrap of a hospital and introduces us.

"Mr. Fields," Judge Adams says. "You're representing Annabelle Nye?"

"That's right, Judge."

"Sad case," Judge Adams says. "Excuse me. Duty calls. It was nice seeing you, Libby."

Daniel Fields suggests we take our seats.

"I would like to see my daughter," Nadine says.

"That's not allowed," Daniel Fields says. "Try to relax."

"That's easier said than done."

"This isn't my first rodeo."

"Come on, Nadine," Mama Libby says. "Let's find our seats before the courtroom fills up and we're forced to stand in the back."

"I wouldn't like that."

"No, you wouldn't," Mama Libby says. She leads Nadine down the aisle, and they take seats behind the defense table. I follow suit.

Annie shuffles into the courtroom in handcuffs when her case is called, flanked by two guards. Daniel Fields joins her at the defense table. Nadine reaches across the bar and squeezes Annie's shoulder.

"Hands back, ma'am," the portly bailiff shouts, and he takes a threatening step forward.

"I was just—"

"Let it go, Nadine," Mama Libby whispers.

Bonnie Nye strides into the courtroom and takes a seat across the aisle from us. She glares at the back of Annie's head.

Everyone rises when Judge Adams enters the courtroom. She asks if Annie understands her charges. Annie nods and offers a feeble "Yes, ma'am." Judge Adams advises Annie of her constitutional rights and records Daniel Fields as her attorney of record.

An intense young assistant district attorney from the prosecutor's office outlines the seriousness of the charges and requests remand. Daniel Fields points out that Annie has no prior criminal record and that the evidence in this case is circumstantial at best. The assistant district attorney objects to every other word out of his mouth. He dismantles her arguments before she finishes speaking.

Judge Adams demands silence in the courtroom, admonishes the assistant district attorney for her inflammatory rhetoric, and suggests that a man of Field's experience should know better than to interrupt his opponent.

"I find many of the arguments presented today questionable," Judge Adams says. "We'll determine at a preliminary hearing if there's sufficient cause to submit the case to a grand jury." She consults her files and suggests a date in a couple of weeks. All parties agree. "Given that the defendant is an upstanding member of her community and has no prior criminal record, I'm setting bail at one hundred thousand dollars."

Bonnie Nye leaps to her feet. "You call that justice?" She points toward Annie. "That bitch murdered my son. I demand you lock her up."

Judge Adams calls for order and reprimands Bonnie Nye for her outburst.

"This isn't over," Bonnie says, "Not by a long shot." She storms out of the courtroom, slamming the door behind her.

After court, Daniel Fields directs Nadine to a bail bondsman and explains the process. Nadine pays the guy his ten percent fee. He processes the surety. Several minutes later, they release Annie.

Daniel pulls his SUV up to the courthouse entrance and we pile inside. On the drive home, Daniel assures us everything will be fine. "The prosecution's case hinges on two circumstantial facts," he explains. "The murder weapon belonged to Christopher Nye and Annie's gun residue test came back positive." He circles the roundabout and takes the third exit. We merge onto the highway. "Should this case go to trial, which I doubt will happen, all I must do is instill reasonable doubt in one juror. I'll hire an expert to refute the gun residue test, and I'll challenge the chain of custody both before and after the weapon came into their possession." He scoffs. "That idiot of a police chief mishandled the evidence. That alone should call into question the integrity of the investigation."

I hope Daniel is right. I refuse to let Annie go down for a crime she didn't commit.

CHAPTER TWENTY-SIX

DAWN PEEKS THROUGH THE CURTAINS. I give up on getting a decent night's sleep and crawl out of bed. If Annie ran a stop sign, she'd turn herself in. She isn't capable of murder. But the evidence against her looks suspect. I tug on a sweatshirt and sweatpants, slip on my sneakers, and take Sparky for a run. A glistening layer of morning dew blankets the lawn.

Sparky bounds around my legs. I rein the dog in and tell her to heel. She trots along beside me down the side of the road. We jog by a pasture where a black-and-white bull grazes. Sparky rushes over to the fence and barks at the bull. The bull snorts and paws the ground. Sparky growls. The bull charges the fence. The dog yelps and retreats behind me.

Beyond the pasture, the woods encroach on the road. I jog down the gravel shoulder. Sparky scampers back and forth before me with her nose to the ground. A skunk scurries under a blackberry bramble. Sparky gives chase, dragging me after her. I dig in my heels and attempt to rein in the dog. A low-hanging evergreen branch slaps my face. I stumble backward and lose my grip on the leash. She bolts into the woods. I groan. Not again.

As I trek along a narrow ridge, the ground beneath my feet

caves, and I tumble into a ravine on my butt. Heavy spring rains have washed away the steep cliff side. I brush myself off and glance around. A vibrant green bush surrounded by thick grasses sprouts out of the otherwise barren earth. I'm no naturalist, but I once guarded a crime scene in Central Park where a jogger had found a dead body. A detective working the case explained to me that plant growth that thrives beyond the limitations of its surroundings often conceals decomposition.

I crawl closer, anticipating that I'll find the remains of a dead animal. Instead, I spot a patch of white rubber. Grabbing a stick off the ground, I whisk aside the dirt and debris and find myself staring at a child's sneaker. Based upon the shoe's condition, it's been buried for a while. Clearing aside more dirt, I uncover denim and—bones. Possibly human. I lurch backward. Scrambling up the hill, I tug off my boot and sock and tie my sock to a nearby tree.

Sparky's barking grows more frantic. She emits a shrill yelp. Slipping on my boot, I rush in her direction and find her pawing at her snout. The skunk she chased disappears under a patch of ferns, save for its bushy black-and-white tail. My eyes water from the sting of its musk. Tugging my sweatshirt up over my nose, I drag Sparky out of the woods by her collar.

"I hope you've learned your lesson about chasing wild animals," I say.

Sparky wags her tail, which I interpret as a no. We jog home where I have cellular service. I dial 9-1-1. Suki answers. I explain what I've found.

"Oh, my! I will let Sergeant Jimenez know right away."

Mama Libby recoils when she smells Sparky. "I'll grab the baking soda and the dish soap. Bring me a bottle of hydrogen peroxide from the medicine cabinet in the bathroom."

I rush upstairs and fetch the bottle. Mama Libby tells me to get the kiddie pool out of the garage. I do so. Taking off my tee shirt and boots so they don't get wet, I fill the pool using the garden hose. Sparky splashes around in the water.

Mama Libby instructs me to mix the hydrogen peroxide, baking soda, and dish soap. I bathe Sparky in the fizzy concoction. After several rinses, Mama Libby passes me a bottle of medicated dog shampoo. I lather the dog's thick coat and rinse her well. She shakes off, showering me. I dry her fur using an old bath towel. Only the faintest musk smell lingers.

Sergeant Jimenez arrives with Officer Reeves. I get dressed and crawl into the backseat of their squad car. We drive into the woods. I keep my eyes peeled for the blackberry bush.

"There," I say. "On the left."

Sergeant Jimenez pulls over. I lead the officers through the woods, something I couldn't have done a few weeks ago. I spy my sock and lead the officers to the spot where I may have found human remains.

Sergeant Jimenez slides down the cliff side and examines the disturbed area. "Secure the location," she says. "I'll radio the sheriff's office."

"What can I do?" I ask.

"You've done enough," Officer Reeves says.

"What is your problem, Reeves?"

"Ever since you came back to town—."

"Drive Nowak home," Sergeant Jimenez says. "You two can hash out your differences in the car."

"I'd rather walk," I say, and I leave before I punch Reeves. Personal feelings aside, I must respect the badge he carries.

AS SOON AS I RETURN, Mama Libby tells me she needs to run errands. She carries a sack of fresh carrots and asparagus from her garden out to the pickup. I toss two bags of donated clothing for the Memorial Weekend rummage sale into the bed of the truck and drive to Annie's house, so Mama Libby can drop off the vegetables.

"I love asparagus, Libby," Nadine says. "I wish it didn't turn my pee green, but . . ." She steps back. "Come in." I follow Mama Libby inside the house.

"How's Annie?" Mama Libby asks.

"She's doing as well as possible, I suppose."

"These things take time," Mama Libby says. "After seven years, I still have moments when I think I see Frank's face or hear his voice."

"I know what you mean," Nadine says. "It took years before I quit expecting Patrick to walk through the door at the end of the day."

"You weren't accused of murdering your husbands," Annie says.

"I didn't hear you come downstairs, sweetheart," Nadine says. "Would you like a cup of tea?"

"I'm going to float away if I drink any more tea, Mom."

"Perhaps a glass of wine, then?"

"I'd like to donate Kit's clothes to the rummage sale."

Annie seems to rapid-cycle through the stages of grief—angry one moment, accepting the next—something social workers cautioned me against doing when I lost my mother.

"Are you sure?" Mama Libby asks. "That's a big step."

Annie nods. "I'll need help, though."

"Cal and I will be more than happy to pack anything you want to donate."

"Mom, can you show them where Kit's things are?"

"Are you sure you'll be—?"

"Quit hovering, Mom."

"I'm only trying to help." Nadine leads Mama Libby and me upstairs. Her eyes tear. "I can't do anything right."

"You're a wonderful mother," Mama Libby says. She hugs Nadine.

Nadine dries her eyes. "I'm tired, that's all."

Nadine and Mama Libby empty Kit's drawers, which are filled with tee shirts, sweaters, and jeans, into plastic trash bags, while I pack his suits, dress shirts, and slacks from the closet. All name-brand designers, which doesn't surprise me. I find ten pairs of shiny dress shoes hanging in a bag on the inside of the closet door and a dozen boxes of sneakers and hiking boots stacked on the shelf above. After we finish, I toss the bags into the bed of the pickup.

"We'd best get on the road," Mama Libby says.

"If you need help with the sale," Nadine says, "let me know."

"Spread the word," Mama Libby says. "We need shoppers."

"Do you have any flyers?" Nadine asks. "I can set them out at my open houses."

"I'll ask Frieda and get back to you."

"Will you be at Helena's show tomorrow night?"

"That's tomorrow?" Mama Libby turns to me. "We should go."

"Then let's go," I say.

Art galleries are not my scene, but I want to support Helena.

"I'll have to wait and see how Annie feels," Nadine says.

After we depart Annie's house, I drive to the Nyes Landing Diner. Mama Libby sends me inside to see Kiki. Kiki asks me to give her a minute and disappears into the kitchen. While I'm waiting, Howie Clark approaches and asks how Annie is doing.

"She has her good moments and her bad moments."

"Tell her to give me a ring if she needs anything."

"You should call her."

"I wouldn't want to be a bother."

I never realized Howie was so insecure.

Kiki brings me two trash bags full of clothing that she collected from patrons of the diner.

Next stop, Helena Potter's gallery, which is a few blocks further down the street. I park in front. Helena waves through her bay window and rushes outside. I leap out of the pickup and greet her on the sidewalk.

"I have two boxes of stuff for the rummage sale," Helena says.

"We look forward to your show tomorrow night," Mama Libby hollers from her seat in the pickup.

"I'm excited for you to see my new designs," Helena says.

I follow Helena inside her gallery. She hands me a cardboard box that contains a lava lamp, a digital alarm clock, a cordless phone, VHS tapes of the movies Practical Magic and The Witches of Eastwick, and several boxes of incense. She follows me out to the pickup with another box, which is filled with dark clothing. I load the boxes into the bed of the truck.

Helena Potter hugs me and lurches backward like she's suffered a shock. "That's never happened before."

"What's never happened before?"

"A dark force—. I don't know how to explain . . . but you're in danger. Promise you'll watch your back."

The concern in her voice, coupled with everything that's gone down the past few days, gives me pause.

"What did you see?" I ask.

"Not see so much as sensed."

Although I don't believe in psychics or spirits, I'd be lying if I said I wasn't a little creeped out.

"If you need help with your preparations for tomorrow night," Mama Libby shouts, "give us a ring."

Leaving Helena's gallery a little shaken, I cruise up a narrow road that winds through a wooded area north of town and cross over Esopus Creek.

"Take the next right," Mama Libby says.

I navigate up a steep hillside driveway and park before an impressive two-story log house. Selling used cars must pay better than I thought. I knock, wait a moment, and knock again.

Suki answers the door wearing a paint-streaked smock. "I'm

getting the nursery ready before my stomach gets too big for me to climb a ladder."

"What a delightful shade of lavender," Mama Libby says.

"We wanted a soothing color that wasn't pink or blue."

"Is it too early to find out the sex of the baby?"

"We want to be surprised," Suki says. "These boxes by the door are for the rummage sale." She leans in and whispers. "I'm glad you came while Joe's at work. I'm donating his comic book collection."

"Are you sure you want to do that?" Mama Libby says.

Suki laughs. "He won't kill me while I'm pregnant."

I load the boxes into the pickup, and we say our goodbyes.

Mama Libby directs me across town to the Kiwanis Club community center, where the Memorial Day weekend rummage sale will take place. She climbs out of the pickup and hugs a bony woman with curly gray hair who wears overalls with clogs. "Cal, this is my friend, Frieda Gladstone. Frieda owns the Stone Witch Inn."

"We met when you lived with Libby and Frank," Frieda says. "I don't expect you to remember." She shows me where I can place the donations we brought for the rummage sale. I unload the pickup while the two women gossip.

On our way home, we stop by the photo lab, and I run inside to pick up Mama Libby's photographs from the orchid show. To my relief, Moira Brighton isn't working.

"You're Annie Nye's friend, aren't you?" the young woman behind the counter says. I nod. "Would you mind giving her these?" She passes me an envelope. "Her husband dropped off a roll of film before—"

"Of course."

I hand Mama Libby her envelope when I get back to the pickup and stash Kit's photographs in the glove compartment.

―――

When we get home, I take Sparky for a run. We near the spot where she chased the skunk. Law enforcement vehicles line both sides of the road. We hike into the woods. Detectives and crime scene investigators comb the area near the ravine where I found clothes and bones.

Officer Washington blocks my path. "No unauthorized personnel beyond the crime scene tape."

"Are the remains I found human?" I ask.

"I can't discuss the case," Washington says.

"What're you doing here?" Officer Reeves asks.

"Making sure you don't botch the investigation."

"Move along, NYPD," Chief Harris says.

Sparky bares her teeth and snarls. The chief steps back and glares at the dog.

"And keep that mutt on a leash or I'll have animal control pick her up."

"You son-of-a-bitch—"

"Watch your step, son."

"Or what?"

"I'll arrest you for obstruction."

Chief Harris glares at me. I want to punch his ugly mug, but I refrain because I don't want to lose my badge.

"Obstruction, my ass. You should thank me for doing your job."

Turning on my heels, I drag Sparky out of the woods and jog home.

CHAPTER TWENTY-SEVEN

MAMA LIBBY EMPTIES the last of the kibble into Sparky's bowl on Wednesday morning and sends me into town to buy more. The feed store is having a sale on dog kennels. I should install one of those in the backyard.

A stocky sales associate with a bushy beard introduces himself as Bob and launches into a spirited sales pitch about the merits and shortcomings of the various models he has in stock. I can't imagine getting that excited about dog kennels. "The chain link with the galvanized steel frame is your best bet," Bob concludes. "The canopy will shield your pet from the elements."

"You've convinced me."

"If you're local, my guy can deliver this afternoon, but he'll need help with the assembly."

"I should ask Mama Libby first."

"This is for Mrs. Goodman?"

"That's right."

"My dad went to school with her. She's right up there with Mother Teresa in his eyes. I'll sell you the kennel at cost."

"You've got yourself a deal."

I pass Bob my debit card. He processes the charge, passes me my receipt, and promises his guy will deliver the kennel after lunch. On my way to the pickup, my cellular phone rings.

"I called the house," Annie says. "Mama Libby suggested I try your mobile phone."

"What's up?"

"Mom's car is in the shop. She needed to show a house, so I loaned her mine because I didn't expect to go anywhere. But the school called, and my paycheck is ready. I can't find the keys to Kit's Mercedes. I've looked everywhere."

"I'll be right over."

Annie is waiting on the porch when I pull up. I drive her to the elementary school and wait in the pickup while she goes inside. She returns upset.

"Evan Langford wasn't in class today."

"Did the school call his parents?"

"His mom's phone is disconnected."

I drive Annie to the bank so she can cash her check and take her home. We find Sergeant Jimenez and Officer Reeves standing on the porch when we arrive.

"We're here for your husband's computer, Mrs. Nye."

Sergeant Jimenez passes Annie a warrant.

"Kit kept his computer at the office," Annie says.

"We searched Kit's office," Officer Reeves says.

"How did you—?"

Officer Reeves jangles a set of keys.

"May we come in, Mrs. Nye?" Sergeant Jimenez asks.

"Of course." Annie opens the front door. "Have a seat. I need to use the little girls's room. It's this medication I'm on. Excuse me. " She goes to the bathroom in the office.

"Have you made any progress on identifying the human remains I discovered?"

"What makes you think they're human?" Sergeant Jimenez asks.

"The sneaker and the scrap of denim I unearthed."

"I wish I could say you were wrong, but you're not," Sergeant Jimenez says. "Given the crime scene is outside the town limits, we surrendered jurisdiction to the sheriff's office."

Annie returns. "Much better." She takes a seat in the armchair. "As I said, officers, my husband kept his ThinkPad at work."

"What about his home office?" Officer Reeves asks. "Did you search there?"

"I assume your detectives did," Annie says, "when they tore up my home."

"I apologize for that," Sergeant Jimenez says. "Would you mind if we have a look around?"

"Be my guest."

Sergeant Jimenez and Officer Reeves search through the drawers of Kit's desk and scour the office.

"I don't understand," Sergeant Jimenez says.

Me either. The last time I saw the computer it was on the desk.

"Maybe someone stole the laptop," Annie says.

"Who would want to steal your husband's computer?" Sergeant Jimenez says.

"The person who shot him?"

"You stand accused of your husband's murder," Sergeant Jimenez says.

"Based upon circumstantial evidence," I say.

"Would you care for coffee, officers?" Annie asks. "Or tea?"

"No, thanks, ma'am. We'll be going now."

As soon as Sergeant Jimenez and Officer Reeves drive away, Annie shows me where she hid the laptop inside a compartment beneath the padded leather seat cushion of the mahogany executive desk chair.

"I can't let them take the computer until we crack the password to Kit's secret email account."

"Let me follow up with my friend in the ITB." I call Dooley

and leave a message on his voicemail. "I should go. I'll let you know as soon as I hear back."

AFTER I HELP the delivery guy install Sparky's kennel, I shower and dress for Helena Potter's show. Moses helps Mama Libby into the Silverado. She slides into the middle of the seat. Moses climbs up beside her. His snowy curls shine, and he smells like coconuts. We arrive a few minutes after seven o'clock and park on the street.

The moment we walk through the gallery door, Gladys Crabtree wobbles in our direction. Wine sloshes over the rim of her glass. She licks her fingers and, leaning in, whispers louder than most people speak, "These prices are ridiculous." I smell more gin on her breath than wine.

Helena Potter waves from across the gallery. Dressed in a black leather corset and lace skirt, with gold glitter sprinkled in her dark curls, she resembles a character from the Harry Potter movies. All she needs is a wand. She shows Elena Fernandez and Daniel Fields around the gallery.

A young woman with strawberry-blond pigtails, wearing an oversized white men's dress shirt with black slacks, passes through the room serving glasses of white wine. Mama Libby and Moses partake. I ask the young woman if she has any beer. She suggests I see her aunt. I find Trixie, the tall woman with the white bob from the farmers market, serving drinks from behind a small bar. She offers me a choice of two local IPAs.

On a table near the bar, Trixie and her partner, Rose, have laid out an impressive spread of local meats and cheeses, grilled vegetables, homemade breads with a selection of jellies and jams, and flaky pastries drizzled in honey. I pile a taste of everything onto a paper plate and grab a napkin and a plastic fork.

Opal Brown gives Helena a silver brooch that's shaped like a spider. "I found this at an estate sale and thought of you."

"It's creepy cool," Helena says. She pins the brooch onto her corset.

Moses claims his bum knee hurts. He fills a plate and takes a seat on a sofa in the corner. The old man can't tell art from shit and only came for the free food.

Helena gives us a tour of the gallery. "My Starry Night dinnerware," she says. She presents a collection of rustic black ceramic plates with silvery white flecks. "They're dishwasher-and-microwave-safe."

"Only a fool would spend thirty dollars on a dinner plate," Gladys Crabtree says.

My sister Mary Catherine and her snooty friends would fork over that much and more if they liked the pieces.

Helena leads us around the corner and pauses before a table with pitchers, platters, and vases that are shaped like dying flowers and ferns. "My Faded Beauty Series." She gestures for us to follow her to a glass case on top of a pedestal that contains a layered pink creation with many folds. "My pride and joy—the Vulva Vase."

Gladys Crabtree gasps and scurries away.

"A vase that repels Gladys?" Mama Libby says. "We could all use one of those."

Brandy Speedman strolls into the gallery on the arm of Bo Satterlee. Helena welcomes the couple. "You're a woman with taste, Brandy," Helena says. "I'd like your opinion of my latest work." She leads Brandy away.

Bo orders a beer from Trixie and grazes off the buffet. Rose passes Bo a paper plate and a napkin.

"The Vulva Vase comes in several shades," Helena says. "From a light pink to a dark reddish brown."

"I'll take three," Brandy says. "They'll spark conversations in the tasting room of the winery." She studies a row of ceramic women's busts with withered breasts sculpted in realistic detail and glazed in a range of shades from ebony to ivory. "Fascinating."

"My Colder Than a Witch's Tit series," Helena says. She laughs. "I suppose I should've given my girls more erotic breasts if I wanted them to sell."

"How much?" Brandy asks.

"The larger pieces are five hundred dollars, the smaller three hundred."

"I'll take one of each size in the light and darker shades."

Helena juggles the four vases in her arms.

"Cal, give Helena a hand," Mama Libby says. She joins Moses on the sofa while I carry Brandy's purchases to the checkout counter.

Joe and Suki arrive and share their baby news. Everyone congratulates the beaming couple.

"Suki can't drink, so she's my designated driver," Joe says, and he asks Trixie for a beer. "Cheers!"

Helena shows Suki around the gallery while Joe argues with Bo over the best starting lineup for the upcoming high school baseball state championship semifinals. If the Fisher Cats beat the Spackenkill Spartans, they'll face off against the Troy Flying Horses for the title. I don't know the players, so I'm lost.

"I pitched for the Spartans back in the day," Demetrius says. I didn't see him come in. He looks hotter than ever in a tomato-red jacket over a white tee shirt with matching slacks and oxblood loafers. Even his bare brown ankles turn me on. I'm glad they're not serving whiskey tonight, because I might make a fool of myself.

Lucille Miller arrives wearing an emerald-green suit. A frumpy woman whose white hair is so thin that I can see her scalp accompanies the mayor. Helena greets the two women and asks if they know me.

"I met the mayor at the diner," I say.

"That's right, you're Libby Goodman's foster son," Mayor

Miller says. "You've had quite an eventful few days in our little town."

"Cloris is our local historian," Helena says. She places her hand on the frumpy woman with the thinning hair's shoulder. "She runs the Nyes Landing Historical Society."

"The mayor and I have a proposition in the works," Cloris says, "that will revitalize our historic downtown."

"We must capitalize on the influx of weekenders from the city," Mayor Miller says. "They have the disposable income our town needs."

I trust politicians about as much as I do criminals, but that sounds reasonable.

Frieda Rosen, the woman who owns the Stone Witch Inn and organizes the rummage sale, bursts through the door. Her clogs clomp across the hardwood floor. "Sorry, I'm late," she says. "This sale is going to be the death of me."

"If you need help," Mama Libby says, "let Cal know."

"Sure," I say. "You know where to find me."

I wish Mama Libby would let me step up to the plate of my own accord. I'm not a child. I excuse myself and ask Trixie for another beer.

"Will I see you at obedience class tomorrow?" Demetrius asks.

"That's the plan."

"I know. I've been sending you mixed signals," Demetrius says. He leans in and whispers. "I've never experienced feelings like this before."

"You're a nice guy, Demetrius. And for sure easy on the eyes. You deserve somebody who'll treat you right."

"What about you?"

"I'm damaged goods."

"Can't we—?"

I walk away before I lose my resolve. Doing the right thing doesn't always feel good.

"Thanks for driving my husband home the other night,"

Brandy Speedman says. "He told you about what happened in Atlantic City?"

"Sounds like you three had a wild night."

"Does Christopher's wife know?"

"I haven't told Annie."

"I appreciate that."

"I'm protecting her, not you."

"I don't need your protection."

"You and your husband have an unusual relationship."

"We're getting a divorce."

"You and Trevor?"

"No, me and George Clooney."

"Sorry, that was a dumb question."

"Trevor's first divorce, my third. Don't say anything."

I mime zipping my lips with my fingers, for I'm in no position to judge.

"What's your story? Anyone special in your life?"

"I'm a lone wolf," I say.

"Who became a cop? How cliché."

"It's a long story."

"I'm all ears."

"I'm strictly hit and run."

"Sounds lonely."

"You're never lonely?" I ask.

"I don't know the meaning of the word."

Mayor Miller gives a speech touting her plans for revitalizing the local economy. Cloris Haney follows up with a rambling but effusive plea for support of the Nyes Landing Historical District. Helena closes by thanking everyone for coming.

The party winds down. We congratulate Helena on our way out the door. Gladys Crabtree takes one last opportunity to complain about the prices. Bo helps Brandy load her bags into her SUV, and the couple leave together. I drive Mama Libby and Moses home.

Mama Libby turns in for the night. I take my whiskey outside and sip on the back porch. The dog kennel went up without too much hassle this afternoon. The guy from the tractor supply knew what he was doing. I followed his lead, and we finished in under an hour. I have blistered fingers and a bruised thumb from a misdirected rubber mallet blow, but Sparky has a safe space to play outside.

Moses joins me. I pass the old guy the whiskey. He takes a swig and hands me back the bottle. "The kennel looks good," he says. "You should reinforce the ground around the base of the chain link, though. In case the dog tries to dig out."

"I'll do that."

"Elizabeth said you found a body?"

"I found bones."

"Do they belong to that foster boy who disappeared last year?"

I shrug.

"I heard they arrested your friend."

"That Smith & Wesson I recovered?"

"Yeah?"

"Belonged to her husband."

"No way."

"If no other viable suspect surfaces, she could get convicted for a crime she didn't commit."

"There's a Vietnamese proverb," Moses says. "Nghịch cảnh là mẹ của trí tuệ. Roughly translated, it means, 'with adversity comes wisdom.'"

"If that's true, I should be a regular Einstein by now."

"I'll drink to that," Moses says. He takes a sip of whiskey and passes me the bottle. "Thanks for the company and the bottled comfort." He stands. His knee joint cracks. He hobbles home.

My brain won't shut off. Except for the terrorist attacks last fall, which were unprecedented, I've witnessed more serious crimes since coming home than I've seen in five years with the NYPD. I'm not sure what to make of that.

CHAPTER TWENTY-EIGHT

Thursday morning, I drive Mama Libby to the hospital. She talks nonstop about how excited she is to get her cast removed. I drop her off at the entrance and park the pickup while she checks in. I find her pacing around the waiting room.

"It's a good thing we rushed to get here. Doogie Howser is running late."

"Did the receptionist say why?"

"She said I should sit down and wait my turn."

An orchid on the cover of a gardening magazine catches my eye. I show Mama Libby. She sits and reads the article and tosses the magazine aside. "That's just flat out wrong. You should never trim aerial roots. They promote healthy growth. Leave them be."

I have no clue what aerial roots are, but I'm grateful Mama Libby is no longer fuming over her doctor's tardiness.

Twenty long minutes later, a stern blond nurse with broad shoulders and thick ankles marches into the room and calls Mama Libby's name.

"Let's get this over with," Mama Libby says. I help her onto her feet.

The nurse leads us down a long hallway and gestures toward an open door on the right. "Wait here. The doctor will be with you shortly."

"I hope so," Mama Libby says. "He's kept me waiting for an hour."

"Babies don't always arrive on schedule," the nurse says.

"Nobody told me Doogie Howser was delivering a baby."

The doctor joins us and studies Mama Libby's chart. "How are we feeling, Elizabeth?" he asks without glancing up.

"Ready for this darn cast to come off."

"Let's take some x-rays. See how the break is healing."

The nurse insists Mama Libby ride in a wheelchair. Mama Libby plops down on the seat, places her feet on the rests, and crosses her arms. The nurse rolls Mama Libby down the hallway into radiology and leaves the room.

"Miserable cow," Mama Libby mutters under her breath.

I wait in the hallway while the x-ray technician scans Mama Libby's wrist. The nurse returns and wheels Mama Libby back to the examination room.

"Those machines are dangerous," Mama Libby says. "They give people cancer."

The doctor examines Mama Libby's x-rays. "Here is the fracture," he says, indicating a faint line on the printout. "It's healing well. I'll see you again in two weeks."

"You expect me to wear this contraption for two more weeks?"

"At least."

"Oh, for heaven's sake. Let's go, Cal."

When we get home, we find Sparky lying down inside her kennel. She doesn't lift her head when we call her name. Foam lathers her mouth.

Hearing the commotion, Moses rushes downstairs from his apartment and examines Sparky. "The dog must've eaten something poisonous," he says. "I need hydrogen peroxide."

Dashing upstairs, I fetch the bottle we used when we bathed Sparky. Cradling the dog's head in my lap, I pry her teeth apart. Moses pours hydrogen peroxide down her throat and massages her larynx. She swallows hard and throws up chunks of raw meat that are tinged with lime-green streaks.

"Her heart is pounding a mile a minute," Moses says. "She should see a veterinarian."

"Let's go," Mama Libby says. I scoop up Sparky in my arms and carry her over to the Silverado. Moses helps Mama Libby climb inside the pickup. I lay Sparky across her lap. She pets the dog and massages her ears while I drive as fast as I dare. We pull into the parking lot of the veterinary clinic. I rush the dog inside. Mama Libby follows us. We explain the symptoms. The veterinary technician rushes us inside an examination room.

Dr. Webb checks Sparky's vitals. "Her heartbeat is elevated." He studies the sample we brought of the meat she threw up. "Most likely brodifacoum," he says. "A key ingredient in many rodent pesticides. By inducing vomiting, you may have saved her life."

"I can't imagine where she could have eaten rat poison," Mama Libby says. "And I never feed her raw meat."

"This may not have been an accident," Dr. Webb says.

"Why would anyone want to hurt Sparky?" Mama Libby asks.

"When I find out who did this, I'm going to—"

"Don't go flying off the handle, Cal," Mama Libby says.

"I won't," I say, "but if whoever did this shows his face again, I'm not about to turn the other cheek."

"What makes you think it's a guy?"

"Odds are . . ."

"Let's wait and see."

I hate it when Mama Libby is right, which is most of the time.

"I'd like to keep Sparky overnight," Dr. Webb says. "I'm already sleeping at the clinic with a cat who ate a child's Ritalin tablet. I can monitor the dog's vitals, too."

I admire Dr. Webb's dedication to the animals in his care.

"You're a good man, Lewis," Mama Libby says. She hugs Sparky. "Behave for the doctor."

As soon as we get home, I call the police. Ten minutes later, Officers Reeves and Lecoq knock on the door. Mama Libby and I share what we think happened.

"Have you received any complaints about your dog?" Officer Lecoq asks. He pulls a notepad from his pocket. His glasses slide down on his nose. He pushes them up and readies his pen to take notes.

"Never," Mama Libby says.

"Have you had any recent altercations with anyone?" Officer Lecoq asks.

"Gladys Crabtree every time I see her," Mama Libby says. "But she'd never hurt a dog."

"Crime has exploded since you came back to town, No Good," Officer Reeves says. "How much longer do you plan on sticking around?"

"I might never leave. You have a problem with that?"

"Watch your step, No Good."

"Or what?"

"Let's go, Reeves," Officer Lecoq says. "We'll file a report, ma'am."

And that will be as far as the case goes. But without witnesses or evidence, I'm not sure what more the police can do.

―――

WHILE CLEANING out the Silverado Thursday evening, I find the envelope of Kit's photographs that the print shop entrusted me with. I call Annie and ask if I can come over. She greets me at the door. She appears listless, but her eyes look less foggy than they did the last time we were together. Perhaps her doctor lowered her dosage. I don't dare ask for fear of sparking another argument.

"Would you like something to drink? I'm having a glass of wine."

"I don't suppose you have any Irish whiskey."

"I might. Kit kept a well-stocked bar. See for yourself."

I'm impressed but not surprised by Kit's taste in spirits. Top-shelf scotches, bourbons, vodkas, gins, and score—a thirty-year-old Bushmills. I pour a generous shot and inhale its floral but peppery aroma.

Annie takes a seat on the sofa in the living room and clutches the envelope of photographs. "What if there are pictures of Kit with another woman in here? I don't know if I can handle that right now."

"Put the envelope away until you're ready to look inside."

"That's what I think I'll do."

Annie stashes the envelope in the bottom drawer of Kit's desk.

"Mom hasn't figured out the password for Kit's secret email account yet," Annie says.

"I can't believe I haven't heard from Dooley. He never lets me down."

"If Kit was hiding an affair," Annie says, "perhaps I'm better off not knowing."

Should I tell Annie about what happened in Atlantic City? If Kit were alive, I wouldn't hesitate. But now that he's dead, I'm not sure it matters.

The phone rings. Annie answers. "I'm fine, Mom." She sips her wine. "Cal brought me some photographs. Seems Kit dropped off a roll of film at the print shop, which he never picked up." She shakes her head. "I haven't looked yet. I'm not sure I want to see what's in there." She nods. "Listen, I need to go, Mom. I'll talk to you in the morning." She hangs up. "I love my mother, but she is driving me nuts."

"Everywhere we go, Mama Libby volunteers my help before I even have the chance to offer."

"If you'd like another whiskey, help yourself," Annie says. "I'm having more wine."

"Don't mind if I do."

"I'm worried," Annie says. "What if a jury indicts me?"

"Let's not get ahead of ourselves."

"I didn't shoot Kit," Annie says. Her eyes tear. "I've never even fired a gun."

"I won't let you go to jail."

"Promise?"

"Promise." I sip my whiskey. "What baffles me is how anyone could've shot Kit and fled the scene without someone noticing."

"I can't think about this right now," Annie says. "Let's watch a movie." She turns on the television and scrolls through the cable menu. "When Harry Met Sally comes on in ten minutes. What do you say? I'll make popcorn."

Annie and I watched that movie on a date our sophomore year.

"May I borrow your phone? I need to call Mama Libby."

"Of course."

Annie goes into the kitchen. Seconds later, I hear popcorn popping. Mama Libby thanks me for calling and tells me to give Annie her love. Annie and I curl up on the sofa and laugh at the banter between Meg Ryan and Billy Crystal.

"Is there anyone special in your life, Cal?"

I shrug. "Maybe."

"I need details."

"I met a guy."

"And?"

"I don't know what's going on," I say. "But he excites me. And not just between my legs."

"Does he live in the city?"

I shake my head.

"Where does he live?"

"I'm not sure. We only met a few days ago."

"Here in Nyes Landing?"

I nod.

"What's his name?"

"Demetrius."

"The owner of the hardware store?"

I nod.

"I don't blame you," Annie says. "That man is too cute for his own good. I didn't realize he was gay."

"I don't know if he's gay or bisexual or what," I say, "but we may have gone on a date."

"What do you mean by may?"

"We went to dinner, and he kissed me afterward."

"That sounds like a date to me."

"A couple of days later, we made out on the floor of the hardware store."

"I don't think straight guys do that."

"Right?"

"So?"

"He doesn't know what he wants. My life is a mess. I'm going home soon."

"He likes you. You like him. What's the problem?"

"This scene on the plane is one of my favorites."

"You're changing the subject."

"I thought you wanted to watch the movie."

"You're right. Forget I said anything."

We sip our drinks and stare at the screen.

"Demetrius has never . . . you know . . . with a man."

"You have enough experience for the both of you."

I can't argue with that.

"So? What are you going to do?"

As long as I'm upfront with Demetrius, what's the harm in fooling around? We're both grownups.

"Mind if I use your phone?"

"You don't need to ask," Annie says. She pauses the movie and goes into the kitchen to refill her wineglass.

I step inside the office and dial Demetrius's number. He picks up on the first ring. "Is everything okay?" he asks. "You weren't in class this afternoon."

I explain what happened.

"I hope Sparky gets well soon," Demetrius says. "She's in good hands with Dr. Webb."

"I can't believe he's sleeping at the clinic tonight. That's dedication."

"What are you up to now?"

"I'm over at Annie's house. We're watching When Harry Met Sally."

"I've never seen that movie."

Demetrius's television plays in the background.

"What are you watching?" I ask.

"Animal Planet."

"You and your nature programs."

"I enjoy learning about the world around me."

"I want to see you."

"Right now?"

"No, of course not. I mean . . . unless you . . ."

"Call me after the movie."

I promise I will and return to the living room.

"Demetrius told me to call him after the movie. I think he wants to get together."

"Are you for real?"

"What?"

"We can watch a movie anytime," Annie says. "Go get your man."

"Are you sure?"

Annie passes me the phone. I call Demetrius back. We make plans to meet at the nature preserve northwest of town. Annie pours me a shot of liquid courage and shows me the door.

When I pull into the parking lot of the nature preserve, I spot Demetrius leaning against the trunk of his car. I park and leap out. He rushes over and takes hold of my hand. "I want to show you something." My head warns me not to venture into the woods after dark. But my dick suggests I grow a pair.

"I've always wanted to bring someone special here," Demetrius says. His smile emboldens me. I follow him down a narrow dirt pathway. Low-hanging branches scratch my arms. I freeze.

"Are you okay?"

"Give me a minute." I take a deep breath and assure myself that I can do this. "Lead on."

"You sure?"

I nod.

Ahead of us, water rushes. We're on the northwest side of town, far from Esopus Creek, but several waterways flow through the Catskill Mountains. I trip over a rock that's buried in the ground. Demetrius catches my arm and steadies my balance. "We're almost there," he says. We slide down a slippery cliff side onto the bank of a shallow brook, which is fed by a lazy waterfall. Moonlight shimmers in the rippling water.

"I was ten years old when my mom got sick," Demetrius says. He skips a pebble across the surface of the water. "My dad couldn't cope and took off."

We may have more in common than I'd realized.

"Mom couldn't take care of herself, much less me and my brother, so my grandma took me in."

"I was seven when my old man walked out on us for good," I say. "He couldn't cope with my mom's mood swings anymore. She'd get drunk and beat the crap out of him. He'd disappear for a few days. She'd track him down and beg him to come home, and he would. But not that time."

Demetrius gazes up at the stars. "I used to hike up here and sit for hours, wondering how I could make the cancer go away."

"Your mom died?"

Demetrius nods. "When I was ten."

"I'll never forgive myself for letting my mother get murdered the way she did."

Demetrius squeezes my hand. "You were—"

"Only a child. I realize that. But I should've—"

"What?"

"I don't know..."

"Is that why you became a cop?"

"Maybe."

Demetrius leads me around to a boulder that overlooks the brook, and we take a seat. He slips his arm around me. I feel the beat of his heart.

A piercing shriek sends me scrambling for cover. Demetrius laughs and says, "Screech owl." He takes off his hiking boots and socks, rolls up the cuffs of his pants, and dips his toes into the brook. He shivers. "That is cold."

"I'm a cop," I say. "We're tough." I struggle with untying a knot in the lace of my boot.

"More like helpless," Demetrius says. "Allow me." He pries the knot loose and tugs off my boot and sock.

I take off my other boot and sock and dunk my feet underwater, only to withdraw them the next second. "Damn! You weren't kidding."

"It gets better, tough guy."

"I'll take your word for that."

Demetrius smiles. I kiss his lips.

"This is nice," I say.

Demetrius pulls away. "The other day, you said I needed to decide what I want." He squeezes my hand. "I can't have what I want."

"I don't understand."

"I can't risk Keisha using this against me in family court. She wants full custody. And she's prepared to fight like hell to get her way."

"We can be discreet," I say, hating myself for slipping back inside the closet for a man. Being out as a cop can be tough, but the officers I've known who've hidden their same-sex affairs either ended up miserable drunks or ate their guns.

"No one can find out."

"Mama Libby knows."

"She won't say anything."

"And I told Annie. But she can keep a secret."

"I hope so."

"Once they clear Annie's name, though, I'll be going home."

"The city is only a few hours' drive away."

"My life is a mess. I can barely take care of myself."

"I don't need you to take care of me," Demetrius says.

"I know, but—"

Demetrius kisses me, and I kiss back. I feel like a teenager again. Although, aside from a brief encounter with my assistant football coach when I was eighteen, I didn't have sex with a man until I moved to the city. Demetrius shucks off his tee shirt. My breath catches in my throat. We make out in the moonlight. I've never wanted anyone more. But I'm not about to screw in the woods at night. I've seen too many slasher flicks.

"Damn mosquitos," Demetrius says. He swats his arm. "We should go back before we get eaten alive."

We dress, and he takes my hand and leads me out to the parking lot.

"I don't know—"

I silence Demetrius with a kiss and whisper, "You don't have to know." We hug, and he drives away, leaving me alone on the edge of the woods, too elated to be frightened.

CHAPTER TWENTY-NINE

Dr. Webb calls the house on Friday morning and lets us know that Sparky feels better and can come home. Mama Libby and I drive into town. She insists on stopping at the bank so she can get cash. I wait in the pickup while she conducts her business and drive her to the veterinary clinic. The sleepy town seems a far cry from the chaos of the city.

When Sparky sees Mama Libby, she gets so excited that she knocks over a magazine rack. I straighten up the dog's mess and tell her to sit several times before she obeys.

"Give her a tablet in the morning with food and another at bedtime," Dr. Webb says. He hands Mama Libby a bottle of pills. She passes him seven crisp twenty-dollar bills. He counts out her change and hands her a receipt.

On the drive home, we pass Chief Harris in his black SUV. The young boy seated beside the chief must be his son. Sometimes I forget that police officers have lives beyond their badges.

When we get home, Sparky has energy to burn. I release the dog inside her kennel. She races around the perimeter of the chain-link fence. I can't believe that less than twenty-four hours ago, she lay on the brink of death.

Before the day gets too hot, Mama Libby waters her garden. The hedges need trimming. I should've taken care of that when I mowed the lawn. The house could use a fresh coat of paint. I imagine the gutters need cleaning. If the rotten floorboards on the front porch aren't replaced soon, someone is going to get injured. I doubt I'll be here long enough to finish all the repairs that must be done around the place. I may need to hire help.

Mama Libby explains how I should trim her asparagus plants and watches over my shoulder while I do as she instructs. "I'm going to make soup," she says. I carry a bundle of the snipped stalks inside and lay them in the sink.

While Mama Libby cooks, I go upstairs and knock back a shot of whiskey. The voice mail light on my cellular phone blinks. I check my messages.

Sorry it took me so long to get back to you.

I recognize Dooley's voice.

My wife had a baby. A little girl. I'm a dad. Can you believe that? Anyhow, I found that password for you. Call me.

Dooley answers on the first ring.

"Congratulations, Dad."

"Thanks, Nowak. Have you got a pen handy?"

"Yep." I scribble the series of letters and numbers he shares on a scrap of paper. "I owe you one, man."

I tell Mama Libby I have to run and will explain later and dash out the door.

———

ANNIE TYPES the password into the form field on Kit's laptop and hits enter. She tries again. "Are you sure that's what he said?"

I check the scrap of paper I scribbled the password on again. "C-J-H-e-1-4-3-0-2-0-0-2."

"It doesn't work."

"Let me try."

Annie and I trade seats. I type the combination in twice before catching my mistake. That's a lowercase l, not the number one. "We're in!"

Annie pulls her chair closer. Aside from spam, we find a trail of saved emails from YourWorstNightmare@hotmail.com. We read through the exchange.

> I want those photographs.

> It'll cost you.

> Don't fuck with me.

> No money, no photographs.

> Let's make a deal.

> Those are my terms.

> You must be nuts. I don't have that kind of money.

> Suppose I make a few phone calls.

> Don't threaten me.

The email trail ends on the day that someone shot Kit.

"Where did you put that envelope from the photo lab?" I ask.

Annie retrieves the envelope and fans out the photographs on the desktop. Random shots of the town and woods. No women, which is a relief.

"That's Evan," Annie says. "My student." She holds a photograph up to the light.

"Are you sure?"

"Positive." She shows me the photograph. In the distance, a scrawny young boy huddles beneath a tree in his underwear. The silhouette of a man of average height and build crouches in the shadows. I can't make out his features. "Here's another shot of the boy," she says, "and another."

Annie calls the elementary school. The secretary confirms that Evan didn't come to class today either and his mother's number is out of service.

"Do you know where the boy lives?" I ask.

"In a trailer park northeast of town."

"Let's go."

———

"Take the next right," Annie says.

Drifting the Silverado around the corner, tires screeching, I speed up a winding dirt road, easing my foot off the gas pedal before each run-down mobile home we pass so Annie can read the name on the mailbox. We drive under a dense canopy of spruce trees.

"There," Annie says. She points toward a beat-up trailer with a flower bed out front that's overgrown with weeds and guarded by two faded garden gnomes. I pull over and park. I've performed many wellness checks. If parents feel threatened, they can go off the rails fast. I gesture for Annie to stand back before I knock on the door and drop into a crouch, prepared to draw my weapon if need be. "Police! Open up!" I rap again. No answer.

"Mrs. Langford, it's Annie Nye. Evan's teacher."

Mrs. Langford peeks out. She sweeps her frizzy blond hair off her sallow face. "Name's Travers. Twyla Travers." A cigarette dangles from the corner of her mouth. "I ditched Stu's name after the divorce."

"Stu is your ex-husband?" I ask.

"Yeah. What's it to you?"

"Is Evan home?" Annie asks.

"Evan is with Stu," Twyla says. She flicks a long ash off her cigarette onto the cinder block stoop. "The prick picked him up Wednesday night."

"Stu is the boy's father?" I ask.

"Who the heck are you?"

"Officer Nowak, NYPD."

"What brings you up this way?"

"Your son hasn't come to class for the past couple of days, Ms. Travers," Annie says.

"Stu better not be smoking crack again." Twyla stubs out her cigarette. "Take a seat . . . if you can find one. I'll call the prick."

I'd rather stand than sit anywhere in the filthy trailer. Dirty dishes crusted with dried food and empty cans and bottles clutter the stained coffee table. A chipped ashtray overflows. I thought I was a slob, but this is next level.

"The school said your phone was out of order," Annie says.

"I changed my number," Twyla says. "Stu? Where's Evan?" She sighs. "What do you mean, you don't know?"

"Fudge!" Annie exclaims under her breath.

"You picked up Evan Wednesday night," Twyla says. She lights another cigarette. "I may be a bitch, Stu, but I ain't crazy."

I open the trailer door to let some fresh air into the stale room.

"Yeah, I'm sure he's not here," Twyla shouts. "Where is my son, Stu?"

"He's my son too!" Stu Langford yells into the phone. "If this is another one of your stunts, I'm going to—"

Twyla hangs up.

"My ex-husband, folks. He's a real prince."

"We must report this," I say.

"I thought you were a cop."

"This isn't my jurisdiction."

"I don't understand—"

"For Pete's sake," Annie says. She snatches the phone from

Twyla and dials 9-1-1. "I'm his teacher." She passes Twyla the phone. "She needs to speak with you."

Twyla takes the phone. "Yeah? I'm Evan's mom." She gives the operator her name. "Not since Wednesday." She chokes back a sob. Her distress appears genuine. "That's right," Twyla says. "My ex-husband picked Evan up Wednesday night. I'm not sure . . . maybe. . . I don't know. Oh, for God's sake, help me find my son!"

Annie takes the phone and shares the location of the trailer. She hangs up. "The police are on their way."

"Would you like a beer?" Twyla asks. "I wish I had something stronger, but I don't."

I know the feeling. I decline her offer, as does Annie.

"Suit yourself." Twyla retrieves a bottle of beer from the refrigerator, twists off and tosses the cap into the ashtray, and takes a swig.

"You didn't speak to your ex-husband when he picked up your son?" I ask.

"I was lying down. I get migraines."

"Me too," Annie says. "They're awful."

"Tell me about it." Twyla takes a long pull on her beer. "Anyhow, a car pulled up outside. Evan shouted that his dad was here. I thought that was odd because Stu wasn't supposed to pick up Evan until Friday. But the asshole sometimes comes early. I thought maybe he'd told me, and I'd forgotten. It happens. When the front door bang shut, I fell back asleep." Her eyes well with tears. "I'm a good mom. I swear."

"We'll find Evan," Annie says.

Sirens wail in the distance. They draw closer. A squad car with its lights flashing screeches to a halt before the trailer. Officers Reeves and Lecoq leap out.

"You have got to be kidding me," Officer Reeves says when he sees me.

"Cal drove me here," Annie says.

Officer Reeves sighs and searches the trailer, while Officer

Lecoq takes Twyla's statement. Twyla shares a school picture of Evan.

"May I keep this?" Officer Lecoq asks. Sweat beads his shiny scalp and bushy mustache.

Twyla nods.

"Do you recall what your son was wearing when he left?" Officer Lecoq asks. He removes a soft cloth from his pocket and wipes the smudges off the lenses of his glasses.

"A red . . . no wait—" Twyla tilts her head backward, like she's looking for answers on the ceiling. Her brow furrows. "A white tee shirt with gray shorts. No, wait a minute . . . they might've been black." She takes a drag of her cigarette. "He took his Snoopy backpack. I know that. I wrote his name on the tag inside the front pocket." Her eyes light up. "And his red Converse hi-tops, a birthday present from his grandmother. He wears those everywhere."

A wiry man in a baseball cap, wearing a greasy sleeveless tee shirt and dirty jeans with scuffed work boots, charges through the front door. I recognize Stu Langford from the elementary school.

"What the hell did you do, Twyla?"

"Calm down, sir," Officer Reeves says. "Are you the boy's father?"

Stu Langford nods. "I had planned to pick up Evan tonight." He takes off his baseball cap and runs his fingers through his greasy brown hair.

"Where were you Wednesday night, sir?" Officer Reeves asks.

"Home with my wife."

"All night?"

"Ask her."

"We will."

"Where's my son?" Stu Langford eyes first one officer and then the other. "Where's Evan?"

"According to your ex-wife, a car pulled up Wednesday night,"

Officer Lecoq says. "Your son told her that you were picking him up and left the trailer."

"Bullshit. I get Evan on the weekends. That's in our custody agreement. My son spends the rest of the school week with her."

"Why would the boy say you were picking him up if that wasn't true?"

"Hell if I know."

"When was the last time you saw your son, sir?"

"When I dropped Evan off at school on Monday morning."

"You haven't seen the boy since?"

"I'm not hiding my son, if that's what you think." Stu lunges at Twyla. "Where is Evan, you—?"

"Let's step outside, sir," Officer Reeves says. He slips his arm around Stu Langford's shoulders and leads the distraught father out the door. His calm under pressure impresses me. In high school, Reeves resolved conflicts with his fists.

"Perhaps we should step outside as well," Officer Lecoq says. Annie and I follow the slight officer out the door. He readies his pen and pad. "So, what brought you here?"

"Evan missed school for the past two days," Annie says. "And we found these." She hands Officer Lecoq the envelope of photographs. He thumbs through the images.

"Who took these?"

I explain how the envelope came into our possession.

"The lab in Kingston may be able to enhance the images," Officer Lecoq says.

"Instead of giving me the third degree," Stu Langford shouts at Officer Reeves, "you should be out there finding my son!" His voice cracks with emotion.

Officer Lecoq asks Annie and me for our identification and jots down our details.

"Here's my phone number." Annie passes Twyla a slip of paper. "Call me if you need anything."

Twyla nods. Annie and I take our leave. Officer Reeves chases us down the hill. "I don't know what your deal is, No Good. But I suspect you know more than you're saying."

"Maybe I do, and maybe I don't."

"I'm watching you," Officer Reeves says. He points two fingers toward his eyes and then at my eyes, then back to his eyes and mine again. He slips his arm around Annie. "You need anything, sweetheart. you call me. Understand?" She nods.

As I drive down the mountain, I punch the steering column. "I don't care if Oakley is a cop. One of these days, I'm going to deck that asshole." The pickup swerves.

Annie clutches her door handle. "Calm down before you get us killed." She and Mama Libby might be the only two people in the world who can tell me to calm down and not piss me off. I take a deep breath and focus on the road ahead.

"Why would Evan tell his mom he was leaving with his dad if that wasn't true?" Annie asks.

"Perhaps it was true," I say. "But my spidey-sense tells me Stu Langford doesn't have his son."

"I agree."

"One thing is certain."

"What's that?"

"If Evan Langford left with someone, he knows them," I say. "And I'll bet his parents do as well."

"I PRAY that they find that little boy safe and sound," Mama Libby says when I tell her where I've been. "His parents must be worried sick."

"They're not the best sort," I say. "But I don't think they'd hurt their son."

"Maybe the boy wandered off and became lost in the woods."

"His mother heard a car engine."

"Perhaps the father is lying."

"Then he's one hell of an actor."

"I'll never understand how anyone can hurt a child," Mama Libby says.

"There are some sick men in this world."

"I'm going to say a rosary for the child and go to bed."

I'm beat, so I knock back a hearty swig of whiskey, and turn in as well. I have messages on my phone. The first is from Dooley. He believes he can trace the origin of the emails on Kit's computer, but he needs more information. I'll call him back tomorrow. I play the second message.

It's me, Demetrius. I'm probably supposed to wait a few days before calling you. But I've never been good at playing mind games. If you like someone, tell them. So here goes. I like you. Last night was . . . different . . . in a good way. I'm rambling. Call me.

I crawl into bed with Chippy and press redial. Demetrius answers on the third ring. He sounds out of breath.

"Did I wake you?" I ask.

"I was working out."

"I had fun last night, too."

I tell Demetrius about Evan Langford.

"What can I do to help?"

"There'll be a search, I'm sure. I'll keep you posted."

We chat for a few more minutes about nothing of consequence.

"I wish I didn't have to open the hardware store in the morning," Demetrius says. "But I do. So I should get to bed."

We say goodnight and linger on the line for a moment longer before hanging up. I chug a shot of whiskey and turn out the light.

CHAPTER THIRTY

UNABLE TO SLEEP because I can't stop worrying about little Evan Langford, I rise at the first light of dawn. Raindrops splatter against my windowpane. A gray day looms ahead. I tug on a sweatshirt and pants.

On my way to the bathroom, I pass Mama Libby's bedroom door and hear snoring. I never wake up before she does. I wash my face, brush my teeth, and venture downstairs, where I start the coffee maker.

I slip on a rain slicker and take Sparky for a walk. After she does her business, I take a cup of black coffee outside onto the front porch and tie the dog's leash to the railing. She curls up at my feet.

A steady rain falls. I hope Evan isn't wandering around lost in the woods in this dismal weather. I'll never forget hiding in the miserable dampness of the abandoned paper mill. The musty aroma of rotting wood. The threatening creak of the floorboards every time I shifted positions. And I was thirteen years old and tall for my age—not a slight seven-year-old. I hate to think of that little boy being out there somewhere, frightened and alone, crying for his mommy and daddy, who'd rather get high than parent their son.

My phone rings. Perhaps the police have found the boy. I herd Sparky inside the house and answer before they hang up.

"Sorry to call so early—"

"That's okay, Annie. I'm awake."

"The police are organizing a search for Evan. Volunteers are gathering at the trailer park in an hour. Mom's driving up from Kingston."

"Count me in."

Sparky bounds through the kitchen and scratches on the back door. I don't have time to take her for another walk. I drag her outside by the collar and release her inside her kennel. The canopy will protect her from the rain. I rush back inside the house before I get soaked.

Mama Libby shuffles into the kitchen and asks, "Who was that on the phone?" I tell her about the search party. She says, "I'll get ready."

"No offense. But with your broken wrist, I don't think you'd be much help."

"I may not be able to hike through the woods," Mama Libby says. "But I can assist in other ways."

I know better than to waste my breath arguing with her.

Mama Libby pours herself a cup of coffee and toasts a slice of bread, while I get dressed. None of my clothes are appropriate for a raining day hike. I borrow a flannel shirt and a hooded nylon jacket from Papa Frank's closet.

After getting dressed, I call Demetrius and tell him about the search.

"I can't imagine what I'd do if Cora went missing," Demetrius says. "I'll close up shop and join you."

MAMA LIBBY INSISTS there's an easier route to the trailer park than the one I take. Figuring she's probably right, I follow her advice. Vehicles line both sides of the rutted dirt road that winds up the mountainside. I drop Mama Libby off as close to the gathering site as possible and park the Silverado several yards up the side of a steep embankment that's inaccessible to vehicles without four-wheel drive.

Two county deputies corral a dozen journalists with their camera crews behind yellow crime scene tape. The woman with the platinum-blond curls who asked to interview me after Kit's funeral shouts, "Officer Nowak! Ernestine Middleton with the *Nyes Landing Gazette*. What made you suspect Evan Langford was missing?"

"The boy didn't come to class on Friday."

"Do you follow up on every delinquent child who skips school?"

"Evan's teacher expressed concern."

"That would be Mrs. Nye, right? The woman who stands accused of shooting her husband."

I walk away before I say something that's not fit for print.

Sergeant Jimenez rushes around, directing volunteers and addressing their concerns. Chief Harris barks orders through a megaphone. He must've cut his chin shaving because he wears a band aid. Officer Washington consoles a hysterical Twyla Travers.

Stu Langford shouts accusations at his ex-wife and raises his fist to strike her. Officer Lecoq steps between the bickering couple. Stu Langford strikes Lecoq. Lecoq's glasses fly off his face. He stumbles backward and steps on the pair, snapping their frames in half.

Officer Reeves leaps into action. "Place your hands behind your back, sir."

"What the hell for?" Stu Langford asks.

"You assaulted a police officer."

"My son is out there somewhere," Stu Langford says. "He

could be injured or—" He clutches his stomach and groans. "And you're arresting me?"

"You're not under arrest, sir." Officer Reeves handcuffs Stu Langford. "You're being detained. Have a seat on the grass."

Stu Langford stands his ground.

"I understand you're upset," Officer Reeves says. "But you can't go around punching people."

Stu Langford plops down and mumbles under his breath, "This is bullshit."

Officer Lecoq digs a roll of tape out of his squad car's glove box and repairs his broken glasses as best he can on the fly.

Detectives wearing rain slickers bearing the logo of the sheriff's office search the area in and around the trailer, aided by a young woman dressed in a K-9 vest who's accompanied by a chocolate Labrador. The alert canine follows a scent from the house to the road, whimpers, and wanders in circles, sniffing the damp ground.

Opal Brown arrives and passes out rain slickers from her thrift store to any of the several dozen volunteers milling about who came unprepared.

Mama Libby tells Annie and Nadine how they should set up the water station. Howie Clark totes and fetches for the women.

Frieda Rosen huffs up the hill. "I have a zillion things to do before the rummage sale," she says between gasps for breath, "but this is more important."

"I'm glad you have your priorities straight, Frieda," Mama Libby says with more than a hint of sarcasm.

Frieda asks what she can do to help.

"Pass out water to the volunteers," Nadine says.

Frieda grabs an armload of bottles and goes to work.

Helena Potter strides up the mountainside wearing a black dress that looks like it's made from plastic garbage bags. Her tattered parasol has seen better days. I almost don't recognize Brandy Speedman in her simple white tee shirt, khaki shorts, and rain boots, with her ebony hair tied back in a ponytail, and no makeup on her face.

"The owner of the trailer park installed a security camera last year," Officer Reeves tells Chief Harris. "Says it was an expensive investment but worth every penny because it discourages drug dealers from setting up shop on his land."

"Smart man," Officer Lecoq says.

"The guy shared his footage from Wednesday night," Officer Reeves says. "It's grainy, but he recognized three of the four vehicles that drove past his camera in the hours around the time the boy went missing. The fourth vehicle—a black SUV—he's never seen before. We can't read the license plate, but we asked around, and none of the neighbors owns an SUV, black or otherwise."

"We showed the father and the mother the footage," Officer Lecoq says. "They didn't recognize the SUV either."

"Do you numbskulls realize how many black SUVs there are around here?" Chief Harris says. "Hell, I drive one. Maybe I took the boy."

Demetrius arrives, holding his skipping daughter's hand. "You remember Cora?"

"How could I forget such a pretty little girl?" I say. I squat so I can look Cora in the eye. At the academy, they taught us we should get down on their level when addressing children. "How are you, Cora?"

"I'm going to find a lost little boy," Cora says.

"I bet you will, too," I say. I stand and smile at Demetrius. "I'm glad you came."

"I can't imagine what the boy's parents must be going through."

Mayor Lucille Miller arrives with her entourage. She poses for pictures and assures reporters the police have the case under control, which is far from the truth.

An argument over jurisdiction erupts between Chief Harris

and Sheriff Jansen, a beefy brute with a buzz cut who barks orders like he's in the military. The trailer park lies within the town's limits, but the county governs the surrounding mountainside. After much posturing, everyone agrees that Harris and his team can lead the search, but if the boy is found on county land, the sheriff and his team will assume jurisdiction.

Mayor Miller grabs the megaphone from Chief Harris. "Thank you all for coming out on this dreary Saturday morning. It's a sad day for our town. No one has seen little Evan Langford since Wednesday evening. As a mother, I can't imagine what I would do if one of my girls disappeared." She slips her arms around the two teenage girls beside her, who share her ginger hair and freckles. "Many of you are parents. Imagine if it were your child who was missing. Let's find that precious boy and bring him home, where he belongs."

I'll bet the mayor stood before the mirror this morning and practiced shaking her head in disbelief, choking up with emotion at the opportune moment, and glancing toward the heavens for answers.

"My winery will contribute five thousand dollars towards a reward for information that leads to the boy's safe return," Brandy says.

"That's most generous, Mrs. Speedman," Lucille says.

"My gallery will contribute a thousand dollars," Helena says.

"My hardware store will as well," Demetrius says.

Their generosity inspires other people to open their wallets. Within minutes, the reward reaches twenty thousand dollars. I'm impressed by how the small town rallies in a crisis. The only time I ever witnessed that sort of one-for-all-and-all-for-one support in the city was in the immediate aftermath of last year's terrorist attacks.

Chief Harris and his team sort the volunteers into four groups. Demetrius, Cora, and I, Annie and Nadine, Helena, Brandy, and Howie, gather around Sergeant Jimenez. Two female nursing students, a statuesque couple with gray hair and ruddy cheeks, a heavyset farmer with a scraggly beard, and a barrel-chested former Marine with cauliflower ears join us.

"If you get tired, Annie," Howie says, "you can take my arm."

"Thank you, Howie."

"Want me to carry your backpack?"

"No, thanks. I'm fine."

The silver-haired couple with the ruddy cheeks suggest that the rain will end soon. The heavy-set farmer with the bushy beard disagrees.

"That's a cool rain slicker, Nadine," Brandy says.

"In case you can't tell, I'm partial to pink." Nadine stuffs several bottles of water into her tote. "If anyone gets hungry, I have energy bars. I've also brought a first aid kit. Insecticide. Extra umbrellas."

"Are you sure the missing boy isn't in your bag?" Helena says.

"You laugh now," Nadine says, "but when you sprain your ankle or get bit by a mosquito, you'll be glad I came prepared."

A wide-eyed Cora tugs on Helena's skirt and asks, "Are you a witch, lady?"

"Cora, that's rude," Demetrius says.

Helena laughs. "I'm Wiccan."

"Like in Harry Potter?"

"Those are wizards, honey," Demetrius says.

"What are—?"

"We'll talk about this when we get home. Right now, we need to find the little boy."

"Can we get this show on the road?" the Marine says.

Sergeant Jimenez shares a photograph of Evan Langford and describes what the little boy was wearing when he left home. "Spread out," she says. "If you see anything suspicious, notify me immediately."

Hiking will never be my favorite pastime. I'd rather go jogging through Tompkins Square Park. I slip and slide over the muddy ground. The dampness of the earth heightens the smell of rotting vegetation.

Cora skips through the woods, oblivious to danger. I could use a dose of the little girl's enthusiasm.

Demetrius points out a patch of poison ivy we should avoid and explains that the nettles we pass can reduce inflammation when they're steeped. His passion for nature may prove too much for me.

"I may have found something," the Marine shouts. He whisks the ground with an evergreen branch.

"Step back, sir," Sergeant Jimenez says. Using a stick, she lifts aside a pile of damp leaves, uncovering a dirty red mitten. "The boy wouldn't be wearing gloves at this time of year. All the same —" She tags the nearest tree.

The silver-haired couple stumbles upon a rusty bicycle frame half-buried in the underbrush. The student nurses trip over a dead animal carcass and shriek in unison. The bearded farmer discovers three marijuana bushes growing in a field of ferns.

"Those are on county land," Sergeant Jimenez says. "I'll tag the location and let their team know."

Around noon, the rain picks up. The farmer makes sure that we all know he was right about the weather. He and the nursing students turn back. The rest of us trudge onward. By one o'clock, we're drenched.

"This is a waste of time," the Marine says. "The boy could be halfway across the country by now. If he's not dead."

"He could be around the next bend," I say. "We just don't know."

"Let's turn back," Sergeant Jimenez says. "Before one of us slips and falls."

―――

MAMA LIBBY and I are seated in the kitchen, eating burgers and fries with shakes from the Jukebox Junction, when someone knocks on the front door. A young man holding a potted pink orchid stands on the porch.

"Delivery for Elizabeth Goodman."

"That's me, young man," Mama Libby says. "Cal, do you mind—?"

I sign for and take the orchid from the delivery guy.

"Let me grab a plant liner." Mama Libby rushes into the kitchen and returns seconds later with a plastic tray, which she places in the center of the dining table. I set the down the pot. She reads the card.

> *Happy Mother's Day, Mama Libby!*
> *Thank you for taking care of me and my brother after we lost our mother. Hope your wrist heals soon.*
>
> *Much love, Mary Catherine.*

"Isn't that sweet of your sister?" Mama Libby smiles. "And what a lovely orchid."

In the chaos surrounding Evan's disappearance, it had slipped my mind that Mother's Day is tomorrow. I can't believe Mary Catherine came through. Perhaps she's not as callous as I'd thought. I need to come up with a plan for tomorrow and pronto. I sneak upstairs and call the Nyes Landing Diner.

"Do you take reservations?"

"Yes, we do," a perky young woman says.

"I need a table for brunch tomorrow."

The young woman suppresses a laugh. "I'm afraid we're booked solid for Mother's Day."

I wish I could say I can't believe I did this, but I can. I'm always putting off until tomorrow what I could do today. Not when I'm wearing that uniform, though. On the job, I possess a sense of purpose that I otherwise lack.

"Mama Libby will be so disappointed," I say. If mentioning her name doesn't score a table, nothing will.

"Elizabeth Goodman placed a reservation for four guests two weeks ago."

"I didn't realize—"

Of course, Mama Libby knew better than to rely on me. She's mothered me longer than my mom did. I should quit letting her and everyone else down.

CHAPTER THIRTY-ONE

ON SUNDAY MORNING, I wake up to an overcast sky, but at least the rain has stopped. I shower, dress, and head downstairs. Sparky scrambles around my feet. I brew a pot of coffee, drop two slices of bread into the toaster, and retrieve the ceramic butter dish and a jar of homemade blackberry jam from the refrigerator. Before Mass, Mama Libby enjoys a light bite.

"You're up early," Mama Libby says.

"Happy Mother's Day."

"You remembered."

"I thought I'd join you for Mass."

"I'd like that."

Mama Libby sips her coffee and nibbles on her toast while I walk Sparky. Mother's Day feels bittersweet. I appreciate everything that Mama Libby has done for me, but I miss my mom. The sun peeps through the clouds. It may turn out to be a nice day after all.

I put on a white shirt with black pants and boots and borrow a dark gray sports jacket from Papa Frank's closet. I may not be walking any runways, but I clean up well enough to accompany Mama Libby to Mass.

"I'll be the envy of all the girls," Mama Libby says. She takes my arm. I escort her down the porch steps and across the lawn, and I help her inside the pickup.

With five houses of worship located within a mile radius of one another, parking on Mother's Day requires persistence and luck. I circle the block twice. A car parked across the street from the Sisters of Mercy Catholic Church drives away. I zoom into their abandoned space, help Mama Libby out of the pickup, and drop three quarters into the parking meter. Taking her arm, I escort her up the walkway.

When my sister and I were kids, our grandfather took us to a small clapboard church on the mountaintop a few times before he passed away. That's the extent of my religious experience. Mama Libby encouraged, but never pressured her foster children to attend Mass. While she was at church, I hung out with Papa Frank, a secular humanist, who impressed upon me the importance of reason and the value of living an ethical life.

Organ music invites us inside. Sunlight streams through stained glass windows that depict rapturous religious scenes, casting an amber glow over the ivory walls.

Mama Libby dips the fingers of her good hand into the font beside the entrance and makes the sign of the cross. I mimic her actions. An usher passes us bulletins and leads us to the front pew. I hope I don't doze off in the middle of the service.

Father O'Reilly strolls down the aisle wearing his vestments, which are what Mama Libby calls the priest's white robes and light blue shawl. He begins the Mass with a prayer. I can't keep up with when to stand, when to sit, and all the responses the congregation must make. Father O'Reilly offers a blessing for the Virgin Mary and all the mothers in the congregation and says a special prayer for the little missing boy.

A choir of six robed individuals sings a dissonant rendition of "Ave Maria." Father O'Reilly blesses the Holy Communion. A line forms to partake in the blood and body of Christ. I remain seated, enthralled by the ritual.

After the service, several people gather around to wish Mama Libby a happy Mother's Day.

"It's a shame that you and Frank couldn't have a child of your own," Gladys Crabtree says, "but at least your foster son is here." Gladys turns to the woman standing next to her, who looks like a younger version of herself. "Calista, this is that handsome police officer from the city that I told you about."

Calista and I acknowledge one another with smiles and nods.

"How long will you be in town, Calista?" Mama Libby asks.

"I have to drive back to Jersey City after brunch," Calista says.

"It must be nice having your daughter with you, Gladys," Mama Libby says. "If only for a few hours."

Father O'Reilly wishes Mama Libby and Gladys a happy Mother's Day and casts a disapproving glance in my direction. I help Mama Libby into the pickup and drive to the diner, drop her off outside the entrance, and cruise around until I find a parking spot on a side street several blocks away.

When I reach the diner, I find Mama Libby seated with Annie and Nadine. Annie looks pinched. As I approach the table, I overhear Nadine say, "I've reached my limit with that woman."

"What did Gladys Crabtree do?" I ask.

"Not Gladys," Nadine says. "That witch, Bonnie Nye." She clenches her fists. "I don't care how much money she has, if she harasses Annie again, I am going to snatch her baldheaded."

Annie excuses herself and heads to the ladies' room. I sense she'd prefer we changed the subject.

"Bonnie Nye attacked us the moment we walked through the door," Nadine says. "Her breath smelled like a distillery. She screamed at Annie, 'I hope you burn in hell!'"

"You heard Judge Adams," Mama Libby says. "The evidence against Annie is circumstantial."

"From her mouth to God's ears," Nadine says.

Kiki approaches our table with a smile and wishes Mama Libby and Nadine a happy Mother's Day before taking our order.

Sergeant Jimenez strides into the diner and orders several cups of coffee to go. She stops by our table on her way out. "No sign of Evan Langford yet. We're gathering at one o'clock to continue our search."

"We'll be there," Mama Libby says. I assume she's including me in that we.

"I'll have to see how Annie feels," Nadine says.

Lucille Miller arrives with her daughters. She strolls around the restaurant, greeting guests and wishing all the moms a happy Mother's Day. Climbing atop a chair, she shouts for attention. Once everyone quiets down, she makes an impassioned plea for volunteers to help in the search for little Evan Langford. Whether she is sincere or grandstanding, her voice carries weight in this town, so I appreciate the interruption.

When Annie returns, she appears calmer, but her eyes look dull. She's taken something. After all she's gone through, I don't blame her. I could go for a double shot of whiskey right about now. Since returning home, a friend has passed away in my arms; someone has poisoned Sparky; I may have discovered the remains of a missing child; and a little boy has gone missing. When was I supposed to get my shit together?

After we finish eating, Kiki brings Mama Libby and Nadine bowls of fresh berries marinated in Grand Marnier and topped with fresh whipped cream.

"I couldn't have asked for a better Mother's Day," Mama Libby says. She squeezes my hand. "Thank you for going to Mass with me." I kiss her cheek and tell her I love her.

MAMA LIBBY and I rush home after brunch and change into our

hiking clothes. I brush off and tug on my boots, which I left in the mudroom yesterday. A light rain falls.

Sparky races around inside her kennel, barking at the squirrels scampering across the lawn. She looks content. I make sure she has a full bowl of food and fresh water.

Mama Libby and I climb into the Silverado and drive to the trailer park. Fewer volunteers have shown up today, but the flock of media vultures behind the crime scene tape has doubled in size.

Sergeant Jimenez greets us. "We may be wasting our time," she says. "With no solid leads, Evan Langford could be anywhere. But we can't sit on our hands."

"The boy has been missing for four days now," I say. "We're running out of time." It might already be too late, but I can't allow myself to think that way.

"We should get a move on," Sergeant Jimenez says.

Mama Libby argues with Gladys Crabtree over how they should arrange the water table. Brandy Speedman offers her assistance. Gladys Crabtree ignores Brandy, but Mama Libby says, "You can hand out water to the volunteers." Brandy scoops up an armload of bottles.

Demetrius jogs up the mountainside and shares that Cora is with her mother. "I'm glad you came," I say, and I reach for his hand. He shies back, averts his eyes, and mutters, "Not here."

Helena beckons me over. Dark circles under her eyes give her pale face a haunted look. "He's over water," she whispers.

"Who?"

"Evan. The little boy came to me in a dream." Helena shakes her head. "More like a vision because I was wide awake."

"It rained yesterday," I say.

"It's more than that," Helena says.

I may not believe in psychics, but I'm desperate to find Evan. "Do you think he drowned?"

Helena shakes her head. "I know this sounds crazy. But water flows under the boy, not over him."

Officers Reeves, Lecoq, and Washington rally their volunteers. Our team gathers around Sergeant Jimenez. I don't see Chief Harris anywhere.

"As a parent," I say, "the chief must take cases like this particularly hard."

"Chief Harris doesn't have children," Sergeant Jimenez says.

"He had a boy with him when he drove past us the other day."

"Probably giving one of his players a ride home. He coaches little league baseball."

Annie and Nadine are no-shows. After that stunt Bonnie Nye pulled, I don't blame them. The two student nurses haven't returned either. Neither has the Marine with the piss-poor attitude. The statuesque couple with gray hair and ruddy cheeks, as well as the heavyset farmer with the scraggly beard, seem eager to help in any way they can.

A pimply-faced uniform with braces on his teeth joins our team and introduces himself as Deputy Fordham. Sergeant Jimenez reminds us of what Evan Langford was wearing when he left home.

"According to the mother," Deputy Fordham says. "A known drug offender who's had Child Protective Services involved in her life ever since the boy was born."

"If you have more substantial evidence to go on," Sergeant Jimenez says, "please share." Deputy Fordham hems and haws. The sergeant smirks. "I didn't think so. Let's roll."

We follow Sergeant Jimenez down a steep, muddy trail overgrown with bushes and shrubs, which proves to be a treacherous shortcut to where we abandoned our search the previous afternoon. From there, we hike southeast through the dense woods.

Demetrius points out a patch of brown mushrooms we should avoid because they're poisonous. I can't tell if he's trying to be helpful or showing off. Perhaps a bit of both.

Deputy Fordham bags everything he finds: food containers,

bottles, and cans; a couple of used condom, a staple at many crime scenes in the city; a creepy doll's head with a crack running down its cheek that has probably lain buried in the dirt for years. Nothing that helps us locate the missing boy.

"I may have found something," the tall man with the gray hair and ruddy cheeks shouts. His wife waves us over. Bits of clothing poke through the leaves piled at our feet.

Deputy Fordham picks up a pair of shorts using a twig. "Too large to belong to the missing boy." He digs out a stained white halter top. "And they're women's garments."

Thunder rumbles in the distance. The sky darkens. We press onward through the drizzle. The rain picks up.

"We should turn back," Sergeant Jimenez says. "Before we get drenched."

CHAPTER THIRTY-TWO

Driving home in the pouring rain, the thought of little Evan Langford lost in the woods, cold and frightened, infuriates me. The sheriff and his team, and the local cops, save for Sergeant Jimenez, have their heads up their asses. The boy has been missing for four days, and they have no leads.

When we get home, I help Mama Libby inside the house. After slogging through the mud for hours, I can't wait to knock back a shot of whiskey and take a shower.

"Where's Sparky?" Mama Libby asks. We search the dining and living rooms, calling the dog's name, and can't find her anywhere.

"Wait a minute," I say. "I left Sparky in her kennel this morning." I rush out the back door, but don't see the dog. I find a hole where she's dug under the fence. She could be anywhere.

"The thunder must've spooked her," Mama Libby says. She shouts Sparky's name several times and receives no response. "That pup is going to be the death of me."

Moses pokes his head out the door of his apartment. "What's wrong?"

"Sparky dug out of her kennel!" Mama Libby shouts over the noise of the storm.

"Was I supposed to be watching her?" Moses asks.

"No, this is my fault," I say. "Let me change into dry clothes, and I'll find her." Although I have no clue how.

"In this weather?" Mama Libby says. "Are you sure?"

I wish Demetrius was here. But he's not. I'm on my own. It's time for me to man up, like Papa Frank always told me to do whenever I complained about facing a difficult challenge. "I'm more afraid of bears than a little rain."

"Bears mostly forage at dawn or dusk," Moses says. "And in this storm, they'll be hunkering down somewhere dry."

I hope Moses knows what he's talking about. "You stay here in case the dog comes home," I say, saving the old guy the trouble of making an excuse for his bum knee.

"Roger that," Moses says.

"Do you mind if I borrow Papa Frank's yellow rain slicker?" I ask. "The one he wore when he worked as a crossing guard?"

"Take whatever you need," Mama Libby says.

I rush upstairs, wash my face, brush my teeth, and change into a sweatshirt and pants. After chugging a shot of whiskey to fortify my resolve, I empty the rest of the bottle into my flask, which I slip into the pocket of the rain slicker.

My phone's voice mail light blinks. I play back the message.

Dooley here. I traced the IP address you gave me. It was sent from a computer at the Nyes Landing Police Station. I hope that helps.

Could a cop have been blackmailing Kit? I'd hate to think so, but that would explain a lot of things.

By the time I get outside, the rain has abated to a light drizzle. I scan the ground. Muddy paw prints lead off through the trees. I take a deep breath and stride into the hemlock grove, while telling myself it's not the woods I should fear, but the men who commit evil acts under its cover.

Without a clear path to follow, I soon become disoriented. I shout Sparky's name. She doesn't answer. I holler again and again without receiving a response. I've seen this thicket of white birches before. I'm wandering in circles. Before I freak out, I knock back a swig of whiskey and remind myself to breathe.

The bushes up ahead rustle. My breath catches in my throat. A dark-brown weasel-like creature scurries across my path. I recognize my old high school mascot. The fisher cat bares its sharp teeth and growls. After a tense standoff, it darts under a pile of dried tree branches and disappears. I sigh in relief, grateful that no one saw me almost piss my pants over a furry creature no bigger than a house cat, who was probably more scared of me than I was of it.

The rain may have lessened to a drizzle, but storm clouds overhead cast a pall over the forest. I grope my way forward, shouting Sparky's name. A slippery patch of damp leaves trips me up. I tumble into a bramble, scramble onto my feet, and pluck the thorns from my sweatpants.

Sparky barks in the distance. I trudge toward the sound, calling her name. Her barking grows louder. She bounds my way. Her fur is soaking wet. She drops a red Converse sneaker at my feet—a child's size thirteen.

"Where did you find this?" I wave the sneaker under Sparky's muzzle. She sniffs the heel and dashes off through the trees. I chase after her. She runs so fast. I fall behind. She waits for me to catch up. I trudge up a steep hillside.

Esopus Creek rushes past. On the opposite bank, the abandoned paper mill where I sought refuge from my mother's killer looms. Could Evan Langford be hiding in there? Helena Potter said the boy was over water. The creek flows under a portion of the rotting structure. I can't believe I didn't think of that before.

Sparky dives into the creek and paddles against the rushing current. She crawls out onto the opposite bank, shakes the water off her coat, looks over her shoulder at me and barks.

Pulling out my flask, I chug a swig of whiskey and take a deep breath. A little boy needs my help. I slip and slide down the hill and traipse over a slippery row of moss-covered rocks that forms a natural bridge across the creek.

Sparky ducks through a door in the side of the abandoned mill, which hasn't produced paper in over a hundred and fifty years. I draw my weapon and follow the dog inside. The pungent stench of brown rot gags me.

"Evan!" I shout. No answer. I ease forward. The floorboards creak. "Evan, if you can hear me, I'm a police officer. You're safe now."

As I side-step around a ragged hole in the rotten floorboards, my boot slips, and a rusty nail tears through my sweatpants and gouges my shin. A sharp pain shoots up my thigh. I crawl forward on my hands and knees. Someone whimpers.

"Evan?" I peer through the cracks in the floorboards. The boy cowers against the wall, wearing nothing but his dingy briefs.

The floorboards behind me creak. I didn't cover my flank—a rookie mistake. Something thick and wooden cracks over my head. I topple forward with a groan. If this gets back to my sergeant, I'll be working desk duty for the rest of my career. A second blow flattens me. I slither forward on my belly. A third whack knocks my lights out.

CHAPTER THIRTY-THREE

I REGAIN consciousness lying on my side in my boxer shorts, with my wrists handcuffed behind my back. My head pounds. I'll be lucky if I don't have a concussion. The swollen red gouge in my shin from the rusty nail stings.

Evan Langford cowers against the wall, shivering so badly that his teeth chatter. What abuse has the poor boy suffered? Will he be able to move on? Or will this experience scar him for life?

"You're Evan, right?" The boy's hollow eyes widen. He nods. "I'm a police officer."

The boy bursts into tears. "Don't tell anyone I'm here."

"Why not?"

"The bad cop said if I told anyone about our playdates, he would kill my mommy and daddy."

I can't believe a police officer would do something this heinous. My faith in the badge I revere is shaken.

"You're safe now," I say, hoping I sound more certain than I feel. I've gotten out of some tight spots before, but I've never rescued a person while unarmed, with my hands cuffed behind my back.

The floorboards overhead creak. "The bad cop is coming,"

Evan whispers. He curls up in a quivering ball. I promise the boy everything is going to be okay, although I have no clue how.

"I warned you to stay out of my jurisdiction, NYPD." Chief Harris peers through a gaping hole in the floorboards above me. "But you wouldn't listen."

Once my initial shock fades, the evidence coalesces in my muddled brain. Chief Harris's build resembles that of the man Kit photographed with Evan. Kit asked the chief about a delivery that afternoon on the street. He knew the chief was abusing Evan, but he kept his mouth shut to serve his own interests.

Chief Harris responded to a call from Gladys Crabtree the night Kit was shot. He drives a black SUV like the one caught on surveillance footage at the trailer park. A black SUV was parked in front of the house on the night that Kit was shot, but by the time Reeves placed me in the squad car, the SUV had moved on. The chief shot Kit and fled the scene, cleaned up, and returned, claiming he'd come straight from the gym. Knowing investigators would find his fingerprints on the murder weapon, he tainted the evidence.

When I drove past Chief Harris on the highway, the boy seated beside him must've been Evan. I had an opportunity to save the boy and failed in my duty.

"Have a drink on you, NYPD."

Chief Harris pours whiskey over my head and drops my flask. I duck my head. The flask falls through a crack in the crumbling floorboards and splashes into the creek below.

"What the hell do you think you're doing?" I ask.

"Apprehending an alcoholic pedophile."

The mill door creaks. Sparky snarls.

"Pesky mutt!" Chief Harris draws his weapon.

"Go home, Sparky!" I shout. "Run!"

Chief Harris fires a shot. The rafters shake. Evan screams. Sparky barks in the distance. The chief returns.

"You shot Kit, didn't you?" I say.

"The prick drew on me," Chief Harris says. "I protected myself."

"Sounds like self-defense," I say. "Why didn't you come forward?"

"You know the answer to that question."

"The remains I found. They belong to that foster kid who went missing last year, don't they?"

"You think you're so clever, NYPD."

"You sick bastard."

"That was an accident—"

"You sure have a lot of accidents. What is the matter with you?"

"Me? I have a spotless record. You're a drunk and a sexual deviant with anger issues who's on administrative leave for assaulting a suspect. You experienced a tragic childhood. That would be enough to push any man over the edge."

"You'll never get away with this."

"Sure, I will. You drew on me. I fired back in self-defense. I didn't intend to kill you. It all happened so fast. And tragically, the boy drowned."

"You're unhinged."

"I'm done talking."

"You stole this boy's future."

"You've seen his parents. Where he lives. He has no future."

"That's not fair."

"Life isn't fair. Of all people, you should know that."

Sparky growls.

"Not you again, you mangy mutt," Chief Harris says. "What is that in your mouth? Oh, shit! Is that his Beretta? Come back here! Give me that holster!" The chief pursues the dog.

"We don't have much time," I say. I scoot over beside Evan. He recoils. It breaks my heart what he must've gone through. "I won't hurt you. I promise."

Turning my back, I fumble with the ropes binding Evan's

wrists. With some effort, I manage to loosen the knot, but not enough to free the boy's hands.

"Let me try," Evan says, his voice a thin whisper. He leans over and pries the knot loose with his teeth. With his hands freed, he unties his feet.

"Climb onto my shoulders."

Evan scrambles up my back like a little monkey. Braced against the wall for balance, I stand and hoist his head through the hole in the floorboards overhead.

"Can you pull yourself up?"

"Yep."

"Make sure the coast is clear."

Evan peers around. "I don't see the bad cop anywhere."

"Be brave, okay?"

Evan nods. His lower lip quivers.

"You can do this," I say. "Climb out and run away as fast as you can."

Evan clambers through the hole. The floorboards creak and bow, but they hold. He gazes down at me.

"Run!" I shout. "Find someplace to hide."

Evan pads across the floorboards overhead. The door scrapes open, and creaks shut again. I'm not a religious man, but I hedge my bets by uttering a silent prayer that the boy reaches safety.

Alone in the abandoned paper mill unarmed, handcuffed, and nearly naked, my anxiety level rises. I take a deep breath and remind myself what's at stake. I must get out of here. But how? I can't climb with my arms handcuffed behind my back.

The floorboards overhead sag and groan.

"Time's up, NYPD," Chief Harris says. He peers through the hole in the floorboards overhead, my holstered Beretta clasped in his fist. "Any minute now, Jimenez will charge onto the scene with her posse." He peers around. "Where's the kid?"

"Safe from you," I say.

"You son of a bitch," Chief Harris says. "I'm going to—" He draws his weapon.

I stomp up and down. The rotten floorboards beneath my feet collapse. I inhale a deep breath seconds before plunging into the creek below. The frigid water stabs my flesh like the prick of a thousand needles.

Rather than fight the rushing current, I float downstream on my back, trying not to think about how dark the night is or how cold I am. Spotting a bend ahead, I brace for impact and collide with the bank. Wrapping my legs around a tangled mass of tree roots, I halt my progress and crawl onto shore, bruised and battered, but alive.

Chief Harris charges out of the old mill, brandishing his weapon. His wild eyes scan the woods. I roll behind a felled tree trunk. I doubt he can see me in the dark.

Sparky barks in the distance.

"I'm going to put a bullet in that mutt's head," Chief Harris says, "if it's the last thing I do."

Over my dead body. I stand and shake my sopping wet boxer shorts loose from my skin. Determined to bring the chief's reign of terror to an end, I tiptoe through the woods, careful to avoid sharp objects, which is no easy feat. Sticks and stones, pinecones and needles, and a plant with wide, serrated leaves that have prominent veins and clusters of pale flowers, which sting like hell when they brush against my bare legs and feet, litter my path.

Sparky's distant barking grows more vicious. She growls like a cornered wolf.

"Make my day, mutt!"

A shot rings out. If Chief Harris shot Mama Libby's dog, I'll kill him with my bare hands.

CHAPTER THIRTY-FOUR

Sparky rushes up and licks my face. The dog is alive! Relief washes over me. I pat her head and scratch her favorite spot behind her ears. She trots off through the dark woods with her nose to the ground.

"If you don't come out of hiding, Evan," Chief Harris says, "I'm going to kill your mommy."

Snatching Sparky's leash, which is no easy feat with my hands cuffed behind my back, I whisper as loudly as I dare, "Heel." To my surprise, the dog obeys. Together, we slink forward through a tangled thicket of spindly birch trees that provide us with scant cover. The swollen red gouge in my shin throbs.

Chief Harris crouches in the center of the clearing ahead, clutching his firearm. He pivots on his heels, muttering under his breath. I must disarm the guy, but with my arms cuffed behind my back and weaponless, I'm at a serious disadvantage.

"There you are you little shit!" Chief Harris cries. Evan screams. Harris chases the sound. I follow the chief. A small shadow that must be Evan bobs and weaves its way through the trees. Harris gains ground. Evan trips. Harris closes in. Evan scrambles onto his feet. Harris leaps forward and grabs the shrieking and thrashing boy.

Sparky yanks free from my grip and charges at Chief Harris, snarling like a rabid beast. The chief struggles to fend off the vicious dog's attack and control the hysterical boy.

"You're a pain in my ass, NYPD," Chief Harris says. He aims his weapon in my direction. The veins in his thick neck bulge. "Everyone knows you're a pervert. It won't take an enormous leap of faith for them to believe you kidnapped the boy, and I shot you in self-defense." He grins. "Thanks to your intervention, however, the boy will unfortunately get caught in the crossfire rather than drown."

Evan bites Chief Harris on the hand. The chief smacks the boy across the face. The boy tumbles into a patch of ferns. Sparky lunges at the chief. The chief staggers backward and fires a random shot into the air. A flock of screeching birds takes flight.

With Chief Harris is distracted, I close the distance between us. The chief glares at me. The rage in his reptilian eyes curdles my blood. Adopting a wide stance, I bend my knees, tuck my chin under, and head-butt his nose with the peak of my brow. The chief reels backward and falls on his ass. His weapon flies out of his hand. I kick the chief under the chin with my heel. His head snaps backward. I leap on top of the twisted prick, wrestle him to the ground, and fumble around until I find the handcuff key on his duty belt. I struggle to fit the flag end of the key into the slot. It slips from my grasp.

A shot fires. My ears ring. I dive for the ground and glance around. A wide-eyed and quivering Evan clutches the chief's weapon in his tiny fists.

"Give me the gun, son," Chief Harris says. He inches toward Evan. "Before somebody gets hurt." Evan pulls the trigger. Harris howls and staggers backward. He hops around on one leg, clutching the toe of his boot. "You shot me in the foot, you little shit. I'm going to kill you."

"Evan," I say, rising onto my knees so I'm on his level. "Whatever you do, do not give the bad cop the gun. He wants to hurt us."

Sparky steps between Evan and Chief Harris and bares her teeth. I try again to unlock my handcuffs. After a couple of near misses, the key flag slips into the slot and twists. I slip off the right cuff and hold out my hand. "Evan, hand me the gun."

Chief Harris lunges at Evan. "That's my weapon, boy!"

Sparky bites Chief Harris on the ankle. The chief kicks the dog. She yelps and tumbles backward. The chief rushes toward Evan. Sparky pounces again. The chief shakes the dog loose. She sinks her teeth into his calf. He grabs her collar. Dog and man tumble around on the ground in a tangle of fur and flesh. I sidle around their skirmish and reach for Evan. He falls into my arms and surrenders the weapon.

Chief Harris tosses Sparky aside and runs off through the woods. Sparky chases the chief. I call the dog's name. She ignores me. I can't pursue the chief and the dog without abandoning the boy, and I'm not about to do that. I place Evan on my shoulders. To my relief, Sparky returns and leads us toward the creek. We traipse across the row of moss-covered boulders onto the opposite bank.

Voices shout. Light beams flicker through the trees ahead. I crouch behind a thicket of shrubs with the boy and the dog.

"This way!" Sergeant Jimenez shouts. She rushes past wearing a headlamp.

I step out from behind the shrubs.

"What the—?"

"It's a long story. Trust me. Harris kidnapped the boy. He ran northeast from the old mill. Here's his service weapon, but he may have my Beretta. Or a backup weapon."

Sergeant Jimenez takes the gun. She studies my face for a moment, eyes the boy, and says, "The chief is likely headed for the highway. He may have a getaway car waiting there." She wraps her windbreaker around Evan's shoulders and zips the boy inside.

"Are you going to catch the bad cop?" Evan asks.

"I am," Sergeant Jimenez says. She tosses me a blanket from her backpack and radios for backup. "Help is on the way." She takes off.

Officer Washington jogs up and grabs her knees. "I'm more of a sprinter than a distance runner," she says. I catch her up to speed and ask her to stay with the boy until the medics arrive.

"Take this." Officer Washington passes me her windbreaker. "And this." She hands me her headlamp. "Give me the dog's leash. I'll keep an eye on her for you, too."

Driven by adrenaline and righteous indignation, I aim the headlamp for the ground and follow Sergeant Jimenez's muddy boot tracks through the tangled woods, determined Harris will never hurt another child. My gouged shin burns. I slip and slide across a pile of damp leaves and race toward the distant sound of traffic.

After fighting my way through the tangled woods for several yards, I emerge onto the shoulder of the highway. The dark night sky has brightened to a deep indigo with the rise of dawn.

Sergeant Jimenez stands several yards away, with her weapon drawn. "It's over, Harris."

Chief Harris dashes across the highway seconds before a car races past. Sergeant Jimenez can't shoot without risking hitting the driver. She shouts for the chief to surrender. He flips her the bird.

Seconds before a semi-truck whizzes past, I dart across the highway and pursue Chief Harris down the shoulder, fighting through the pain in my gouged shin. Harris limps down the shoulder a few years ahead of me. I gain ground and, leaping through the air like a defensive lineman, tackle his sick ass to the ground. We grapple around. I gain the upper hand and raise my fist, prepared to pummel the sick son-of-a-bitch to a bloody pulp. A faint voice of reason inside my head stays my hand.

"No," I say. "I'm not giving you a reason to challenge the legitimacy of this arrest."

Sergeant Jimenez joins me and produces a set of handcuffs. The chief worms loose from our grip and draws his backup weapon from his ankle holster. He fires a shot. We drop to the ground. He flags down a passing car. The driver slams on the brakes and swerves onto the shoulder. She and her three kids scream. Harris tries but can't open the locked passenger door. The hysterical driver speeds away.

Officers Reeves and Lecoq screech to a halt in their squad car. Reeves leaps out and draws his weapon. Lecoq strides onto the highway, arms raised, and halts oncoming traffic. Reeves fires a shot. The chief yowls and grabs his ass. He returns fire.

Officer Lecoq clutches his arm. "I'm hit."

Officer Reeves ducks behind a tree and shouts into his radio, "Officer down!" He confirms our location by referencing the mile markers along the highway.

Sergeant Jimenez fires a shot. Chief Harris tucks and rolls into a ditch. Sergeant Jimenez and Officer Reeves surround and apprehend their raving boss. Rather than exercise his right to remain silent, he blames me and the boy for his crimes.

Sparky runs up, dragging a wheezing Officer Washington. Evan rides on the husky officer's shoulders.

"Sparky, you're my hero," I say. The dog wags her tail and barks. "You deserve all the treats in the world."

An ambulance arrives on the scene. A paramedic takes Evan Langford from Officer Washington and climbs inside the box. She checks the boy's vitals. Her partner shuts the doors. The ambulance speeds away with its lights flashing and sirens blaring.

Sergeant Jimenez wraps another blanket around my shoulders. "You're shivering and no wonder. You're nearly naked and soaking wet."

My fingers tingle. I rub my arms to stimulate my circulation, while I share what the chief told me in the old mill.

"The evidence was right in front of me the whole time," Sergeant Jimenez says, "but I failed to connect the dots."

"Don't beat yourself up. Nobody suspected the chief."

A second ambulance arrives. Paramedics slide Officer Lecoq inside the box on a stretcher.

"You need medical attention, Nowak," Sergeant Jimenez says.

"I'll be fine once I get warm."

"Humor me." Sergeant Jimenez summons the paramedics. They check my vitals. She takes Sparky's leash from Washington. "I'll see that the dog gets home safe and sound."

"What about Harris?" I ask.

"He can wait for the next ambulance."

"Are you sure he won't bleed out?"

"We should be so lucky."

Paramedics insist I lie on a stretcher. They slide me inside the box with Officer Lecoq. I take a deep breath. My head aches. My shin is on fire. I break out in a cold sweat. The paramedics ask me a battery of questions and give me something for pain. I doze off.

CHAPTER THIRTY-FIVE

BY THE TIME the ambulance reaches the hospital, my adrenaline rush has subsided, and I'm shivering from head to toe. Orderlies whisk Officer Lecoq and me inside on gurneys and roll us down a long hallway into an examination room. A triage nurse assesses our conditions and shares her findings with a husky doctor in his fifties. The doctor suggests we be transferred to an inpatient room and then joins us there.

"You're lucky you weren't in the frigid water any longer than you were," the doctor says. He examines the bump on my head. "You suffer quite a blow. I'll order a CT scan."

A young nurse cleans and bandages the gouge in my shin, gives me a tetanus shot, and bundles me in blankets.

"How's Evan?" I ask. "The boy we rescued."

"Aside from a case of mild hypothermia, his body will be fine. His psyche is another matter."

I'm relieved the boy is alive and hope for the best.

Annie rushes into the room and bursts into tears. "You could've been killed."

"Evan's safe," I say. "That's what matters."

"If you can't trust the chief of police," Nadine says, "who can you trust?" She tosses her tote onto the chair beside my bed.

"How are you feeling, sir?" the doctor asks Officer Lecoq. "Are the painkillers doing their job?"

"I'm grinning and bearing."

The doctor turns to me. "And you, sir?"

"I'll be fine once I get warm."

The doctor checks my temperature. It's still too low. He tells the nurse to monitor my progress and continues his rounds.

Nadine tucks the blankets under my chin. "Would you like a cup of coffee? Or tea? I can ask if they have hot chocolate if you'd prefer."

"I'm not thirsty."

"I'll get you a coffee," Nadine says. "Milk and sugar?"

"Black is fine."

"Annie, what would you like?"

"I'll take a bottle of water if they have one."

Nadine grabs her wallet from her tote. "Be right back."

After her mom leaves the room, Annie asks me what happened. I share what I recall, omitting the more sensitive details.

"That poor child."

Nadine sails into the room, juggling two paper cups and a bottle of water. "Here we go." She passes Annie and me our drinks. "What did I miss?"

"It's a long story, mom. I'll fill you in later."

"I blame the mother," Nadine says.

"What about Mr. Langford?" Annie asks.

"The boy wasn't living with his father."

"If it isn't Doogie Howser," Mama Libby says from out in the hallway.

"Elizabeth Goodman," her doctor replies. He sounds surprised, and not in a good way. "You're not here to see me, are you?"

"Relax," Mama Libby says. "I'm visiting my foster son. He rescued that missing boy. Surely, you've heard."

"You must be proud."

Sergeant Jimenez swaggers through the door. "Tell you the truth, Nowak. I didn't think you had it in you."

"I'll take that as a compliment."

"You should," Mama Libby says as she steps into the room. "The sergeant had nothing but good things to say about you on the drive over."

I'm so used to being in trouble that I'm not sure how to react to praise.

"When I took the dog home," Sergeant Jimenez says, "I mentioned I planned to drop by the hospital, and Libby asked me if she could tag along."

"Moses offered to watch Sparky and make sure she doesn't chew up any more of my quilts."

"Who's watching Moses?" I ask.

"Lord, I hope those two don't burn down my house."

"Sparky may be a handful," I say, "but we might never have found Evan without her help."

A grim nurse pokes her head through the door. "You're only allowed two visitors at a time."

Sergeant Jimenez flashes her badge. "Perhaps I should speak to your supervisor."

The nurse narrows her eyes. "That won't be necessary."

"Reeves recovered your Beretta," Sergeant Jimenez says, "and Washington found your clothes. Detectives booked Harris. As soon as he gets released from the hospital, they'll transport him to the county lockup. He admitted he killed Christopher Nye but says it was in self-defense. He claims you abused the boy."

"I can't believe how wrong I was about that man," Mama Libby says. "I worry about how many other boys he's abused."

"You think he's done this to other boys?" Nadine says.

"Predators don't strike once and done."

"Harris same as admitted that he killed that missing boy last fall," I say.

"You're shitting me," Sergeant Jimenez says.

Officer Lecoq pulls back the curtain that separates our beds. His taped together eyeglasses rest askew on his nose. "That would explain why the chief discouraged us from searching in that area."

Annie steps out into the hallway. Nadine follows her daughter.

"I just—" Annie gasps. "Kit knew Mom. My husband knew Chief Harris was abusing Evan, and not only did he not tell anyone, but he tried to blackmail the chief. Who did I marry?"

Sergeant Jimenez and I do our best to ignore their conversation, but we're cops. We're trained to listen.

"Sweetie, you're not responsible for any of this."

"I should've known, Mom. That poor little boy."

"Don't get yourself all worked up."

"I'm not . . . give me a minute, okay?"

Nadine returns. "This is all too much."

"All things considered," Mama Libby says. "Annie is holding up remarkably well."

Annie returns.

"Your mother's right," Sergeant Jimenez says. "None of this is your fault."

Annie dries her eyes on a tissue and nods.

"I need to get back to the station," Sergeant Jimenez says. "This case is going to bury me in paperwork."

"I suppose that means I should say goodbye," Mama Libby says.

"We can give you a ride home if you'd like," Nadine says.

"I'll take you up on that offer."

"Thanks for interfering, Nowak," Sergeant Jimenez says.

"Anytime," I reply.

"Heal fast, Lecoq," Sergeant Jimenez says. "Reeves misses you."

"He does?"

"Seriously, Lecoq?" Sergeant Jimenez says. "Have you met your partner?" She chuckles and swaggers out the door.

"When do you get released?" Mama Libby asks.

"The doctor wants to run a CT scan. If that looks good, I can check out in the morning."

"I'm proud of you, Cal," Mama Libby says. She sets a shopping bag on the windowsill. "I brought you a change of clothes." She holds up Chippy. "I thought you might want your little buddy."

"I'm not a child," I say. But I take the sock monkey.

"Moses sends his best wishes. He would've come, but—"

"His bum knee."

"How'd you guess?"

I chuckle and clutch my side. "It hurts to laugh."

"We should go," Nadine says. "I have an open house tonight." She fluffs my pillows and tucks my blankets under me. "If your pain worsens or your temperature drops any further, ring the call button for a nurse. Don't wait for them to check on you."

"I shudder to think what might've happened to Evan if you hadn't found him when you did," Annie says. She kisses me on the cheek. "Thank you."

Mama Libby squeezes my hand and whispers, "I love you, son." Coming from her, that means the world.

After everyone leaves, I realize how exhausted I am. A nurse offers me painkillers, which I decline. I'm on the verge of dozing off when I hear a familiar voice.

"I came as soon as I heard."

Demetrius stands in the doorway. He smiles and gives me a bouquet. No man has ever brought me flowers. I'm not sure how I feel about that. I smile and say thanks.

"Are you okay?"

"All in a day's work."

"You're on vacation."

A cop is never on vacation. Not really. But I don't tell him that.

"I wasn't sure what you'd like, so I brought you candy, too." Demetrius hands me a box of chocolates. "And reading material." He slips me a copy of *Men* magazine. The "Men in Uniform" issue. The cover model looks like a guy I trained with at the academy. I slip the magazine under my pillow.

"If anything ever happened to Cora, God forbid, I'd want you working on her case."

"Cora is safe with you and Keisha," I say, because that's what Demetrius needs to hear. But it's a load of bunk. Evil people commit unthinkable acts every day.

"I told Keisha that I was seeing someone."

"How did she react?"

"When she thought you were a woman, she was not a happy camper," Demetrius says. "But when she found out you were a man, she laughed and said that explains a lot of things." His brow furrows. "She wasn't as surprised as I thought she'd be."

"They never are."

"I don't want to hide who I am anymore."

Officer Lecoq snores. Demetrius closes the curtain that separates our beds, and we fool around until the nurse announces visiting hours are over.

CHAPTER THIRTY-SIX

Monday morning, my CT scan looks good, so the doctor releases me. Before I leave the hospital, I stop by Evan Langford's room. The boy looks better than he did the last time we saw one another, but that's not saying much. His mother sits beside him on the bed. He hugs me and won't let go.

"You're safe now," I say, prying the little boy's scrawny arms from around my neck. "That bad cop won't bother you anymore."

"Promise?" he asks.

"Promise," I say. "I brought you a gift." I pass Chippy to Evan. I hope the worn-out sock monkey will comfort this little boy the way he did me when I was a child.

Twyla nudges her son. "What do you say, Evan?"

"Thank you, mister."

"Call me Cal."

"I know I messed up, officer," Twyla says. "I'll do better. I swear."

I do not doubt that Twyla loves her son, but she doesn't seem stable enough to keep him safe. I'd hate for her to lose custody, but I hope for the boy's sake she gets help.

Annie picks me up from the hospital. "Have you seen the

newspaper yet?" I shake my head. She passes me a copy of the *Nyes Landing Gazette*. The headline reads, "Lost Boy Saves Another Lost Boy's Life." Seems I've redeemed myself in the eyes of Ernestine Middleton.

On the drive home, Annie tells me she plans to go back to work this afternoon. "I can't believe I didn't see the abuse that was going on right under my nose."

"No one suspected Chief Harris."

"Kit knew, and he did nothing. Worse than nothing. He blackmailed the chief."

"Kit wasn't perfect," I say. "But he loved you." I don't know if that's true, but I'm not sure what else to say.

"The district attorney dismissed my case."

"As she should."

"Kit's life insurance policy will cover his funeral expenses and pay off a few debts. But I may have to sell the house, which might not be so bad. After everything that's happened, I'm not sure I want to live there anymore."

"If I can help, I will."

Annie drops me off and drives away. I find Mama Libby seated at the dining room table when I get home, thumbing through old photo albums. "I miss all my babies," she says, dabbing her eyes with a tissue. "The ones Frank and I helped, and the ones we couldn't."

"I shudder to think about how my life might've turned out if you and Papa Frank hadn't taken me in."

"You're a good egg, Callum Nowak. It makes me sad that you can't see that."

After I take a long shower, I call my sergeant. He sounds annoyed when he answers the phone, but that's nothing new. I summarize what's happened since we last spoke and inform him that I plan to return by the end of the month.

"You've gone through a lot the past few weeks," Sarge says. "Are you sure you're ready?"

"Positive, sir."

"I'm placing you on desk duty until you've proven to me that you can control your temper."

That stings, but I have no grounds for argument.

Tuesday morning, I drive into town and purchase three dozen concrete bricks from the garden center, which Moses helps me place around the perimeter of Sparky's kennel. And by help, I mean he shares war stories while I work.

That evening, Moses flips burgers on the grill while Mama Libby makes potato salad and coleslaw, and I set up the picnic table in the backyard.

After dinner, Demetrius calls. I retreat to my room for privacy. "You're a hero, man," he says.

"I'm a cop."

"How're you holding up?"

"All in a day's work."

"Don't give me that tough guy act."

"I'll be fine."

For the first time in years, I mean that. I've still got my share of issues, but I'm going to be okay.

"Guess I'll see you at the park on Thursday," Demetrius says. "Only two more classes left."

"Sparky and I will be there."

I should tell Demetrius I'm returning to the city at the end of the month, but I don't want to spoil the mood.

Mama Libby keeps me busy running errands for the Memorial Day rummage sale on Wednesday. That afternoon, the same detectives who interviewed me about Kit's shooting track me down and take my witness statement regarding the chief with a deference their tones lacked the last time we spoke.

"It's never a good look when an officer of the law turns to the dark side," Detective Davis says.

"We appreciate your cooperation," Detective Moore says.

"When can I retrieve my weapon and belongings?"

"They're evidence until after the trial, unless Harris takes a plea deal."

"I guess that gives me an excuse to go gun shopping," I say.

The detectives shake my hand and thank me for my time. As they drive away, Moses joins me on the lawn and asks me if everything is all right. I fill him in.

"They owe you big time," Moses says.

"That a member of law enforcement who took an oath to serve and protect could do something so heinous blows my mind."

"You never know what darkness lurks in a man's heart."

EARLY THURSDAY MORNING, I take Sparky for a run. I have a little over a week before I return to the city. Mama Libby won't get her cast off before I leave, but she assures me she'll be fine, and Annie promises she'll drop by every day before and after school. Moses will do his part too. Still, I feel guilty.

When I return to the house, I'm drenched in sweat. I tug off my tee shirt and hang it over the fence to dry. Having a few hours before I need to leave for obedience class, I plug the extension cord for the trimmers into an outlet inside the mudroom and prune the tangled hedges that border the old house.

Mama Libby greets me in the mudroom afterward and tosses me one of Papa Frank's old bathrobes. "Take off your dirty clothes. I'm about to do laundry." She goes outside and picks a head of lettuce from her garden. I undress, slip on the robe, and pad upstairs. I could go for a shot of whiskey. I haven't had a sip since I lost my flask.

After I shower, I trim my beard and splash on some of Papa Frank's Old Spice. I put on my usual black tee shirt with jeans and polish my boots.

Sparky leaps into the Silverado. I drive into town and buy a bottle of whiskey. We reach the park early. I take Sparky for a walk so she can burn off some energy before class starts. We pass two women who thank me for finding Evan. To the first, I'm a hero, and to the second, I'm a saint. Of course, I'm neither.

Sparky drags me over to the fountain and laps up the water. Before I realize what the dog is doing, she leaps into the fountain and splashes around. I haul her out. She shakes off, showering me. I tell her to sit. She does. I pass her a treat.

"Hey, handsome," Demetrius says. Flower squiggles in his arms. The puppy appears to have doubled in size. Demetrius sets Flower on the ground. Flower and Sparky get tangled in their leashes. By the time we separate the pair, the rest of our classmates and their dogs have arrived.

Sparky and I haven't practiced, so she's fallen behind in her lessons. She's eager to earn treats, though, so she watches the other dogs and catches on fast. A squirrel dashes by, distracting the class, and we finish early.

"Would you like to have dinner tonight?" Demetrius asks. "If you're not busy. You're probably busy—"

"What time?"

"Seven o'clock?"

"Where should we meet?"

"I'll pick you up."

"Are you sure? People might see us together."

Demetrius leans in and kisses me. "I'm sure."

When Mama Libby hears I have a date—a word that sounds foreign coming out of my mouth—she asks what I'm planning on wearing.

"Jeans and a tee shirt, I suppose. That's all I brought with me."

"I'm sure Frank has a jacket you can borrow."

I follow Mama Libby upstairs. She sorts through Papa Frank's closet. I wonder why she doesn't donate his clothes to the rummage sale.

"What color jeans?" Mama Libby asks. "Blue or black?"

"Black."

"Try this on." Mama Libby hands me a charcoal-gray wool sports jacket. I'm taller than Papa Frank, so the sleeves are too short, but the jacket fits through the shoulders.

"What size shoes do you wear?"

"Twelve."

Mama Libby passes me a pair of shiny black calf-skin loafers. "Frank only wore these to weddings and funerals." She leaves me alone so I can get ready.

Before brushing my teeth, I chug a generous shot of whiskey for fortification. I haven't been drinking as much as I did in the city and my skin looks healthier.

Demetrius pulls into the driveway a few minutes early, but he waits until seven o'clock to knock. Mama Libby beats me to the door and invites him inside. She asks about his daughter.

"Cora lost another tooth," Demetrius says. "She was with her mother, so I didn't get to play tooth fairy."

"That's too bad," Mama Libby says. "But you'll share other milestones."

"We should get going," I say before Mama Libby brings up any embarrassing stories from my teenage years.

Demetrius opens my car door, a gesture that catches me off guard, and tells me I look nice. It's like I'm learning a foreign language.

"Our options are limited," Demetrius says. "Besides the diner, there's the pizzeria, the Jukebox Junction, a questionable Mexican hole-in-the-wall, and a vegan bakery that closes at eight o'clock. Where would you like to go?"

"Not the questionable Mexican hole-in-the-wall or the vegan bakery."

It's a pleasant night. Clear skies. Not too hot, not too cold. We try Maestro's Pizzeria first. They have a thirty-minute wait for a table. We drive past the diner. Patrons pack the sidewalk outside. The Jukebox Junction looks packed too, and a dozen cars idle in line for the drive-through.

"Looks like the weekenders from the city have arrived early," Demetrius says. "There's always dinner at my house, if you're game."

"I'll wash the dishes."

CHAPTER THIRTY-SEVEN

DEMETRIUS LIVES in a cabin in the woods outside of town. Bullfrogs croak in a nearby pond. Crickets chirp along the stone pathway that leads to the porch.

"I have a couple of steaks thawed in the fridge," Demetrius says. "I'll light the grill."

"What can I do?"

Demetrius kisses me. I kiss back. We grope like horny teenagers. He shoves me backward onto the couch and climbs on top of me. We devour one another's mouths. There's a hunger behind his kisses. I'm so turned on. He loosens my fly and tugs my jeans down around my knees. His tongue teases me. He takes me into his mouth. I close my eyes and clutch the cushions. My toes curl inside my boots. It's not long before he drives me over the edge.

"I've wanted to do that ever since I met you," Demetrius says.

"I can't believe you've never . . . that was—"

"I should fire up that grill," Demetrius says. He steps outside onto the back deck.

Down the hallway, I find the bathroom and wash up. I could use a drink. Hearing whining and scratching, I open the bedroom door. Flower tumbles out, panting hard, and bounces around my feet.

"I see somebody escaped," Demetrius says.

"He had help."

"Care to take a walk?"

Demetrius snaps Flower's leash to his collar and takes my hand. We step outside. Flower chases a squirrel up a tree.

"You enjoy living all the way out here?"

"I enjoy the woods. They're peaceful," Demetrius says. "But I wouldn't mind sharing... with the right person."

I doubt I'll ever be ready to take that step with anyone.

Flower does his business. Demetrius carries the squirming puppy inside and washes his hands. He asks how I'd like my steak cooked.

"Medium-rare."

"Same here. I have a ribeye and a T-bone. Which do you prefer?"

"Either is fine."

"We'll share."

If this is what it's like to have a boyfriend, maybe I should give dating a chance.

"Baked potato sound good?"

"Steak and potatoes," I say. "You're my kind of guy."

"I hope so."

I hug Demetrius from behind and rest my chin on his shoulder. I can't find the words to express my feelings right now. He takes my hand. We entwine our fingers. I nibble on his neck. He giggles. His head turns toward me. We kiss.

"I should check on the grill."

When Demetrius steps outside, I explore his living room. A bearskin rug covers the floor. I've never seen one of those up close. Simple wooden furniture. Wrought-iron fixtures. Antlers on the walls. Very rustic. Peering through the glass front of the locked gun cabinet in the corner, I spy a Smith & Wesson .357

Magnum revolver, a Remington bolt-action rifle, and a Winchester bolt-action rifle. Demetrius must hunt.

Framed photographs of Cora from the time she was a baby until now cover the walls. Several include a gorgeous Black woman with shiny beaded braids—Keisha, I presume. A cedar chest filled with toys rests beside the couch. Our lifestyles could hardly be more different.

"Grill's almost hot," Demetrius says upon his return. "We need music. I lost the stereo in the divorce, but I have a boombox."

Static dominates the first few stations Demetrius lands on. A fire and brimstone preacher decries the sin, but not the sinner. National Public Radio hosts a debate on the war on terrorism, a conflict without end.

"I get limited channels," Demetrius says.

"Here's Toby Keith's hit single 'You Shouldn't Kiss Me Like This,'" an announcer with a twang exclaims.

I have no clue who Toby Keith is, but his lyrics about getting a funny feeling when we kiss and thinking about lots of crazy things hit home tonight.

Demetrius sprinkles a liberal dash of seasonings over the steaks and tosses them on the grill. He pops a couple of potatoes into the microwave. I watch him cook and wonder if I'll get an invitation to spend the night.

"There's beer in the fridge," Demetrius says. "Help yourself."

"Would you like one?"

"Sure."

"Sam Adams or Stella?"

"Whichever you're having."

I open two Samuel Adams lagers and pass Demetrius his.

"To new experiences," Demetrius says.

We clink bottles.

"I can't get over the fact that the police chief abused that little boy," Demetrius says.

"It's not the first time, either," I say. "He same as admitted that he killed that missing boy last year."

"What a monster."

"The worst kind," I say, clenching my fists. "Hiding behind a badge while he preyed on children. Makes me so mad I could punch my fist through the wall."

Demetrius steps backward. "Please don't."

"Oh, I wouldn't—. I'm sorry. It's just—"

"I'm sure you've seen some awful shit as a cop."

"Policing is not all doom and gloom. My partner and I helped deliver a baby last month. In the back seat of a cab that was a stuck in traffic."

"Good thing I wasn't there," Demetrius says. "When Keisha went into labor, the nurse sedated me."

"My partner deserves most of the credit. She's had two kids. I merely followed her lead."

Demetrius slices the steaks in half, retrieves the potatoes from the microwave, and sets a plate before me. The meat has a seared outer layer and a pinkish-red center. I slather butter on my potato and clean my plate so fast you'd think I hadn't eaten in a month.

After dinner, Demetrius suggests I spend the night. While he puts Flower to bed, I clear the table and call Mama Libby. She tells me to play safe.

"Leave those dishes," Demetrius says. "I'll do them later." He takes my hand and leads me down the hallway toward the bedroom. We pause in the doorway. "Who's going to do...?" he asks. "I mean . . . I've never . . . with a man." He rests his forehead against my shoulder. "I sound so lame."

"You have a condom?"

Demetrius digs through the drawer on the bedside table and pulls out a box and a tube of lubricant. "After my divorce finalized, a buddy of mine gave me these."

"Put one on."

He does. We lock lips and do what comes naturally.

CHAPTER THIRTY-EIGHT

FRIDAY MORNING, Demetrius brings me coffee in bed. I pull him down onto the sheets, and we make out for a moment before he disentangles himself and says, "I have to get ready for work." I follow him into the shower, and we explore one another's bodies with soap and water. After we dry off and dress, he drives me home.

"I don't need to ask how your date went," Mama Libby says when I walk through the door. "That smile on your face says it all. Are you hungry?"

I shake my head.

"Sergeant Jimenez rang," Mama Libby says. "She left her number."

"Did she say what she wants?"

"No, and I didn't ask."

I pour a cup of black coffee and return the sergeant's call.

"Can you drop by the station today?" Sergeant Jimenez asks.

She must have an update on the case.

"Sure. What time?"

"The sooner the better."

When I reach the police station, I find Officer Lecoq seated behind the front desk with his arm in a sling. "First day back on the job," he says. "Jimenez is expecting you. Her office is—"

"I'll find it."

I round the corner and walk down the hallway toward the interrogation room where Chief Harris interviewed me. As I pass the men's room, Officer Reeves steps out, and we collide.

"Nowak." Officer Reeves steps back and allows me to pass. "Listen . . . sorry for giving you a hard time."

"Keeps me on my toes."

"You're looking for Jimenez?"

I nod.

"Last door on the left."

"Thanks, man."

I find the office and knock.

"What is it?" Sergeant Jimenez shouts.

"You asked to see me?"

"Come in, Nowak," Sergeant Jimenez says. She stands. "Have a seat."

"You have an update on the case?"

"I do," Sergeant Jimenez says. "But that's not why I called." She plucks a piece of candy out of a jar on top of her desk. "Dulce de coco," she says. "My abuela sends me care packages from San Juan." She offers me one. I shake my head. She unwraps and pops the candy into her mouth. "So good."

I lean back and cross my arms.

"I'm sure you realize Chief Harris won't be returning to duty."

I nod.

"He's claiming self-defense. Said Christopher Nye drew on him. He blamed you for Evan Langford's abduction, but the boy fingered his abuser."

"I figured Harris for an asshole, but never suspected he'd do anything this twisted."

"Me either," Sergeant Jimenez says. She sits forward. "So, here's the deal. The mayor and town council appointed me interim chief."

"Congratulations."

"I'm not sure if the job is a blessing or a curse."

"I guess you'll find out."

"I'm appointing Reeves to sergeant. He can be a jerk, but he's good at his job." Chief Jimenez leans forward. "That leaves me down an officer. This is a long shot, but . . . I don't suppose you'd consider joining our ranks?"

I was not expecting that.

"We need officers who are familiar with the town. You grew up here. This is your home."

"Not in years."

"I can't pay you what the NYPD does," Chief Jimenez says, "but I can offer more flexible hours. And despite what's gone down the past few weeks, we have one of the lowest crime rates in the state."

"Reeves and I are oil and water. How do you think he'd feel about this?"

"It was his idea."

"Say what?"

"You heard me."

I could not be more surprised.

"I'm flattered, but—"

"I understand you've had some issues in the city," Chief Jimenez says. "Might be time for a fresh start."

For the past five years, the NYPD has been my life. I've never considered working anywhere else.

"Can I have the weekend to think it over?"

"Of course."

ANNIE FINISHES TEACHING in a thirty minutes. I drive to the elementary school and wait for her in the parking lot. A group of rowdy boys roughhouse on the playground. I hope none of them fell victim to the former police chief.

The bell rings. Shrieking children stream out the doors of the school. Annie emerges, holding Evan Langford's hand. I didn't realize the boy had returned to school. I get out of the pickup and say hello. He leaps into my arms.

A stout woman in a stained white blouse and rumpled brown skirt rushes up. "Sorry, I'm late."

"No worries," Annie says. "School just let out." She turns to me. "Cal, this is Francine. Evan's social worker. Evan is staying with a nice foster family for a few days."

"That sounds exciting," I say, because that's what the boy needs to hear.

"I wish I could stay with you," he says.

"No, you don't. Trust me."

I Evan on his feet. Francine leads the boy away.

"I talked to Zelda," Annie says. "She said to tell you hello. She couldn't believe it when I told her what Kit did. Who did I marry?"

"People like Kit and Harris are masters of deception."

"What brings you by?" Annie asks. "Not that I'm not glad to see you."

"You'll never believe what I'm about to tell you."

"With everything that's happened the past few weeks, I'm not sure I want to hear this."

"Sergeant Jimenez offered me a position on the local force."

Annie suppresses a shriek of joy. "What did you tell her?"

"That I would think about it."

"You should."

"It would be less money than I'm making now. But I'd be living in Nyes Landing, so my expenses would be lower."

"Much lower."

"I'm not sure I'm ready to leave the city and chase raccoons out of grocery stores."

"You saved a little boy's life."

"With any luck, that's a once-in-a-lifetime occurrence."

"Mama Libby is not getting any younger," Annie says.

"Are you laying a guilt trip on me?"

"Yes."

"I'd need a place to live. I can't stay with Mama Libby forever. And I'd have to buy a car."

"You can stay with me until you get on your feet. I have plenty of room."

"I'd pay rent, of course."

"I would loan you Kit's Mercedes, but it's being repossessed. Seems the bank has been threatening take the car back for months."

"I'm sorry."

"Promise you'll consider the job offer."

"I'd be a fool if I didn't."

―――――

WHEN I GET HOME, I share the news with Mama Libby. She tells me to have a seat and pours me a cup of coffee. "Moses and I baked a blackberry pie. Would you like a piece?" I shake my head. She cuts me off a slice anyway and asks if I'd like ice cream. I nod. "So, how do you feel about this offer?" she asks.

"Three weeks ago, I would've turned the job down without a second thought."

"And now?"

Mama Libby takes a bite out of my pie and ice cream.

"In the short time I've been home, I've made more of a difference than I did in five years with the NYPD."

Demetrius calls. I retreat to my room.

"I had a good time last night," he says.

"Me too."

"I know you're going back to the city soon. I hope we can get together before you leave."

"I may stay."

"What do you mean?"

I share the news.

"Are you taking the job?"

"Maybe. I don't know. It's a lot to process."

"I'm a good listener," Demetrius says.

"I wouldn't be able to keep my hands off you."

"What's wrong with that?"

"I'M NOT sure what to do," I say. I pass Moses the whiskey bottle. He takes a long pull. We sit on the back steps and stare at the moon, which shines full and bright.

"A lot of boys in my platoon got drafted," Moses says. "Not me. I enlisted to save the world from commies." He takes a swig of whiskey. "Different times." He passed me the bottle. "Most of my buddies came home in body bags. When I returned not only alive but with all my limbs intact, I figured I must be invincible." He chuckles. "I soon learned that wasn't the case when I went skydiving, and my parachute malfunctioned. After I recovered from my injuries, I volunteered at the Veteran's Hospital and touched far more lives than I did in Nam." He takes a long pull on the whiskey bottle and wipes his mouth on the back of his hand. "That's when I realized it's not where you are, but what you do that counts."

"You're saying I should take the job?"

S. F. WILLIAMS

"I'm saying use your head, but listen with your heart."

CHAPTER THIRTY-NINE

On Thursday, I drive down to the city with Demetrius, and we pack up my apartment. As we're leaving with our last load, Miss Tawanda LaRue opens her door. "You're moving out?" she says. "Hallelujah!" Spying Demetrius, she smiles and fluffs her wig. Demetrius kisses me. Her jaw drops.

At the precinct, Sarge seems disappointed when I break the news that I'm leaving, which surprises me. I thought he'd be relieved. I introduce Demetrius to the squad. Fagan asks Demetrius why he's dating an asshole like me, which I take as a win.

The captain calls me upstairs and asks me why I'm resigning. I share everything that's gone down over the past few weeks and confide that I've met someone. He tells me he respects my decision and wishes me luck.

On our way out the door, Tran whispers in my ear, "Don't screw this up."

SATURDAY MORNING, I meet the crew from the monument company at the cemetery and make sure they place my mother's headstone in the correct location. The maintenance crew must have received my message because they've mowed the grass. I chose a headstone with lots of birds and flowers, and I hope my mother finds peace in the afterlife, if there is one.

After the crew from the monument company drives away, I plop down on the grass and listen to the birds chirping and the squirrels chattering in the nearby treetops. The warm sun caresses my skin. For better or worse, this is my home.

Now that I'm on the local police force, I can access my mother's cold case files. "I won't give up until I catch your killer, Mommy," I whisper.

The alarm on my cellular phone rings. I must go. I'm on patrol in thirty minutes.

―――

SUITED UP in my NLPD gear, I patrol the perimeter of the Memorial Weekend rummage sale at the Kiwanis Club meeting hall, keeping an eye out for thieves. Locals and weekenders up from the city rummage through piles of donated merchandise. Tomorrow, I'll cover Family Day at Turtle Creek.

"Officer Nowak?" A woman around my age, blond and dressed in a halter top, shorts, and sandals, approaches. "I'm Sandy Higgins. I read about your heroism in the newspaper. I'm glad you've decided to stay and serve our little town." She passes me her phone number on a slip of paper. "If you're ever patrolling in my neighborhood, drop by. I make a mean martini."

"I'm a whiskey man myself."

"I'm flexible."

I bet she is. I excuse myself and load the purchases of a woman who's using a walker into her car. When I return, Mama Libby offers for me to help Gladys.

"I hate to be a bother," Gladys Crabtree says. I lug the overstuffed armchair she bought outside and cram the bulky item into the rear of her AMC Pacer. She slips a dollar bill into my fist and thanks me for my help.

"I can't accept this." I hand back her money. "I'm on duty."

Demetrius shouts my name. I turn around. He smiles and waves. I rush to his side. "You look so handsome in your uniform," he says. "I'm proud you're my boyfriend."

"I'm the lucky one," I say. I want to know everything about Demetrius. To keep him safe and make him happy.

"I brought lunch," Demetrius says. He holds up a Jukebox Junction bag. "Are you hungry?"

"Starving."

ABOUT THE AUTHOR

S.F. Williams is a member of the Alliance of Independent Authors (ALLi), the Mystery Writers of America (MWA), and the NYC Writers Critique Group. His diverse portfolio ranges from short stories and poetry to reflections on fatherhood as a single gay man, but his roots lie in the theater. Williams holds a BFA from the University of Oklahoma and membership in the Actor's Equity Association, and he has acted in, directed, produced, and written over a hundred productions for the stage.

Williams's novels, characterized by their fast-paced narratives and resilient protagonists, reflect the diverse tapestry of our world.

MAKE AN AUTHOR HAPPY TODAY!

If you enjoyed *The Lost Boy*, please consider leaving a review on Goodreads, Amazon, or the bookstore platform of your choice. Even a sentence or two would be a huge help and most appreciated.

Sign up for my newsletter at https://sfwilliamsauthor.com and I will notify you about upcoming book releases and giveaways.

If you think your followers might enjoy *The Lost Boy*, please spread the word on your social media platforms. You can follow me at @sfwauthor on Facebook, Instagram, and Twitter.

www.ingramcontent.com/pod-product-compliance
Lightning Source LLC
LaVergne TN
LVHW041907070526
838199LV00051BA/2528